ANTI-C

V.J. James

TRANSLATED FROM THE
MALAYALAM BY MINISTHY S.

VINTAGE

An imprint of Penguin Random House

VINTAGE

USA | Canada | UK | Ireland | Australia
New Zealand | India | South Africa | China

Vintage is part of the Penguin Random House group of companies
whose addresses can be found at global.penguinrandomhouse.com

Published by Penguin Random House India Pvt. Ltd
4th Floor, Capital Tower 1, MG Road,
Gurugram 122 002, Haryana, India

First published in Vintage by Penguin Random House India 2021

Copyright © V.J. James 2021
Translation copyright © Ministhy S. 2021

10 9 8 7 6 5 4 3 2 1

This is a work of fiction. Names, characters, places and incidents are either the
product of the author's imagination or are used fictitiously, and any resemblance
to any actual person, living or dead, events or locales is entirely coincidental.

ISBN 9780143457718

For sale in the Indian Subcontinent only

Typeset in Adobe Garamond Pro by Manipal Technologies Limited, Manipal

www.penguin.co.in

To my late parents, Antony Joseph and Marykutty Joseph.

—V.J. James

To Mattayamma, who loved books.

—Ministhy S.

Preface

Very often, 'writing' enters a person unknowingly. At least I can vouch for it from my experience. There were no writers in my family or circle of friends. In retrospect, it was the schooldays spent in the picturesque Kuttanadu that furrowed the fertile fields for storytelling. Since I had opted to study engineering after my pre-degree, I never expected to become a writer. My lone creative endeavour in engineering college was to read aloud a story I had written, for an association called 'Sahitya'. The name of the story was 'Sangham Chernnavarude Sankeerthanam' or 'The Hymn of the Gang'. Who knew then that the theme of the story was destined to be my third novel, *Dattapaharam, The Retrieval of Offering*, years after.

In my final year at Mar Athanasius College of Engineering, Kothamangalam, I happened to visit an isle in Cochin to attend the wedding of my friend Patris's sister. One could see the majesty of Cochin town from that small island. But the residents of the isle were deprived of basic infrastructure. In order to get drinking water, they were forced to cross the waters, to access the tap situated on the opposite shore. That island was waiting for the writer in me, readying the backdrop for my first book: *Purappadinte Pusthakam*, aka *The Book of Exodus*. I visited the island several times to learn more of its rural customs, peculiar language dialects and myths.

I had already been appointed as a scientist at ISRO by that time. My family was reeling under a huge financial crisis then. One's entire salary was insufficient for even the monthly interest. It was but natural that I was sorely tempted by the cash amount associated with the Maman Mappila literary award organized by *Malayala Manorama*. I started writing my first novel in order to participate in the competition—a thought which makes me smile today. The novel could not be completed and I eventually didn't compete for the award. Indeed, that particular award ceased from the following year.

My situation became like that of a hopeful person who went swimming to grab a bundle of wool in the water, only to have it clasp him in return. It was rather late by the time I realized that the bundle of wool was in reality a bear. The novel grasped me in its clutches and travelled with me for twelve long years. After rewriting and editing it endlessly, when I finally tried to get the book published, all the bitter experiences of a first-time writer awaited me. I became frustrated when the magazine which had promised that 'it is a good novel and we shall publish it very soon', kept it in abeyance for a long time. However, I had implicit trust in the power of words. That was how I submitted the manuscript for the DC Books Silver Jubilee Novel Award in 1999.

It turned out to be 'the path' nature had kept aside for me. I received the award from the famous author Arundhati Roy, and all the renowned wordsmiths of Malayalam were present on the stage. Madhavikutty, T. Padmanabhan, O.N.V. Kurup, Adoor Gopalakrishnan, M.V. Devan, Paul Zacharia, Punathil Kunjabdulla, Asha Menon, M. Thomas Mathew and C.V. Balakrishnan were among the stalwarts who graced the function—almost inconceivable for a naïve first-time writer. The icing on the cake was the award sculpture which was designed by O.V. Vijayan, whom I silently revered as my guru. That day I realized that writing would never be subdued by anything else. When *The Book of Exodus* became award worthy, writing overcame money.

When I joined Vikram Sarabhai Space Centre as a scientist, my attention was drawn to a coffin shop near Palayam Church in Thiruvananthapuram. That was the genesis of *Anti-Clock*. Death seemed to be lying in wait within its dark innards. Electronic media was not as commonplace then, and the shop also functioned as a rental place for video cassette recorders and televisions. The coffin shop evoked the conjoining of opposites, where the colourful sights of the television and the darkness of death merged into one other. The seed the shop sowed inside me blossomed into a story which was published in a Malayalam weekly magazine. But my mind insisted it should not be restricted inside the shell of a short story.

Anti-Clock was written after the publication of six novels; many decades had passed since the beginning of my writing journey. Time had been particular about that waiting period. Nature knew that *Anti-Clock* could not be written until the dilemmas associated with life, death and time were affixed in one's mind. In truth, the writer never selects the writing; the writing comes to the writer, searching for him compassionately. Words have such a mesmerizing beauty that many unplanned thoughts flow in when you sit down to write. And thus, I believe that no writer should ever feel too proud about his or her writing.

The discovery that even in a place of death, where no one expects anything of beauty, the loveliness of life was still strewn around became the catalyst for *Anti-Clock*. The unpredictability of the writing process forced the book to traverse many landscapes. To understand the life of a coffin maker, it became necessary to meet those practising the profession and spend a lot of time in coffin shops. I experienced the lives of gravediggers by spending time with them in the cemetery. I too had some terrible memories of the cemetery from when I was a primary school student of a church school at Changanacherry, which made its way into the narration.

When an imaginary village called 'Aadi Nadu' situated near the Neyyar dam became the canvas for the novel, it became an arduous task to find someone who had witnessed the construction of the dam. I started off in my car, with my friend V. Shaju, to Neyyar dam and the interior villages alongside it. After being guided my many different people, we finally reached an old man who had been a teenager when the dam was built. I listened to what the locals had endured during that time. Those stories were of Neyyar being filled with the tears of all who lost their homes, livelihoods and farms. The old man's voice broke while speaking of how he had transformed from a prince to a pauper overnight.

It is no coincidence that one of the greatest curses of our time, environmental degradation, became a major theme in *Anti-Clock*. The ruthless exploitation of nature wreaks havoc in not only a specific region but also on the balance of earth as a whole. When man, urged by his avarice, scoffs at nature's warnings, she strongly intervenes as floods, droughts and pandemics. The anxieties of a common man about the relentless destruction of nature takes a prominent place in this novel. Satan Loppo is not just a person but a metaphor for the rotten system which is intoxicated by power, materialistic pleasures and conceit.

The pandemic has shown us how the 'deep consciousness of nature' sets out to battle against a tyrannical system which stops at nothing to reign over everything. From nature's viewpoint, we humans have transformed into a virus which is destroying her. Maybe COVID-19, the microscopic virus, is the anti-virus which nature has designed against us, to annihilate the arrogance of mankind. Nature can survive only when we turn back from our attempts to vanquish, exploit and poison the air, water and earth. The ultimate revolution the present demands is nothing but protection of nature.

History tells us that when the 'great consciousness of nature' steps in, the needles of the Kalachakra—the wheel of time—turn into arrows that fly in the direction of all dictatorships. It is the same thought which is symbolically portrayed through the Anti-Clock—a time machine which moves in the opposite direction—which contains within itself the idea of a 'return to nature'.

My colleague at V.S.S.C., James P. Thomas, has a collection of ancient clocks. It astounded me to see him painstakingly search for old, dysfunctional clocks and try to breathe new life into them, spending a good deal of his life immersed in that task. I acknowledge with gratitude that my imagination was inspired to create the characters of Pundit and Anti-Clock because of that friendship. Devarajan Pillai and Mathew Sebastian are colleagues who helped to kindle many philosophical discussions; and I remember them with warmth.

After an effort of almost five years, moving through different surroundings, the novel assumed its present form. The main character of the book, the Anti-Clock, haunted my dreams with its ticking. Sometimes dreams can provide answers to many troubling questions. I have had many experiences where stories came to me in the guise of dreams. Once, I got up halfway through a dream. Frustrated at not knowing the end of the tale, I went back to sleep again. Oddly enough, the rest of the dream came back! In short, a writer is someone who has to face the time when the past, present and future get inexplicably entwined. Probably that is the reason why 'time' has made its presence felt in this novel, both in a palpable and impalpable way.

Human beings who lived in different times faced different challenges. But 'death' and 'time' have forever stayed beyond the reach of human comprehension. These phenomena have driven the novel *Anti-Clock* forward and forward; nay, backward and backward. Accompanying them is a different perspective about the philosophical elegance of the Holy Bible.

As an engineer, one works with great precision and planning. But writing is not wholly a planned activity. However, the writer in me gets full support from the engineer in me, both complementing each other. That has influenced the way in which I write.

After *Chorashastra: The Subtle Science of Thievery*, *Anti-Clock* is my second book to be published in English. I would like to congratulate Ministhy S. for having translated this book with much care. My heartfelt gratitude is also due to Penguin Random House for the very graceful presentation of *Anti-Clock*.

Welcome, dear readers, to this reverse rotation even as the moments trickle from the Kalachakra enfolding the time.

May the time be auspicious, for everyone.

V.J. James
Thiruvananthapuram
18 April 2021

Translator's Note

V.J. James's books entered my life serendipitously. Struck by the depth and finesse of the writing, I eagerly wrote to him to express my interest in translating these gems. The author, humble and affable, responded warmly. Apart from *Anti-Clock*, we have completed two other books together, which we hope to publish soon; and have started working on a fourth.

Anti-Clock came my way when I needed to do some forgiving myself, and every page I translated seemed to speak to me directly. I told James I had been feeling bitter about the hundreds of hours I had lost on another project which got stalled. Ironically, that book was based on the Holy Bible too. James responded, 'No effort goes waste, ever. He will answer in His own time, you know!' I bowed before that wisdom.

Anti-Clock made me pore over both the Malayalam and English versions of the Holy Bible and left me convinced that if ever there were masterpieces of translations, I was reading those. How beautiful the lines were! Sheer poetry greeted me in both the languages. I grew as a translator, as a human being, and developed the habit—much like Hendri—of opening the Holy Bible randomly and reading it.

The challenge in translating *Anti-Clock* was to keep Hendri's ruminations as close to the original as possible without losing the cadence in English. Hendri drifts between the past, present and the future, and I struggled initially to capture the tenses accurately. Slowly, the voice became clear and steady in my head. I had to explore many Christian rituals and rites, and read further on Kerala's dams and quarries. The Medical Sisters of St. Joseph at Lucknow helped clear many doubts and James was always ready to answer my queries.

This book is a labour of love. I have been fortunate to play the role of translator and sincerely hope that you enjoy reading it.

Ministhy S.
13 April 2021
Lucknow

1

The Carpenter's Son

'How deserted lies the city, once so full of people. How like a widow is she, who once was great among the nations. She who was queen among the provinces has now become a slave. Bitterly she weeps at night, tears are on her cheeks. Among all her lovers there is no one to comfort her. All her friends have betrayed her; they have become her enemies. After affliction and harsh labor, Judah has gone into exile. She dwells among the nations; she finds no resting place. All who pursue her have overtaken her in the midst of her distress.'

(Lamentations 1: 1-3)

As usual, I am about to go to sleep, after reading the Bible and contemplating its words.

It was Appan who ingrained in me the nightly habit of opening the Bible to any page, and skipping seven lines before starting to read, no matter what the circumstances. Since he had insisted that I shouldn't desist from the routine even if he lay dead, I followed his instructions even on the day death visited my house.

By no means should anyone jump to the conclusion that I am an ingenuous saint. I have a wicked intent that goes against the teachings of the Scriptures. I want to kill Satan Loppo, either by tying a noose

1

around his neck, bashing his head in with my mallet, or stabbing him through his heart. It is that lone desire that keeps me going.

The bloodier and more dishonourable ending I can think of for Loppo, the better! What he deserves is much more than what I desire. The only way I sustain my life is by keeping a coffin ready for him and waiting for death to ensnare him.

At a mere glance, a coffin maker can assess the body measurements of a person and visualize a fitting casket. It is a place where life is lidded before being sent off on its final journey. Only the coffin maker and those who have experienced death can appreciate that the dead are not merely dead. If someone believes that the dead crumble into dust beneath the earth, he is wrong.

It was Appan who told me that the coffin is just a temporary retreat.

I used to frequent Appan's sweaty workplace in my childhood. I became his favourite child as I loved helping him at work, pasting black varnish paper or saffron strips over the panels of the coffin with wheat flour glue. I continued to assist Appan even after my siblings got bored and stopped working. The many nuggets of wisdom that he shared with me in his boundless affection turned my notions on life upside down.

It is hard to believe that there exists a mathematics of life that adheres solely to a coffin. Appan revealed the truth about the hollow tents that interred the lifeless on a foggy December night.

'But only Christians use coffins. What about the others, then?' I questioned naively.

'Who told you that? The pyres of the Hindus and the tombs of the Muslims are all boxes,' Appan said. 'I am sure each religion has something similar. I don't know much about those, my child.'

Appan always confessed his ignorance. He would never besmirch his soul by telling lies. My poor Appan! He would often advise me that whenever others tried to harm us, we should light a candle and pray to the Lord. Whenever I forget my tender-hearted Appan and get into a frenzy about murdering Loppo, a turbid guilt congeals inside me. Truth be told, my vengeance has no leg to stand on.

Despite my ferocious obsession with Loppo, I doubt whether I would be able to land a stinging slap on him, let alone kill him. Who does not know that a coward's revenge is nothing but a mulishness that dies within himself? However, to convince myself otherwise, I repeat my death wish for Loppo often, and deceive myself. Preparing for murder, I have built a coffin and wait for my enemy to step in it.

Like a moron, I continue to dream that one day, Satan Loppo's sturdy body will fall right into the box I have propped up against the wall. Having crafted it for my arch-enemy, I should be feeling affection instead of hatred for the coffin. It is my heart's beloved creation: A refuge made of wood, the culmination of a lifetime's desire.

If one were to think expansively, it is an act of benevolence too. Though I treat him as my nemesis, there is nobody but me for creating Satan Loppo's final resting place. People build magnificent mansions to live in. But why is it that nobody builds a shelter in advance for their sleep after death? It is such a good deed that I have done for Satan Loppo! Isn't it a marvellous gift when one fashions a luxurious home for someone's last slumber?

Though I pretend to don a saint's robe and justify my intentions, that fluttering mind of mine refuses to be fooled.

'You are deluding yourself that building a coffin is an act of kindness. Wishing to see your enemy lying dead inside is a sin in the eyes of the Lord.'

Like a deflated balloon—punctured during its sojourn in the sky—I then shrivel up and succumb to the pull of the earth. That is my true state of mind right now.

As is my wont, when feeling guilty after transgressing in my thoughts, I place a candle before the picture of the Sacred Heart on the alcove. In some unforeseen future, if I do end up killing that wretched Satan Loppo, the lighting of this candle might serve as some kind of redemption.

If the Lord accumulates all the candles I have lit till now, the heavens would be flooded with the light of a veritable afternoon sun. As the matchstick flickers and the candlewick lights up, I remember my Appan again.

Appan started making candles after he was no longer able to sustain his household by crafting coffins. It was a small cottage industry, not entailing much capital. I was my Appan's helpmate in that endeavour too. The 'Saint Anthony' brand candles had mediated all the prayers in the parish church and neighbourhood during that time.

Appan would collect the molten teardrops of wax coalesced on the candle stand and transform them into new candles. He earned a decent profit from the candle business. Though we sold our candles at a much cheaper rate than the market price, when the profits started arriving, my pure-hearted Appan suspected an inadvertent sin in that too.

My Appan knelt in confession and muttered in extreme contrition:

'Father, I have made excess profit from the candles.'

'How much did you make, my son?'

'Five times my investment, Father.'

'From whom did you make the profits, child?'

'That would include the sales for this church too . . .'

'Levied a profit from the Lord himself, you rogue?'

The Reverend Father stared at my Appan through the netted separation that filtered out the sins. Fearing the perdition of hell fire, Appan cringed, even as Father burst into hearty laughter. He kindly reduced the debt of my father's sins. After all, the Lord was bound to forgive my Appan, who was generosity incarnate to his own debtors.

Appan made profits so that he could feed his children. Still, if he felt guilty about it, his heart must have been as pristine as that of an angel. The same gentle soul had carved the heart of the rosewood into an elaborate candle stand and nailed it on the alcove.

When he opened his shop in the morning, Appan would light the candle in front of the Sacred Heart and pray with his eyes closed. Minutes would tick by . . . Appan wouldn't budge even if a customer arrived. It was a holy communion between the coffin shop and the heavens.

When I became older, Appan allowed me to light the candle. At the first instance of that burning flame, I realized that a candle wasn't a mere wax light. Usually, all shopkeepers lit lamps before their favourite Gods at the start of day and prayed for munificent profits. In Shashankan's tailoring shop opposite the road, the lamp is lit before Vighneshvara, with his long trunk and broken tusk. I do not know if the God with the human body, elephantine face, and mouse-vehicle is pleased with Shashankan. Somehow, I am unable to pray the way others do. Isn't it similar to praying for an acquaintance's death?

'*Lord, thy will be done.*' That was the prayer my Appan taught me.

Cogitating on the past, I lit the candle, and a mouse leapt down from the candle stand fixed on the wall. When it started crisscrossing the floor frantically, I left the Lord and Appan to their own devices and chased it.

I had been after that little terrorist for a while!

Not only did the mouse disturb my sleep with its ceaseless squeaking, but it also gnawed at the coffins. It dared to exhibit an indecent acuity, and taunted me by appearing and disappearing suddenly.

The mouse was driving me nuts, evading my traps every time I tried to catch hold of it.

Determined to finish it off this time, I grabbed a piece of wood and gave chase, scattering my work tools in my wake. In the welter of coffins and implements, it was easy for the mouse to play hide-and-seek while dodging me.

I angrily turned each coffin around and peeped beneath. The scamp must be hiding under one of these. Either I would maim it with a wooden chunk or strangle it with my own bare hands!

There it was: A dirty black tail could be seen twirling from within a chink in the coffin made for Satan Loppo.

'You night raider!'

The mouse, which had made an ill-timed entry inside the casket meant for someone's posthumous sleep, deserved a solemn death. I moved ahead cautiously—like Yama trying to lasso a soul—without making a sound. The mouse had no clue about the impending disaster.

The Yama in me was struck by a mischievous fancy then.

I caught hold of the tail which was extending through the coffin's fissure and yanked it. Dreadful squeaks emerged, as the creature thrashed around for its life. It evoked a stink of putrefied fish curry. Since the box was meant for Satan Loppo, I had always imagined his body inside. His body too was forbiddingly dark and furry like that of a mouse. Satan could assume any form, couldn't he?

Brother Romario, while delivering Bible classes for children, had gone overboard one day while describing Satan. He had ascribed to him horns and a tail, along with an abhorrent, repulsive body.

'Just like Loppo here,' Manas cried out. Everyone burst out laughing.

As Lopez's hard fist connected with Manas' face, four blood-streaked teeth broke in his mouth. Lopez blazed fierily, very much like Satan. Thus, he was christened with his nickname—Satan Loppo—in the precincts of the church.

The humiliation associated with that name followed Loppo unremittingly and made him a rebel. There was no day in school when he did not get into fisticuffs because of his name. When he grew up, everyone obsequiously called him 'Lopez Muthalali'* to his face but jeered at him, calling him 'Satan Loppo' behind his back.

---

* Boss

Imagining Loppo as a mouse, I became excited.

With Satan Loppo having entered the coffin meant for him with inimitable precision, the emerging squeals acquired the exquisiteness of spicily roasted meat. Though it was an illusory joy, I could not help relishing the moment. If one cannot directly fight with someone, imagining retribution soothes one's frayed nerves. The rare occasion when a trifling person like me could torture a powerful man like Loppo deserved celebration.

But the one-to-one fight between man and mouse did not continue for long.

Unexpectedly, I lost my foothold and fell backwards among the coffins.

In my hand was a twitching black tail.

Drops of blood were dripping from it.

The mouse scrabbled desperately between the coffins with its bleeding butt, screeching wildly. Its heart-rending curse rang out more lucidly than any in a human tongue. Then it bolted from my sight and vanished inside an obscure mouse hole.

It came to my notice that I had fallen inside a coffin. Like an undersized corpse, I was lying inside a rather large box. I felt amused at my pathetic position. It was shameful, this ghostly status that I had brought upon myself.

'Lord, you boxed me in, didn't you?' I looked at the Sacred Heart lit up by the candle and chuckled, 'Alive and kicking!'

Though I laughed for quite a while about landing inside that coffin, my eyes soon welled up with tears. My sight was shrouded by a moistness which could be claimed by neither happiness nor misery. My laughter unexpectedly turned into wails, and tears started flowing uninhibitedly. Nowadays, a thin line separates my laughter and tears.

Recollecting my Appan's words that men should desist from crying, I slowly regained my composure. Then I wished to brag about my latest adventure.

Whom should I disclose it to?

If only my Beatrice and my children were here, I would have showcased the tail and been lauded for my achievement.

'Finally, I trapped that bratty mouse, my dear! Look, how dark its tail is.' I would be a coxcomb indeed.

'Huh! What bravado in your dotage!' Beatrice would tease.

'Appa, how did you cut off the mouse's tail?' my young daughter Roselyn would lisp.

Then I would enact the battle scene between man and mouse. After catching the second show of the movies in the village theatre, I would often mimic the emotional scenes for the benefit of my family. Actors like Sathyan, Kottarakkara, and Sankaradi would travel afar with me. I am a master of facial expressions. Even when I would act out the tragic scenes, my family members would shake with laughter. Since my poor Rosarios was blind, he would laugh on hearing the laughter of others.

It would be at that juncture, when the talented actor in me would bring to life the human-animal conflict, that my eldest son Alphonse, the scholar under training, would put forth the question on genetic science: 'Appa, was the mouse male or female?'

I would be irritated at not having determined the mouse's gender. When it came to mice, it was difficult to guess grandchild or progenitor, let alone male or female! Yet I would reply like this:

'I did not check, Alphonse.'

'Likely to be female. Suppose it is a male, will it have tailless children?'

'Perhaps . . .'

Then my sightless Rosarios would sigh deeply, 'Poor creature, how it must have suffered when its tail was severed! If a hand is cut, wouldn't we hurt?'

The long-sightedness of my blind son often left me speechless. Though he could never watch my enactments, I perceived that amongst all of them, Rosarios understood me the best. Sometimes I felt that both his sightless eyes were lit up by candles.

My dearest family would talk about the next generation of tailless mice running amok among the coffins. We would have our supper. Then we would embrace one another and go to sleep.

Ah, those were just my crazy dreams!

It was on a tepid Friday that the augury had descended from the skies, accompanied by thunder and lightning.

'*Carpenter's son! Build a tent for four.*'

I built the tent without complaining. When my Beatrice and children were resting—in a coffin crafted by my own hands—in the third row of the weed-infested cemetery, with whom could I talk about the tailless mouse?

Leaving behind unceasing rains and an everlasting Good Friday, when everyone took off for the graveyard, my life was sucked into the pits of hell.

No, I do not need these unbearable memories.

I don't want to remember Appan either, the one who left after reminding me to uncomplainingly light candles before the Lord. Neither Appan nor the Lord will understand the plight of someone who wishes himself dead but is forced to continue living. If I am holding on, it is only from the desire to see a human-shaped ghoul lie inside a coffin that I have built.

With a heart that bled continually, I retreated to the coffin workshop. I found my tools and started hacking away at the wood. Collecting the chopped-up pieces, I built the world's smallest coffin. It had all the attractions of being small and beautiful.

Observing all reverence due to a corpse, I placed the tail inside and covered the top with a wooden lid. I nailed the lid in, and then carrying it on my shoulders, walked towards the southern part of the house. By the side of the shivering macaranga tree, I dug a pit with my bare hands and buried the box.

To invoke the atmosphere of an elegant funeral, I recited a requiem silently and cast a fistful of earth over the box.

'May the soul rest in peace.'

It felt as if I had buried a disgusting organ of Satan Loppo. Though a battle was raging in my mind, I felt a sense of victory. Yet, when I returned to the coffins, my mind was melancholic, like an orphan's grave. There was a trail of blood left behind by the mouse's posterior all the way to the box made for Loppo. It was the largest among all the coffins in my shop.

My life, which dragged on without anything to share with anyone, was not even worth a mouse's tail. Rather than stretching it meaninglessly, it was better to put an end to it. It could then be kept inside a box and buried in the earth to make it fertile.

Wasn't my shop a big coffin, housing someone who was long dead?

2

The Death Knell

'Vanity of vanities, saith the Preacher, vanity of vanities; all is vanity. What profit hath a man of all his labor which he taketh under the sun? One generation passeth away, and another generation cometh: but the earth abideth forever. The sun also ariseth, and the sun goeth down, and hasteth to his place where he arose. The wind goeth toward the south, and turneth about unto the north; it whirleth about continually, and the wind returneth again according to his circuits. All the rivers run into the sea; yet the sea is not full; unto the place from whence the rivers come, thither they return again.'

(Ecclesiastes 1: 2-7)

The bane of a coffin maker is the absence of a regular income. Hence, he fights a losing battle with a life lacking stability and security. A stretched calendar, seeming longer than twelve penurious months, is his working life. The black and red colour variations on the calendar hold no meaning for him and he passes through life unaffected by holidays or working days.

Coffins are not products whose sales can be increased through a special offer on Onam or Christmas, are they? Neither is a coffin shop an enjoyable tourist destination. If no one dies, a coffin maker would be easily forgotten.

I often grieve the despicable condition of having to wait for someone's death to earn my bread. A coffin maker is likely to celebrate Christmas or Easter only if some families, owing to a loved one's death, are deprived of the festivities. It cannot be any death: there is an angle of religious discrimination involved, as it has to be a Christian death!

While studying in the church-run primary school, tortured by hunger pangs, I would wish fervently for everyone to purchase coffins, irrespective of their religion. I would allay my hunger by breathing in the delectable scent of cooked meat emanating from the kitchen behind the rectory. Analysing the heady smell of the food, I would try to guess whether it was chicken curry, beef fry or mutton roast. I would close my nostrils and inhale through my mouth, as I wanted the air to reach my stomach instead of my lungs. Later on, I was disappointed to learn that air goes to the lungs whether inhaled through the nose or the mouth.

I used to drink water from the pond beyond the rectory and the kitchen. Climbing down a few steps, I would wade into knee-deep water, shove aside the shimmering green foam with my elbows, and bend down to drink straight from the pond. Since other kids scooped the water with their hands, my style of drinking invited much ridicule.

'Look, he laps up water like a buffalo!'

Having laid me on a bed of arrows tipped with the poison of their sharp-edged mockery, they bestowed on me the nickname 'Buffalo'. I never felt bad about the name-calling. When I hesitated to answer questions in class, the teachers also hailed me as 'Buffalo'. Since I ended up hearing 'Buffalo' more often than my own name, Hendri, I sometimes believed that was my true name.

But Saraswathy teacher, who taught me Malayalam, never used that nickname. Malayalam was the only subject in which I always scored well. As I loved reciting poems melodiously, she would often make me sing Changampuzha's lines: '*Aaaru vangum innaru . . .*'[*] For me, Saraswathy teacher was the incarnation of the Goddess of Letters.

Perhaps the attention she paid to my recitation triggered my fondness for reading in those days. I became acquainted with the books of Basheer, Kesavadev and Thakazhi stocked in our village library. On reading Dev's *Odayil Ninnu*[†] I wept. I adored *Pathummayude Aadu*[‡], and Karoor's *Marappavakal*[§] became a favourite. But except for Malayalam, no other subject lingered in my head.

Somehow, I managed to reach the tenth standard, but could never surmount that formidable barrier. When I failed to clear the obstacle in my second attempt, Appan told me kindly, 'You can join me now, son.'

Thereafter, language also abandoned me. My Appan's coffin shop circumscribed my life. The death knell from the nearby church became my life's tempo. Whenever the bell chimed death, a ray of hope arose in our hearts. For Appan and me, the pealing of that death bell came as auspicious tiding of the next business opportunity.

When fifteen lives were lost in a sudden landslide, we got an unexpected deal. It is indecent to refer to that as a 'deal'. Though we fished a bountiful harvest from the sea of tears of fifteen families, Appan's turbulent mind was far from peaceful. I felt uncomfortable wearing the new garments that Appan purchased to clothe my thin body. It seemed that the warp and weft of the cloth had been woven with the thread of death. My heart was heavy with the realization that it carried traces of lamentation for the departed.

---

[*] Who will buy the gift of the garden today?
[†] *From the Gutter* by P. Kesavadev
[‡] *Pathumma's Goat* by Vaikom Muhammad Basheer
[§] *Wooden Toys* by Karoor Neelakanta Pillai

When the exultations of the Perunnal[*] were cut short by the agony of a mass burial, I pondered deeply. Why did my Appan, who could not bring himself to harm an ant, turn into a coffin maker? Why did he anoint me as his heir? Had Appan pursued some other decent business, I too could have followed suit.

What could be done? My grandfather was also a coffin maker. The profession had come to me in the form of a legacy. There is no one to blame for certain facts of life. Which branch of knowledge can explain why some are born in palatial bungalows and others in squalid hovels? We can only accept it placidly. Nowadays, coffins having become an intimate part of my life, I tend to adopt the impassivity of a mature philosopher.

If not I, someone else was bound to wait with his mallet and chisel on this karmic path. It is all nature's selection.

'Indri, it is not feasible to have a world where everyone holds a top-notch job. The Lord has entrusted us with making homes for the dead. It is a holy task, my child.' Those were Appan's words to anchor my unsteady mind.

It astounded me that Appan had such an unconventional perspective on every matter. Some of that blood must be flowing in my veins too.

* * *

I have known tears, love, happiness and even the humour of life through coffins.

One of the best jokes that I enjoy in life is hiding myself behind vertically placed coffins. I imagine myself as a corpse then. It is a highly amusing flight of fancy.

While mutating into a corpse, under persuasion of an asinine mind frame, it is possible to traverse the skies and even land on the

---

[*] Feast day of the Saint

stars! Or else, one can join the cohorts of those diving beneath the seas, searching for pearls and rubies. Since ghosts are not deterred by doors or walls, the journeys are unhindered.

Nobody will believe me if I say that I have travelled in that manner. Not only have I travelled, but I have also reached my dead Appan's abode.

Anyone can travel to the land of the dead in this way. But how many, while alive, have laid down in coffins like me? After death, when they are buried in the coffins, they shall realize the worth of my words. However, they cannot return to reveal it to others. You can reach the land of ghosts only when you lie down in a coffin, unleash your mind and allow it to travel untrammelled.

If you can harden your heart a bit, there is another thing you might attempt. Especially if you bear an unsatiated vengeance inside you. You can step out of the coffin, and with your vampire fangs, step into the compound of your opponent. You can bite into the veins of his throat, suck his lifeblood and kill him!

I can state facts so objectively because I have done all of the above. In my case, there is also a dark dog destined to die a dastardly, horrific death.

Satan Loppo's pet dog.

By that time, Appan's words ring a note of restraint in my ears: 'When others harm you, light a candle before the Lord and pray . . .'

Appan's gullibility is rather hard for me to digest. But he being my father, if I dishonour him, it would be the violation of the Fifth Commandment.

Restraining myself, I transfigure back into a wretched ghost, no longer thirsting for blood, cowering behind an upright coffin. Then I stare through the crevices of the planks and view the street in front of my shop. I can see the corroded posterior of the board which proclaims 'Coffins for sale' and the human souls who walk past, ignoring it. They never see me.

When you observe the world, hidden, you can starkly comprehend its hypocrisies. How lazy human beings are! They are petty souls who fritter away their lives.

Their customs are so weird.

They are so glued to their lives that they never cast a glance at the coffins meant for them. And they live so arrogantly as if they shall never die! Yet, most human lives rust away like the board of my coffin shop.

See, someone has a cancerous growth inside him.

Another's heart is due for a failure at any moment.

That third man nearing the street corner is sure to die under a speeding vehicle.

Yet these humans . . .

The riddle about the coffin, rather popular in usage, is full of perspicacity:

'The one who needs it does not buy it, the one who buys it does not use it, the one who uses it does not know it.'

* * *

In the olden days, when I gazed at the afternoon sunshine, my Beatrice would make her way down the road with my lunch box. Unknown to her, I would watch, captivated, every sensuous movement of her body. I would be breathless with desire. Beatrice was such a beautiful woman! When she would step in with her seductive, intoxicating fragrance, I would emerge like a ghost from the coffin and pull her towards me. Her loving protests would be muffled in my close embrace.

A gorgeous woman like Beatrice should never have been the life partner of a coffin maker. Though my looks weren't all too bad, my personality was mediocre compared to hers. Her father, in dire circumstances, had proposed marriage with my family. During the formal visit to 'see the girl', I did not have the confidence to look into her face. I had stared at her in awestruck admiration from a safe distance, in the church of St. Anthony. She resembled an angel. My fear was about the angel accepting an asura who cohabited with coffins.

Yet she liked me.

It was Beatrice who showed me that the measuring stick of a woman's love was unique. The markings on that instrument, throughout its length and breadth, were unpredictable and utterly beyond a man's imagination. On the day she revealed that she liked my manly perspiration and the hands that were callused from holding the chisel, I wanted to open heaven's doors and windows for her.

In the beginning, Beatrice was afraid to look at the coffins.

'How can you live among these coffins?' she asked.

'But what is there to be scared about?' I retorted.

'Coffins mean death . . . aren't you afraid?'

'The only truth we can be sure about in life, Beatrice, is death—the inevitable reality that occurs in the lives of both the rich and the poor.'

'Whatever you say, I am terrified of both death and coffins.'

As she said that, black scorpions of dread slithered across Beatrice's fair face.

Reaching out from behind, I gently held her close. When my breath grazed her neck and my lips touched her ears, forgetting about death and coffins, Beatrice started blooming.

I kissed her ears softly and murmured, 'Were you afraid when you slept in your mother's womb, Beatrice?'

'Hardly. That is the soundest sleep.'

'When you dozed off listening to a lullaby inside the cradle, were you afraid?'

'Why fear anything then? Lying in a cradle is fun, isn't it?'

'Yes, why be afraid? A coffin keeps you safe like a womb and rocks you to sleep like a cradle. Poor coffin! Why hate it or be scared?'

While I spoke, I hugged Beatrice closer. The scent of soap, along with her body heat, intoxicated my veins.

'This is our livelihood, Beatrice,' I said.

'If people don't die, or lie inside coffins, how will we buy food? How will we pay the children's school fees? Death puts bread on our table. Death keeps us alive. So, we should not hate coffins.'

Beatrice blossomed all over and pressed softly against me.

'Are you still afraid?' I whispered into her ears tenderly.

'All my fears have gone,' she responded sweetly. 'A coffin is actually a poor creature, isn't it?'

'Yes, inside each coffin is the name of the one destined to recline within. Imagine that every coffin has a Guardian Angel allotted to it. Very beautiful angels. Anyone who sleeps inside the coffin is guarded by one. Beatrice, you are also an angel. My own Guardian Angel.'

Listening to me, Beatrice turned into the kind of beautiful sculpture depicted in the pages of the Old Testament. Smooth as wax and soft as butter, her body rested against mine. She caressed the coffin which leaned against the wall, next to us. Then she lifted her head and gently kissed it. When I saw that gesture, I embraced my angel along with the coffin and gently nibbled at her rosy lips. Beatrice slipped away from my hug and ran away like the heroine of a romantic movie. Mirroring a love-struck hero, I chased after her amongst the coffins.

Standing on the opposite sides of a vertically placed coffin, we laughed at each other through the slits. When I extended my hands, she stretched out hers too. With the casket between us, we forked our fingers together, and looked passionately at each other. Unable to control my feelings any longer, I made my way to her side and took her lovingly in my arms. We made a coffin lying on the ground our love nest.

On many occasions, we found space for two inside a coffin designed for one. All of my children—Alphonse, Roselyn and Rosarios—were probably conceived inside these coffins.

Oh Lord, then . . .

The children of the coffin returned to the same place . . .

No, I cannot think any further.

Without my Beatrice and children, the place was darker and emptier than the prison of death. Panting with fatigue, I stood behind the coffin like an undead man who was truly dead.

3

Wounds

'Now will I sing to my well beloved a song of my beloved touching his vineyard. My well beloved hath a vineyard in a very fruitful hill: And he fenced it, and gathered out the stones thereof, and planted it with the choicest vine, and built a tower in the midst of it, and also made a winepress therein: and he looked that it should bring forth grapes, and it brought forth wild grapes. And now, O inhabitants of Jerusalem, and men of Judah, judge, I pray you, betwixt me and my vineyard.'

(Isaiah 5: 1-3)

'Making boxes for the dead, you got trapped in one!'

Once again today, Antappan rained his reproaches at me.

His admonishments occur at regular intervals. He is perhaps the lone man on earth who worries about me. Even so, I was not inclined to respond. I stood silently, as if drained of energy, physically and mentally.

My silence provoked him further.

'Step out a bit or you will also end up as a corpse! Been a while since our last get-together in the cemetery, remember?'

I stood like a man who had lost count of the days.

'Say, shall we plan one today?'

I did not feel like replying even then.

'Still pig-headed? I won't come to see you again!'

Antappan turned on his heels. I knew he would take a backward glance on reaching Pundit's watch shop.

I did feel sad about what happened. How simple-minded my Antappan is! His likes and dislikes are very impulsive. Even if he goes away annoyed, raining a volley of abuses at me, he will not be able to resist visiting me again. We are two bodies but one soul, waiting to end in a single grave. Ours being a rustic bond, shorn of artificial, polished façade, if he is hurt, I feel the sting; and if I am hurt, he feels the pain. The old villagers of Aadi Nadu often chortle that we defecate through the same orifice.

In truth, we inherited our friendship. Antappan's father, Philippose, and my Appan were the best of friends. The close friendship of a coffin maker and a grave digger was replicated through us. Philipposachan and my Appan occasionally used to drink together in the graveyard at night. They would crack jokes amidst the souls around them and return with their arms around each other's shoulders, singing the popular movie song, '*Samayamam radhathil njan . . .*'*. That was the only song they sung whenever they left the cemetery. On hearing it, one recognized the homecoming from the graveyard.

For them, the graveyard was a second home, which they could enter in the middle of any night. In the course of time, both reached their ancestral resting place, accompanied by the same song. The friends were buried next to each other. Who knows whether the best pals are making merry and drinking away there too! Antappan and I have carried on the tradition laid down by our fathers. His recent visit was to express his peeve at the breakdown of the ritual.

Even though we are thick friends, Antappan is unaware of the coffins I have secretly kept aside. If I reveal the truth, I would have

---

* In the chariot of time—a song for the final journey

to disclose the reason behind it. Since that revelation would only lead to a disgrace that would heckle me till death, why bother with a confession? I am not under any obligation to convince anyone in this regard—neither the world nor God.

I suspect that God too is partial to the rich. Otherwise, would the fiends thrive like lush trees while the poor are mercilessly trodden to the ground? I could never untangle the knot of that popular proverb about the wicked flourishing like a palm tree. If you argue that after the careful tending of the tree, the trunk would be felled with a single blow at the roots, I do not have the patience to wait for God's messenger to arrive with the sharpened axe. The wounds festering inside me and the coffins earmarked for those who caused them are the only truths before me. The first wound opened on the day my darling son hurt his forehead.

* * *

A mango drops beyond a wall, a little boy picks it up. 'Who the devil?' A diabolic shout . . . That was what happened.

Stumbling in panic, our son broke his forehead, and Beatrice wept while smothering sugar over the gash. I saw the sweet specks, stained with blood, glisten red that day. But the fact that Loppo was behind the injury was hidden from me like the inner secret of a Sacrament. Beatrice trained the child to explain that he had stumbled on the door frame and hurt himself. She worried that I would pick up a fight with Loppo. Even if I didn't challenge him, I would burn with shame at my inability to do so, and that my wife found unbearable.

It was much later, when the emotions attached with that incident had cooled, my son unknowingly revealed the truth. Though I flared with indignation, I had no option but to suppress my rage. I consoled myself by interpreting my submissiveness as the divine gift of forgiveness. The clemency I showed was a smokescreen for my incapability. Mercy is the act of letting go when you can easily crush somebody. The restraint shown in fighting an undefeatable opponent is not mercy, but cowardice.

Even cowards can be stirred to aggression at times.

Once, just once in my life, losing all control, I had emerged from the slinking mudhole of my cowardice. Even now I am scalded by the tongues of fire erupting from that memory. My body drips with heavy perspiration, as if drenched by a keening night rain.

That day, work had stretched till the middle of the night. It was Satan Loppo who came to my shop and ordered a splendid coffin decorated with lace and special motifs. It was the magnanimous contribution of the local landlord for the burial of an accident victim, Anthonios. Satan Loppo insisted that his largesse be displayed prominently on the coffin. Though the villagers had scoured the surroundings, there had been no evidence of the vehicle which had come rushing into the night to mow down Anthonios.

'Damned fellow,' Loppo was vehemently cursing the driver when he arrived.

The rain had wet his shoulders despite the umbrella, and the *jubba* he wore stuck close to the body. His lips held a thick cigar, Hercules brand, which spewed curling smoke. It was an expensive, imported item.

'Anthonios needs a coffin,' Satan Loppo rasped, clouded in cigar smoke. 'Money does not matter. Make it really good.'

'How charitable,' I thought, 'and considerate he is of the destitute.'

Lured by the promise of money, I got busy giving finishing touches to the coffin. I wanted to make a nice profit by adding to the fineries. Even when the coffin was ready, the rain thundered on. I set off for home, getting thoroughly soaked, treading over the fast-flowing water on the road. In that cold and shrivelling atmosphere, thick black smoke billowed from a coconut tree struck by lightning. When I opened the front door, I saw Beatrice lying face down on the cot, weeping bitterly. The acrid smell of smoke from the burnt tree filled my nostrils.

'What's the matter?'

Beatrice did not answer my frantic query. When I lifted her chin, a thunderstorm broke inside me, spearing me with lightning. I gazed, panic stricken, at the bluish-black clot of blood on her lower lip. Realizing that I had seen it, Beatrice murmured, 'I tripped over the door frame.'

She was repeating the same lie which had been used to conceal my son's wound. The same lie, however, could not cover up two wounds.

I had caught the whiff of a strong smell in the room by then. It wasn't the smoke from the burnt tree. It was the noxious stink of a Hercules cigar that was polluting the air. My heart shuddered as if the cigar had stabbed me with its fiery end. Struck by an inner lightning, my soul separated from my body, ascended and slowly traced its way back to me as if returning to a stranger. I have been living without a soul since.

Beatrice could not stop me that night.

As I rushed out into the inebriated monsoon night, she cried helplessly.

'Please don't go. Nothing happened! He stepped on to the porch when the rain turned heavy. And then . . . ran away when the lightning struck the tree.'

Was it the Lord's own lightning sword which was sent down for her protection? Except for casting a blue-black stain, he could not sully the purity of my woman. Yet the distasteful smell of cigar on her lips caused Beatrice the same agony as of an aggravated assault. Shaking off my timidity, I kicked open Loppo's mansion gates with blood lust that night.

'You bloody swine!'

I stood challenging him, like a battle-ready bull. I had no idea that I had such inner fortitude. The fact that none of Satan Loppo's henchmen were there to aid him that night doubled my confidence.

I had a sharp chisel used for building coffins tucked away at my waist, to combat his brute strength. There was only the distance of a chisel's sharp edge standing between Satan Loppo and his death-box.

Satan Loppo did not seem in the least taken aback. I was incensed on seeing that he was openly sneering at me. Edging closer with my raised chisel, I unleashed a hurricane from within, aiming for Satan Loppo's stomach.

'Hitler . . .'

That was all I heard.

Satan Loppo's German hound, spawn of a demon, bounded towards me and sank its monstrous teeth into my right leg. It was a devil's grip which would not let go until the victim died. When its fangs pierced the shin bone and reached the marrow, all my vengeance oozed out through the wound and I thrashed around in mortal agony.

The hound had bitten through my veins and I could not defend myself. As my lifeblood splattered on the ground, I, who would get dizzy at the sight of blood, became faint with weakness. When the bone-shattering pain overwhelmed me, Satan Loppo called out again.

'Hitler.'

The hound let go of my leg as if a switch had been turned off.

The drooling tongue flicked, tasting human blood.

Blood dripped relentlessly from my leg and the dog's mouth. The dog continued to snarl menacingly at me, as if possessed by the evil spirit of an extremely malevolent dictator. Its name was apt.

I had rushed in like a mad elephant and by twice hailing 'Hitler', Satan Loppo had tranquillized me. As I struggled to stand steadily, Loppo spat contemptuously on the ground.

'Pthbuu! Do you know why I am sparing you, filthy dog? I shall need many more coffins in the future. And you shall make all of them! I am hell bent on ordering the coffins of my enemies! That includes the one which you made today.'

At the thought of death, far agonizing than a dog's bite, I froze. Burning both inside and out, I limped my way back in the torrential rain.

When Antappan found me, I was wandering about lost, leaving a betraying trail of blood behind me.

I lied to him that a street dog had bitten my leg, causing the deep wound. How could I disclose to him that my Beatrice's purity had been tainted by Satan Loppo's bite? Beatrice is an angel. I am determined that no one should denigrate her even in their thoughts. Hence, I cannot share the reckless adventure of setting out to wreak vengeance on Satan Loppo with anyone else. It stays as a dark deal between Loppo and me. It shall continue to be so until one of us loses his life.

Even when the bite wound healed, it affected my stride, and I betrayed a permanent limp.

Yet, the first thing I did, on walking to my shop, was to create a death trap for my sworn enemy. A vitriolic hatred took hold of me, embittering me to the tip of my tongue. Like a vengeful serpent, I accumulated that venom within my glands. At a fitting time, I would send my enemy back to the abode of Lucifer by spitting that poison into his veins.

How quickly had I, who hated to hurt even an ant, sunk to a perverse sinner! What had happened to the holy dictums that I often preached? When I chipped away with my mallet and chisel, carving out the humungous death container, a mad obsession stretched taut my shoulder bones. In those intense moments, I imagined that every slash of the chisel and every smash of the mallet were assaults on Satan Loppo's body. Except for the images of my bitterly weeping Beatrice and son, all the remnants of my sanity were forcefully banished.

Life has become an inexorable wait for my enemy's death. Despising myself, and withdrawing into myself, I have been lying in wait for Loppo since that day.

It is that unfounded belief, that Satan Loppo's lifeless body shall one day lie inside the tomb that I have created for him, that has sustained me over the years. Why can't the Lord, who could turn even water into wine, perform a minor miracle for me? If a poor coffin maker infers in his frenzied moments that even the Lord is biased towards the rich, can he be blamed for it?

* * *

Satan Loppo, with his head held high, visited my shop umpteen times afterwards. Every word and glance from him were hurled like knives at me.

He could easily purchase coffins from Joppan's shop in the west market. In fact, he crosses that shop on his way to mine. Yet, for a perverse kick, he travels to my shop and commands me to sell him coffins. Unable to fight him, I surrender abjectly, with my tail between my legs. Any attempt to stand up against him would attract the attention of others and tarnish Beatrice's purity. Even otherwise, I do not have the wherewithal to react. The very memory of my mangled leg makes me weak and dizzy.

So, I end up labouring like a helpless slave and craft the coffins which Satan Loppo demands, even when vengefulness foams inside me. My mind laments that my coffins are reaching the homes of 'accident' victims. Even when that isn't the case, I cannot bring myself to believe it.

Satan Loppo is an evil soul infested with sickening thoughts. One day, he shall appear in front of me and demand a coffin for a dead man called Hendri. He will be the epitome of generosity while insisting that the coffin be decorated with lace and motifs, regardless of the cost.

Before that happens, I shall . . .

Lord, was it to ensure that no evil eye fell on your perfect creation that you affixed on my body a life that cannot utter even a word of resistance?

The mighty do as they please. What can the lily-livered do except wait for an opportune moment? I shall continue to wait. Like Samson the Israelite, trapped in the dark dungeon of his blindness, I shall wait for my moment of retribution.

4

The Pool's Secret

'If only my anguish could be weighed, and all my misery be placed on the scales. It would surely outweigh the sand of the seas—no wonder my words have been impetuous. The arrows of the Almighty are in me, my spirit drinks in their poison; God's terrors are marshaled against me. Does a wild donkey bray when it has grass, or an ox bellow when it has fodder? Is tasteless food eaten without salt, or is there flavor in the sap of the mallow? I refuse to touch it; such food makes me ill.'

(Job 6: 2-7)

The horrid, grating noise of metal woke me up with a start in the middle of the night. When I peeked out through the door, I saw a demoniac vehicle straddling the road, before trundling away. I was bemused whether a war—which was something other countries experienced—had descended upon the village of Aadi Nadu. It alarmed me that a police jeep was escorting that monstrous vehicle. If the devilish vehicle waved one of its claws, my coffin shop would be shattered. Never in my life had I seen such a strange vehicle. Its metal armours, flashing emergency lights and rasping rollers were intolerable.

I held my breath until it turned the corner, crossing Pundit's watch shop. I recalled that over the past few days, the branches of trees extending on to the street had been lopped off and sagging electricity wires tightened. They had even shifted a few electric posts. It was clear that these preparations were made in expectation of the iron-ogre's arrival. What then was the aim of this night trip? It seemed to be an ill portent, considering the reckless way it moved.

I could not sleep that night. Overcome with anxiety, I yearned for dawn so that I could discuss the monstrous vehicle with another human being. My mind was turbulent when David stepped inside my shop around forenoon, with a casual greeting: 'Uncle, how are you?' It was hardly twenty-four hours since Antappan had showered me with curses. It was good that father and son had not arrived together. The growing distance between them had become all too evident over the past few years.

I smiled at David.

'You seem to be terribly busy nowadays?'

'Yes, lots of work at the bungalow.'

'What sort of work?'

'Cannot divulge the goings-on in Muthalali's bungalow. Strict orders!' David grinned at me.

It had disturbed me no end when David became Satan Loppo's driver and then turned into his acolyte. On the day that he drove the lorry named Dragon, I heard a crackle inside me, as if the veins of my heart had started to rupture. Yet I could not dissuade him from the relationship with Satan Loppo. He needed a job to sustain himself. All he had inherited from his grave-digger father was a dilapidated hut on the outskirts of the village, wherein reigned the goddess of poverty. If he thought that there was nothing to be gained from the ancestral occupation, and was fascinated by Satan Loppo's gleaming money, I could not blame David. I had seen the airs he put on, pretending to be a close confidante of his Muthalali.

Recently I had relinquished the assumption that David's frequent visits were due to his fondness for me. It dawned on me rather late that he was interested in the girl working in the tailor shop opposite.

Shari is a decent girl. However, Antappan has been at loggerheads with David since his girl isn't from a Christian household.

I consider Antappan's son as my own. I was there in church when he was christened David. How can I forget the way he bawled that day, attracting the attention of the churchgoers as well as the angels above? It was an auspicious time when the blessed saints—depicted in the paintings on the church's ceiling—bestowed their noble glances on those beneath. During a child's baptism, it is said, heaven descends to earth.

But Gracy Mamma, the grand old doyenne of Aadi Nadu, had a different take: 'Ah, the devil's intervention! That's why the child screams.'

I could not believe that the devil would interfere with church matters. Had things turned as disorderly as that? Gracy Mamma declared that the devil, abhorring the fact that the child would soon walk the godly path, was upsetting him to prevent the baptism. Closing my eyes for a moment, I prayed that the crying child's heart opened to the blessings of heaven. I chanted the benediction to the Holy Ghost to step down from the skies and grace him. Instantaneously, little David, safe in the arms of his godmother, started smiling sweetly, as if seeing angels. How can I be separated from David, who became a part of my life with that toothless smile?

Yet that David ended up in the clutches of the man I hated the most. Perhaps because he trusted David, Satan Loppo had allowed him access to his secret hideout. That was how I came to hear about the mysterious goings-on inside the forbidding four walls of his house.

It was a bungalow gifted by the Sayyip—the white man—to Jerome, who worked as his pimp, before he left the country. It was a reward for setting up an environment for his carnal sins. Later, Satan Loppo, who had a similar propensity, had purchased that property. Only the most trusted cronies were allowed entrance inside that place concealed by massive stone walls. The villagers had never seen the architecture of that bungalow.

The guard dog was brought in by air from Germany in a special air-conditioned container. Eight German cows arrived as companions via ship, in air-conditioned containers. Loppo built air-conditioned cow sheds for those bovines. Like the others, I too was curious about the morbid mysteries inside Loppo's bungalow. However, I could do nothing about it except to return half-dead, after being bitten by the German hound, when I set off to exact revenge.

'That dog cannot sleep without air conditioning.'

When David blurted this out, I was initially disinclined to believe it. I helplessly glanced at my right foot. The revulsive remnant of a past nightmare lay indelibly imprinted as a scar. No one knew that it was the German hound's gift to me. I hid the truth from everyone by lying that a street dog had bit me. When well-wishers advised me to visit a hospital to avoid a possible rabies infection, I contained myself by throttling that hell hound in my imagination.

The dog, which was born in Germany, preferred a cold climate. That was why Loppo had emptied an air-conditioned room for its stay. The comforts in that room would have stoked the jealousy of Aadi Nadu's pariah dogs sky high. There was a mattress to lie down on and a sanitized plate for its food. David sniggered that the toilet-trained dog was fastidious about its cleanliness. Its intelligence was more acute than that of humans. When David announced that the dog belonged to a breed which fetched lakhs of rupees in international markets, I wondered whether I would fetch a miniscule part of that amount if auctioned off in a sale. I felt a sharp envy for the dog that was more valuable than a human being.

'Better to be born as a German hound then,' I commented wryly when David waxed eloquent about the dog.

One could live a royal life, enjoying delicious repast, without much responsibilities. Just by wagging the tail and barking occasionally to please the master, one could enjoy a nutritious breakfast, growth-enhancing vitamins, and the freedom to sit anywhere without restrictions! Aren't those the same traits we observe in those who jostle in the backrooms of power? There were so many helmsmen who felt a wag start from an unseen tail at the bottom of their spines when they saw Satan Loppo.

The dog with German citizenship did not have a mate. The lack of a female affected its male glands acutely. The frenzy exhibited by the dogs of Kerala in the month of September, the German hound displayed as early as July. As per its German genetic disposition, the month for lust must have coincided with the July weather of the Malayalam-speaking land.

Satan Loppo was quick to notice the sexual frustrations of his dog due to his matchless expertise in the field. He never observed any discrimination on the grounds of religion or caste when it came to releasing his own tensions. Since it was not possible to procure a German bitch, Satan Loppo stuck to his own practice of arranging for a local substitute.

The poor bitch panicked on seeing the size and attitude of the foreign hound. But there was no escape. Like the Portuguese who had arrived to conquer the land, raising the flagpole, the German dog chased after the creature. The bitch tried every route to flee that compound. It tried, unsuccessfully, to wriggle through the gate and jump over the walls. The colossal stone wall, with its sky-high arrogance, defeated the creature's efforts. Finally, after a bloody battle, the foreign power hoisted its victory flag over the local land. Satan Loppo relished the episode thoroughly. On account of the dog displaying the true colours of his master, in due course, three mixed-breed puppies were born outside the gates.

Whenever I meet street children with traces of Satan Loppo on their visages, I remember the cross-bred puppies.

A dog and a master of the same breed!

Every time such thoughts rise in me, I feel an equal measure of hatred for the dog as I feel for his master. I have sworn to destroy the abominable creature which crippled me. I wish to bash in its horrid fangs and shatter that leering face. Once, I thought of throwing poisoned meat inside the compound. However, I recollected David speaking about the dog declining all temptations of the flesh, except his own home-cooked special meals, and retreated from that strategy.

It was not just the dog but also the cows belonging to Satan Loppo who had artificially cooled sheds. They were fine breed cattle, purchased from abroad, by his only son Timothios who worked in Germany. Timothios occasionally visited Aadi Nadu, showing off his foreign grandeur. No one in Aadi Nadu had a clue about what he was doing in Germany to make him so filthy rich. I presumed he must have attained success owing to his mother Philomenamma's pure heart. Otherwise, the fruit sprouting from Satan Loppo's terminator seed would have also exhibited a destructive streak.

'Uncle, what are you thinking about?' David interrupted my ruminations.

'Nothing.'

'Annoyed that I did not tell you the secret?'

I was, but pretended otherwise.

'Well, if you promise not to tell anyone . . . There is an artificial pool inside the bungalow.'

'Pool?'

'Yes, the one which the Sayyip enjoyed to the hilt. The earth digger was for deepening that.'

The secret behind the mysterious vehicle which had terrified me at night was disclosed.

'There is another marvel being installed using cranes. A suite which can be lowered inside the water.'

'Suite? What do you mean, suite?'

'Like a room in our houses. Chairs, tables, bed . . . Muthalali's son sent it from Germany.'

I listened open-mouthed with wonder at what David narrated. The suite worked on electricity and floated on water like a boat. Once you entered it, closed the door and switched on the electricity, it would dive to the depths and station itself there.

After the work was completed, Satan Loppo would travel to the ends of the water for his drinks and amusement. When the water received him, there would be no trace of the suite's existence. Through the glass walls one could kiss the fish swimming about. David frightened me by mentioning that poisonous snakes, flashing multiple colours, were present in the pond. I imagined Satan Loppo as another venomous serpent slithering among the snakes.

Lord, which of them would be more deadly?

Being terrified of snakes, I immediately prayed to St. George and promised a small contribution to the divine coffers to overcome my agitation.

To hide my fear, I cracked a weak joke.

'Vamana could have banished Mahabali to a similar container, what do you say, David?'

'Oh yes.' David grinned at me.

I surmised that 'Pathal',* invisible to human eyes, might be a container buried inside the earth. A lyrical article in Malayalam that we had studied in the ninth standard stirred in my memory. It had played a significant role in making me a lifelong fan of King Mahabali. While perusing those captivating lines, which I learnt by heart, I would wish to possess similar writing skills. I also made a few futile attempts in that direction.

I used to scribble my lines on the middle pages of my Malayalam notebook; easy to rip away. Saraswathy teacher happened to notice them and praised my linguistic abilities in the class. This made me momentarily dream that I might become a writer someday. My confidence stemmed from the truth that my most beloved author, Vaikom Mohammad Basheer who wrote *Pathummayude Aadu, Shabdangal* and *Premalekhanam,* was not highly educated.

Fool . . .

---

* Netherworld

It never struck me that there were no coffin makers who were writers. The only one who could have been one was me. But after failing the tenth standard examinations, renouncing both language and the desire to write, I was anointed as my father's successor in the coffin business.

In my wild imagination, I visualized Satan Loppo's suite as a giant coffin. As if in a motion picture, I enjoyed watching him suffocate to death inside it.

After two days when I saw David, I noticed that he seemed to be on edge.

'What's wrong?' I inquired.

'I'm feeling suffocated because I haven't told anyone yet!'

'About what?'

'When we dug up Muthalali's pool, we saw human skeletons!'

'Skeletons?'

'Yes . . . seven in number.'

'Lord.' I was thunderstruck. I burnt in the agony of not knowing who it was that lay buried within the depths of the pool. Who would have been the brutal murderer who pushed them inside the cavernous death pit?

'The skeletons were old and decayed . . . almost disintegrated. Well, to avoid any legal wrangles, Muthalali bribed the police.'

Suddenly I had a flash of intuition. Appan used to narrate an event related to the freedom struggle. It was about the unexpected disappearance of a group of young revolutionaries, seven in number. The viceroy was supposed to visit the Sayyip's bungalow for his recreation and the young men had heard the news. They conspired against the viceroy and set off to complete their plan. No one in Aadi Nadu heard of them again.

As per the news, Satan Loppo was planning to establish his playhouse by digging away the same mud which had accepted the bodies of the revolutionaries. I wanted to announce it to the whole world. But David restrained me.

'Uncle, please don't! Muthalali knows that apart from him, I am the only one privy to that information. Anyway, what's the use of digging up the past now?'

I silently mourned the seven souls who had vanished in time.

Since he was confident of my silence, after the lapse of a week, David excitedly gabbled away about the completion of the water suite. I saw that he was bursting with pride at being the right-hand man of a Muthalali who possessed a home under the water. Apparently, there was an emergency switch to make the contraption ascend in case something went wrong with it. David was hopeful that one day he would be entrusted with the manipulation of all those intricacies.

'There is a bar inside the room.'

The open craving in David's face disturbed me.

'The best foreign brands are stocked there. I went under the water yesterday with all of Muthalali's stuff. I was offered foreign scotch that I never could have dreamt of tasting in my life. Uncle, I have no words to explain the sheer pleasure . . . it is nothing like our local brands.'

David's face reddened as if he was diving inside a wine jar. As he struggled to articulate the intoxication he had felt, I soberly remembered the sour local toddy his father and I had gulped down, seated on a gravestone in the cemetery. We had never touched foreign liquor in our lives. If Loppo had condescended to give such expensive drinks to David, it meant that Loppo had accepted him into his inner circle.

The shameful fact was that, fired up by all those extravagant descriptions, I felt a stirring of desire to board that water suite myself. It was not meant for a poverty-stricken man like me. Forget the suite, setting foot inside Satan Loppo's compound was a forbidden venture.

I loathed stepping inside that foul man's house anyway! Once I had stormed my way in there, only to return hobbling. Now, in my helpless state, it was a sin to think about the pond and the room which would descend into its depths.

Whenever I imagined Loppo, liquor within and liquid outside, ecstatically watching the swimming creatures through his glass doors, an intense jealousy galled me. Those like Loppo, given to celebrating conquests, would be few even among real devils. Though the name of the man who reigned over both fertile properties and female bodies was Satan Loppo, he was more privileged than cherubs in heaven.

What about me? My life's goodness has been buried under the dead earth.

My God, my God, why do you sow seeds of injustice in fields that are ill-suited?

5

Pundit's Watch Shop

'Jonah had gone out and sat down at a place east of the city. There he made himself a shelter, sat in its shade and waited to see what would happen to the city. Then the Lord God provided a leafy plant and made it grow up over Jonah to give shade for his head to ease his discomfort, and Jonah was very happy about the plant. But at dawn the next day God provided a worm, which chewed the plant so that it withered. When the sun rose, God provided a scorching east wind, and the sun blazed on Jonah's head so that he grew faint. He wanted to die, and said, "It would be better for me to die than to live."'

(Jonah 4: 5-8)

Antappan did not visit me for many days. I don't think he has progressed to such an extent as to harden his heart against me. When Antappan left in a huff, after having quibbled in front of my shop, my own heart started murmuring mutinously. 'Come on, time to step out now,' I told myself. Isn't it natural to feel stronger when you deliberate with the hand over the heart?

After ages, that was how I decided to step out of the precincts of the coffin shop.

One of the streetlights, standing guard in the night, flickered on and off intermittently, as if it were jolting awake after dozing off. Shashankan had left after shutting his shop. Though the environment was suitably desolate for my sojourn, I kept to the dark side of the street, not wanting to be seen. The neighbouring watch shop's bulb was still burning. The oldest watch shop in that area, it had a board dangling in front that said *Pundit's Watch Works*.

I know the owner only as 'Pundit' and have no clue what his real name is, even after all these years. Ever since I have known, the old man has been addressed as Pundit by everyone around. Though I have often felt that it is a name at odds with a Christian, I can't exactly pinpoint the reason behind it. I have heard that the owner was an ardent fan of Pandit Nehru during the Independence movement and later named his shop 'Pundit's Watch Works' to commemorate that memory. There is another story: that Pundit was a member of Subhas Chandra Bose's Indian National Army.

As I scurried along, I could not help peeping inside the brightly-lit shop. Pundit was hard at work even at that hour, bent over the table. The magnifying glass, worn over the left eye like a monocle, was straight out of a yesteryear detective movie. What was incomprehensible to me was why the man worked so hard even in his declining years.

Pundit lifted his face and saw me through the glassless right eye. I tried to slink away sheepishly but did not succeed. Without removing the monocle, Pundit ushered me in with a wave of his hand. I could not dawdle any more.

In the shop where hung hundreds of clocks, I entered hesitantly, like a man out of step with time. The rhythmic tick-tock was as surreal as earth's heartbeat itself. Most of the clocks were antique. A few, devoid of the strength to keep pace, carried the burden of time wearily. Suddenly, as if to announce my arrival to one another, all of them started ringing together. It was a mélange of tunes.

'Did you hear that welcome song?' Pundit asked with a smile.

I stood dumb, an insignificant mortal on the face of earth, undeserving of any welcome.

Each clock was announcing hoarsely that it was eight o'clock!

The uncorroborated village gossip was that Pundit was at least one hundred and twelve years old. All the inhabitants of Aadi Nadu, including me, were witness to the fact that Pundit's five children had enjoyed full lives and died of old age. He has a troop of grandchildren, great-grandchildren and their offspring. The centenarian has set up residence inside the watch shop for many years now, conversing lovingly with his clocks. One of his many grandchildren provides him food regularly. There is nothing wrong either with his sight or his hearing. In the midst of the ancient clocks inside that archaic watch shop, Pundit's heart, too, beats like an old pendulum.

The world has changed; no one goes in search of a watch shop anymore. Who cares about getting his watch repaired in this busy new world? Most people prefer automatic watches on their wrists. Besides, people of Aadi Nadu can be seen with mobile phones held close to their ears, chatting away all day. The need for torches, cameras and inland letters disappeared after the arrival of mobiles; and the same is true of watches too. Probably Pundit and I are the only two human beings without that instrument in Aadi Nadu. Sometimes, though, people bring their old clocks to Pundit. Even in his hundred and twelfth year, Pundit applies himself to repairing them with total dedication. As if he had the 'key of time' with him, the time machines follow Pundit's diktats implicitly.

One similarity between us is that we are both reticent. Perhaps Pundit has a soft corner for someone who lives a solitary life like himself. He has witnessed the deaths of his wife, his children, their spouses and many more. In the history of the world, there will be few like him who have endured the deaths of so many close relatives in a single lifetime. Long life bestows that fate on a human being. There is nobody from Pundit's generation still alive. It is an existential dilemma when everyone around is several generations younger.

Those who cannot find compatible people to interact with, being unable to forge attachments, are likely to be lonely. Who knows whether this was the reason behind Pundit's decision to limit himself to his watch shop? Maybe he is the oldest living person in the world, having seen many a generation come and go. Neither he nor the world realizes it though! If he proceeds in this manner, Pundit might reach the ultimate limit of a human life: hundred and twenty years.

I was gaping at the different types of time machines in that shop. Though he had a wide collection of clocks, Pundit was never seen wearing a watch on his wrist. Does the keeper of time need a watch of his own?

As I stood deliberating, Pundit requested me to take a seat.

It was then that I noticed that Pundit was examining the internal organs of a clock on his worktable. It looked like a body from which the heart had been plucked out. Some clock wheels, tiny springs, metal pieces and other accoutrements were scattered on the table.

Seeing my doubting look, Pundit quipped, 'The heart and liver of an old clock. I am trying to see if the heart might beat again. Just for curiosity's sake.'

His voice indicated no ailments attributable to a hundred-and twelve-year-old man. I merely listened and did not respond.

'These are the internal organs of a grandfather clock,' Pundit continued.

'As ancient as that?'

Pundit laughed on hearing my silly question.

'Any clock taller than six feet is called a grandfather clock. Anything between four and six feet is referred to as a grandmother clock. There is also a granddaughter clock. Its height is less than four feet. I am trying to give life to this grandfather. Not sure if it will work! The brains are a total mess. Clocks, too, are like humans. Once the brain gets afflicted, it loses sense of time. But I don't feel like giving up.'

On seeing me looking intently at the clock, Pundit resumed his speech. 'What has been designed inside this clock is as intricate and complicated as the interior of a human body. One cannot help admiring the white men, the Sayyips of yore. I am trying to transplant some organs with the material available with me.'

I grinned. The interactions of laconic people are bound to be brief. It was time to exhibit some encouragement from my side.

I liked the simile which Pundit used: *Every human being was a clock.* Every clock was a dead body hanging on a nail, its life having escaped the noose of time when the heart stopped beating. The way they ticked together was a cadence which resonated at intervals: *Body, be not proud. Life, be not proud.*

I attempted to read the labels on the clocks.

SETH THOMAS, USA.

I managed to unravel the yellowing English letters on the clock nearby.

'That one is older than me,' Pundit said, 'the other one was purchased by my grandfather from Madras. He bought it from Khalid Yusuf Brothers. It has a history attached to it. A history which saw me become a repairer of time! See, there is an exquisite mechanical arrangement which indicates thirty-one days. Every night, sharp at twelve, the movement occurs. Now, that is much tougher than a digital clock. My uncle inherited the clock purchased by my grandfather. His sons discarded it as scrap when it became faulty. Since it was associated with my grandfather's precious memory, I assumed ownership of it. When it came into my possession, the small needle was stuck between 9 and 10, while the big one was stranded at 7. An irretrievable moment in time, frozen forever! Since I loved my grandfather very much, I wished to retrieve that memory. It was by rectifying that clock that I turned into a surgeon of time! Did you see its numbers? I, II, III: in that Roman number pattern, instead of IV, it is inscribed IIII. There are more oldies here: Japanese Seikosha, American Ansonia and such . . .'

In those living moments when I was cohabiting with the clocks, I almost forgot myself. I felt that ending up in the watch shop was not a mere coincidence and it would lead to something which would redefine me. If I left that place, deep-rooted agonies would instantaneously snake around me. I wanted to stay put in the shop. But life had never bestowed me with the authority to make such choices.

'Don't you attend the prayer sessions any more? Those conducted by Mother Gabriel?' When Pundit asked that question unexpectedly, I felt flustered, as if I had slipped down from the branch of time.

'Not for a long time now.'

'If you wish, you can continue, perhaps . . .?'

I wondered about the turn in conversation. It was a swift journey from 'time' to 'prayer'. I could not respond as the question brought back repressed memories. My mind bid goodbye to Pundit's watch shop even before I did. Following my mind, I too walked out.

On reaching the church steps after a long time, I gazed at the Holy Cross with its hands spread wide, embracing the skies. How many times have I bowed before you, and how many times have I kissed you, dear cross?

In between the cross and the collection box was an 'Ardhana petti', aka 'The Box of Appeals'. In it, the representations to heaven were posted. The box was part of a quaint history that only Aadi Nadu could lay claim to. Whenever I saw the Ardhana petti carrying heartfelt yearnings influencing the lives of Aadi Nadu, I remembered Saint Gabriel. This box, with its pact with the soul, could narrate many tales of tears and woes.

For the villagers of Aadi Nadu, the fact that Father Gabriel, or Gabriel Acchan of the parish, and Mother Gabriel, or Gabriel Amma of the convent, had the same name was amusing. We celebrated the coincidence as if Saint Gabriel had assumed both male and female forms while coming to our area. Father Gabriel, the parish priest, was like the caretaker of salvation, being filled with the grace of benevolence. His voice sounded feminine, but when he melodiously sang the Qurbana, I found it charming. When certain missionaries recite the Qurbana, my mediocre mind wishes for a quick ending and wanders wildly.

For us, Mother Gabriel's arrival was equivalent to receiving the blessings of heaven. She showcased her zealous missionary spirit by organizing a prayer group. As a prelude, she established the Box of Appeals next to the church of Saint Anthony, the saviour of Aadi Nadu. Anybody who had tasted life's bitter draught could submit his grievance within it. The box would be opened only on Thursdays. All group members who were present would beseech the Holy One, who calmed the seas and the storms, on behalf of the applicant. There was a rule that details of the petitioner should not be publicized by the prayer group members. All the group members were expected to fast on Thursdays.

Obeying my Appan's instructions, I had attended the evening prayer sessions, after fasting during the day. Instead of fatigue, an inexplicable energy used to course through me. That was how I came to realize that the main reason behind the intensity of hunger was the awareness of missed meals. The impact on someone with no meal to hope for would be deadly! More than the body, it was the mind's desolation that kindled hunger. Consequently, when we feed the hungry, not only his stomach, but the One Mind which encompasses his mind and ours gets satisfied too.

But I was shocked by the disaster which awaited Mother Gabriel, who tirelessly endeavoured to make our lives fulfilling. A few years after the prayer sessions began, a debilitating knee pain took hold of Mother. Initially she ignored it, but diagnosis revealed festering pus inside. Even after the amputation of her leg, seated on her wheelchair, Mother continued to transmit her indomitable will power to the Lord. Her disability only strengthened her resolve, leading to far more intense prayers for many more people.

'I begged for this wheelchair. This is my share of His suffering,' Mother murmured, looking at us, who were caught in anxiety's inescapable noose.

'Love, compassion and suffering encompass all ages. Anyone, in any age, can find his way to Him through these paths. Do you know why He had to die after enduring such excruciating suffering? He compassionately took on Himself the sins of all who approached Him: the crippled, the deaf, the paralyzed and the destitute. Since that was against the law of nature, He had to suffer their pain in His own body. Martyrs in many revolutions underwent similar experiences.'

Those were words which could burn you the moment you heard them! I could never have expected that perspicacity from someone confined within the boundaries of a convent. In my life, I had heard a comparable, scorching statement only from my Appan. When Appan uttered the lines, in the guise of a folk song, it imprinted itself into my consciousness with the sharp edge of an ancient writing tool.

> *'Petti, petti, nalla shinkara petti*
> *Petti thurakumbol kayam manakkum.'*
> *'Box, the box, so very alluring:*
> *An asafoetida smell on opening.'*

Just two sentences, easy to memorize, sung in an upbeat tempo! Since I had a natural proclivity to singing, I absorbed the lyrics like a sponge.

'Hendri, do you know the meaning of those lines?' my Appan asked me like a master examiner.

'Er . . .' I was stumped. It sprung to my mind that it could be the box of asafoetida used for making sambhar, and I eagerly blurted out the answer.

'Wrong,' Appan smiled broadly.

'Then it must be a jewellery box.'

'There might be fools who think like that. Wrong again.'

My meagre brain could not unlock the key to the puzzle. Something flashed in my brain and I ventured:

'Is it a coffin?'

'You are getting closer to the answer.'

'Then what is it?' I could not contain my curiosity.

'Deeper meanings might hide in trivialities.'

'What meaning?'

'Imagine a body in the place of a box.'

'Can we open a body?' I gasped in wonder.

'If I say yes, you might not appreciate it now. When you acquire understanding, Appan will explain.'

I became agitated imagining an open body baring bloodied kidneys, liver, heart and intestines. But the promise that the secret of the open body would be revealed one day remained unfulfilled. Leaving behind a riddle, Appan went journeying to the churchyard in a coffin which he had crafted himself. Appan, who had built coffins for different generations, was buried in the cemetery's backyard, which was overrun by scraggly weeds. The rich had auctioned to themselves the front yard and the stone graves.

Satan Loppo had taken over the cemetery's front row for his family vault at an exorbitant price. He bargained for prominence both in the cemetery and the church. After accumulating coffers of sin, he and his heirs would sleep there.

I often wonder whom the Lord shall prefer on his right on Judgment Day: the wealthy souls who sleep in stone vaults, or the poor who are received by the earth? Dear Lord, who bestowed hell fire for the rich man and offered redemption for the beggar Lazarus, whatever be the ways of your divine justice, please let my poor Appan and Beatrice stand on your right. Let my innocent children be by their side, holding on to their hands.

My fate is one I am unsure of.

If I reach the Lord's presence with the stain of having violated the Fifth Commandment, He will have no other option but to order me to stand on his left and condemn me to hell fire. I know that while doing so, His eyes would be overflowing with tears and His body would be sweating blood.

'I have set my rainbow in the clouds, and it will be the sign of the covenant between me and the earth.'

Lord, I am waiting still, not having opened my body. Appan will surely arrive one day to unlock the inner secret of the alluring box. On that day, dearest Lord, bless me with the vision of your dwelling place.

Glory to my father, the maker of coffins.

6

The Well of Bones

'My enemies speak evil of me: "When will he die, and his name
perish?" And if he comes to see me, he speaks lies; his heart gathers
iniquity to itself. When he goes out, he tells it. All who hate me
whisper together against me; against me they devise my hurt. "An evil
disease," they say, "clings to him. And now that he lies down, he will
rise up no more." Even my own familiar friend in whom I trusted,
who ate my bread, has lifted up his heel against me.'

(Psalm 41: 5-9)

Perhaps it is the similarity of our trades that holds fast the soul
connection between Antappan and me. I am the coffin maker and
Antappan, the grave digger. The glue that binds us together is the
corpse that connects the coffin to the grave.

Isn't that a special kind of chemistry?

Antappan was four years senior to me at school, but dropped out
after sixth standard and started assisting his father at the cemetery.
I left school much later, after the tenth standard. It was Appan who
insisted that I study till tenth standard, saying, 'All that education
might come in handy, son!'

Since I studied at the church-run school, during the lunch breaks when I went hungry, I would visit Antappan in the cemetery. Sometimes, sitting there, we would share his meagre lunch of boiled tapioca and crushed green chillies. That was the most exquisite taste I had experienced until Beatrice stepped into my life. After marriage, how many times must I have recaptured that taste by asking her to prepare the boiled tapioca and chilli mixture!

Along with digging graves, Antappan doubles as a caretaker of the cemetery. His apprenticeship with his father started with clearing the grass over the graves. He was careful not to let the marauding weeds take over the graveyard. Not only that, he also made a small garden by planting flowers in that aridness. He said the corpses should feel like having a sound repose on seeing the place.

Having seen from a young age lifeless bodies arriving for their eternal sleep, he not only lost all fear of corpses, but also developed an empathy for them. *Antappan's view was that dead bodies weren't scary, and one needed to be afraid only of human beings whose souls were dead.*

True, man is the only living being that betrays with a smile!

When his father fell ill, the responsibility of the cemetery and its inhabitants came to rest on Antappan's shoulders. He carried out those heavy duties with utmost earnestness. Like a man possessed of a vast field of his own, he toiled on the 'Land of the Dead'. He dug holes, planting the corpses as seeds. For him they were the 'Trees of Life', which would bloom again on the Day of Judgement.

Some rich people offered money to the humble gravedigger during the burial of their relatives. Or they paid him tips when he cleared up graves before death anniversaries. Antappan was adept at making attractive square-shaped partitions with sparkling pebbles and white sand. Those who wished for special decorations for the graves, to impress the onlookers, paid a visit to Antappan. Whenever he made extra money, Antappan would invariably make an appearance outside my coffin shop in the evening.

'Indri, tonight we should have a get-together.'

A get-together did not mean the luxury of a sophisticated bar or even a toddy shop. We would walk to the cemetery with a bottle of the local brew. There is no other place on earth that has such peace and serenity. The burial ground does not possess the egotism of guarding the royal sleep of great heroes. An open space, unhindered by huge trees, is the most attractive feature of the cemetery. Two close friends could spend time there, listening to the chirping of the crickets and smelling the periwinkles also known as the corpse-stink flowers.

We would sit atop a grave in which the dead slept, and guzzle liquor in the potent presence of the souls. Before starting the drinking ceremony, Antappan would indulge in a rite dedicated to both our fathers. My Appan had gone away first, followed by Antappan's father. Antappan had been vigilant about burying them side by side. Although he loved his father a lot, he had dug the grave without much grief. It was as if he was gently guiding his father to another room in the house to lie down. Later, after he buried his father next to mine, Antappan wept on my shoulder: 'Let both friends sleep shoulder to shoulder. Unknown to others, I have opened up a little byway between the graves.'

Whenever we got together for our drinks, Antappan would pour an ounce each in two coconut shells for both the fathers. It was a prayer. Then, before clinking our glasses together, we would wish peace to the new soul, the one which had added its name to the Book of Death that day.

This one for Clément's eternal peace.

This for Clara's repose.

When Antappan gulped down his drink after his toasts, I would cooperate heartily. At frequent intervals, he would ask questions about those for whose purported happiness we were drinking. He would ask the questions, and also provide the answers. I was just supposed to give him company. He hates drinking alone. Neither have I shared drinks with anyone else. Truth is, for me, the get-togethers with Antappan were as much a ritual as the Sunday Qurbana.

We would stay in the cemetery, unknown to others, till the wee hours. It is not correct to say that it was not known to others. My Appan, Antappan's father and many other erstwhile lives were our witnesses. Since we were aware of that, we would make our way through that dark, ghostly yard to the spot where both our fathers slept and pray silently before departing.

'Indri, do you think our fathers are also opening a few bottles in their world? Weren't they best friends like us?' Antappan would ask.

Whatever be the answer, neither of their graves exists today. It is impossible to maintain graves forever. When you pay for space in the graveyard, it is on the condition that one would relinquish it when the new tenant arrived. The stay is for a maximum of three or four years. After that the cross—engraved with the address and age—is uprooted from the grave. It was Antappan's job to extract the remains of the dead. The one who went to sleep all decked up and handsome, would emerge, gathered up in Antappan's basket, as skull and bones. Antappan would dump the remains in the 'Well of Bones' situated at the back of the graveyard. The remains would disappear among a pile of bones, erasing all traces of any individual existence.

Those who came to light candles or offer flowers the next day would be at a loss, seeing a new occupant in the home of their beloved one. A cry would be stifled inside their throats. Everyone unquestioningly accepted the new flowers, new candles and the new cross. The thought that they too would end up in the tomb one day might silence them for a moment too.

It was Appan who had told me that the existential truth dawned on human beings when they saw the cemetery: *Chudala Jnanam* or the Wisdom of the Graveyard. The same men who stood pondering on the transience of life forgot about it as soon as they crossed the walls of the cemetery. Emerging outside, they would take their places back in the world of hatred and competition.

This is the drama of worldly illusions. The man or woman who tries to commit suicide after the death of his or her partner, gets remarried even before the first death anniversary! What is this existence, if not worldly illusion?

I was baffled by what Appan told me once: *Those who know the secret of the alluring box would never get entangled by the quirks of time.*

I had foolishly inquired once more: 'How do you open it?'

'When the time comes, you will find the key,' Appan gave his usual reply.

Apparently, my time was yet to arrive! My father and his weird notions!

I could never understand how my Appan knew so much philosophy. To be truthful, I am averse to the complicated, knotty Vedanta. No one has ever appeased his hunger pangs by ingesting it. It cannot palliate, even a tiny bit, the burning revenge within me. For that, the dead body of my enemy should be inside the coffin I have prepared for him. The bony remains should vanish inside the cemetery's Well of Bones. I am willing to accept nothing less.

If what my Appan left unsaid was something that would have doused the flames of my vengeance, it was better this way. Some learnings can make us inert by reminding us about the futility of action. Perhaps that is why the wise hide the key from us until it is time.

* * *

I had seen the horrors of the Well of Bones when I was a child. The pit was surrounded on all sides by a wall of red bricks. One had to struggle to climb atop that barrier. While my classmates clambered up rather easily, I found it tricky. I was in the sixth standard at that time. When I looked down from the top of the well, I felt dizzy. The grotesque sight of bones and skulls entangled in a steep pile was devastating. There was no difference between the rich or the poor, the wise or the foolish in that heap. One person's skull was stuck to another's humerus. A femur lay next to someone else's ribs. Generations had deteriorated into mere skeletons whose identification was impossible. They had all merged with the earth, corroborating the impermanence of life.

One could have created a mixed human from someone's skull, a second person's limbs and a third person's ribs. It was a terrifying epiphany that finally everyone, including me, would have to lie in that well one day, having relinquished our ego. I clutched frantically at the red stone wall, trying not to slip inside the pit. The thought of falling into that ghastly mound of bones was scarier than death itself.

The clawing and clutching, so as to not fall into the Well of Bones, is synonymous with 'life's fear'. Even when one knows that falling in one day is inevitable, irrespective of how tight your grasp, one hangs on to frivolous desires. I have a hunch that this sticky urge should be overcome in order to open the alluring box that Appan spoke about. *It is an opening which happens from within.* Every such reflection over the Well of Bones reminds me of what a great man my Appan was.

During our childhood, it was Antappan who sat on the red brick wall fearlessly. And once, he even dared to descend to its depths. He stomped through the remains of the dead and picked up a glistening skull. It was flawless and not even a tooth was amiss. It must have belonged to a beautiful woman. He held that skull in front of his face and tried to scare me witless.

'Bbhee . . .'

Horrified, I lost my grip of the wall. With my heart in my mouth, I barely managed to hold on and avoid a tumble into the heap of bones. Antappan was bold as brass. Like a grave robber, he emerged from that death well, holding the skull aloft.

'Why do you want to keep the skull?' I squeaked in terror.

'It is meant for the vaidyan,' he replied nonchalantly.

'For the vaidyan?'

'Yes, for making medicinal oil. Take a look!'

He turned his head to show me the back of his neck. It was then that I noticed a protuberance, the size of a laurel nut, on Antappan's neck.

'The oil is for curing this.'

I had not known a prescription like that before. From the next day, Antappan started applying a dark oil prepared from the skull. Whenever he came close, I smelled death, remembering the oil. Perhaps the oil worked, because the swelling dwindled in size. But it never disappeared totally.

After all these years, whenever I catch a glimpse of that bump on Antappan's neck, like a fading memory, I recall the Well of Bones. It was after that incident that I acquired the ability to sniff out death, which lurked around the corners to absorb everyone. When I see certain people, I get a whiff of that distinct scent which tells me that their deaths are imminent. Since all such forebodings always turn out to be true, nowadays when that smell wafts close, I pinch my nostrils, trying to turn away from death's presence.

* * *

I am befuddled why Antappan, so daring otherwise, gets jittery before his son. David is more audacious than his father. He evaded taking over the ancestral task of digging graves. He was not good at studies and could not succeed in any alternative trade either. In my opinion, the driver's uniform which life had set aside for him suited his severe nature better.

Presumably, like all dictators, Satan Loppo also indulged his cronies liberally. It was like the master's caress enhancing the enslavement of the pet dog. On hearing David praising Satan Loppo to the skies, I realized that there were many who were willing to die for a villain. It was hard to digest. I surmised that David was counting on his Muthalali's support for his love life with Shari.

Love is really a disease.

Initially, it clouds the sense of sight. Then it infects the ability to think properly. People lose all powers of discernment overnight. Like a man entrapped in an illusory world, he assumes a mental fortitude for sacrificing everything for his beloved. His sojourn is through the present, having scant regard for future consequences. Life enmeshes him in all its romanticisms.

Indeed, love is a disease which distracts human beings from reality. Some carry the mesmerizing diversions of that disease all through their lives. Some get cured eventually but continue their lives nursing the wounds left behind. *Without wounds, love has no existence.*

I have accepted the pain caused by love's wounds too.

When Beatrice joined me, I lost my desire for material objects. The coffin seemed a treasure trove to me. Our children were my precious gems. Why did the handyman of Lucifer step into that blissful world of mine?

How can I convince David that the enticing world hides a deadly betrayal? How will I persuade him that Satan Loppo is my nemesis, and his sword is aimed at my chest? To disclose the murky details of the past would be as abhorrent as digging up Beatrice's remains for evidence.

If someone digs out seven, or seventy, or even seven hundred skeletons from Loppo's swimming pool, I would not be surprised. Across the ages, many dead bodies have accumulated in the backyards of absolutism and tyranny. Every dictator's empire stands upon heaps of corpses.

All Satan Loppo could do was to imprint the stink of his cigar on Beatrice's lips. Even if the crime was proven, no court in the world would sentence him to death for that! Beatrice had tearfully pleaded with me to never divulge the story of that stain to any creature in the universe. Yet I could not restrain myself then. A wild animal had bayed for blood inside me.

And what had I achieved?

A bite mark on my leg and a cripple's hobble.

First Loppo and then his dog, two animals had attacked Beatrice and me, leaving behind their fang marks.

After that, didn't the Lord too turn his face away from me?

Dear Lord, why did you sow pestilence in my life and gather the bitter harvest? Why did you uproot the tamarind tree that bent over my home?

I only want to die . . . I only want to die . . .

But before that I want to tame Satan Loppo's feral strength and inter it in a coffin. Only after relishing that sight shall I vanish amid the tangled mass in the Well of Bones.

I wouldn't mind if afterwards someone were to make a special oil with my skull for curing a lump in their neck.

7

The Lacerations of Love

'I compare you, my love, to a mare among Pharaoh's chariots. Your cheeks are comely with ornaments, your neck with strings of jewels. We will make you ornaments of gold, studded with silver. While the king was on his couch, my nard gave forth its fragrance. My beloved is to me a bag of myrrh that lies between my breasts. My beloved is to me a cluster of henna blossoms in the vineyards of Engedi.'

(Song of Solomon 1: 9-14)

I have never returned to that compound after the tamarind tree crushed my home. From outside and inside, thunderstorms haunt me without respite. I loathe that dead land which could not safeguard my Beatrice and children.

During the nights when the monsoon creates havoc, monstrous trees bide their time to flatten the huts. But I had never suspected that the strongly-rooted tamarind tree would ever harm my abode. The inhabitants of Aadi Nadu whispered that the newfangled machine brought for Loppo's latest quarry had eaten away the topsoil and weakened the mother root of the tamarind. I ranted to myself that the crashing of the tree and the ensuing deaths were lies spread by a malicious gossip monger.

Dear Lord! Why does misfortune lead a war solely against certain lives and fell them with its foul sword?

Not even a floor was left for four bodies to lie side by side, as everything was shattered to smithereens. While Antappan and others created a tarpaulin shed in my wasted yard, I raced like a madman to my coffin shop. The one who earned bread through the deaths of other people had to create the final tent for his own loved ones. Like a weaver who weaves the best clothes for his dear ones, I was in a hurry to make the most beautiful coffin.

I ignored everyone who followed in my wake. Antappan stopped me when I took up my mallet and chisel to carve a casket.

'Indri, what are you doing? Let us go home. I will arrange everything.'

'No, I shall make it myself. Very quickly!'

Antappan might have thought that I had lost my mental balance again. His baffled gaze made it evident. I saw his eyes tearing up at my frenzied state.

'Antappa!' I cried, 'We always slept with our arms around one another. My children will be terrified to sleep alone. Let them sleep next to their mother!'

Antappan stared at me, stunned into silence. He knew me inside out. We had grown up together, never keeping secrets from each other. He would be gutted, yes.

I started making a coffin large enough for four to rest side by side. Such a casket had never been heard of before. Only with a unique gift could I bid farewell to my darlings. As if by building a spacious home, I created a beautiful dwelling place.

'Antappa, what are you gaping at?' I asked my friend who stood hunched up by my side. 'You should dig their home's foundation. There should be enough space for a box that can house four people.'

When Antappan, who never blanched at anything in life, burst into tears while hugging me, I pressed my face against his shoulder and consoled him tearfully.

'Don't be sad . . . don't be sad!'

It was a consolation where neither of us knew who was supporting whom, and where neither could support the other.

Using exquisite lace, special carvings and adornments shaped like jasmines, I polished the lovely resting place. I gave it a beautiful look, providing ten inches depth to the casket's bottom and two and a half inches to the top lid. Instead of two holding bars, I made four, and pasted a cross of the Mar Thoma congregation in between pictures of doves on the top lid. Everything was easy as I had recently purchased many accessories from a trader in Vaikom. All the precious stuff that I possessed were used to create that coffin. On seeing four people sleep within it, a cry emerged from my broken heart and tore open the skies. My blind Rosarios, my Roselyn with her tender serenity, my Alphonse who loved books and my Beatrice, as lovely as a Holy Angel . . .

My God, My God, why have you forsaken me?

Of what hard material has the foundation of your justice been forged?

How can you blame me if I doubt that God is the name of a heartless, deaf, blind entity?

When Satan Loppo arrived with four red wreaths, one for each, and placed them over my loved ones, I questioned the universe as to why no massive tree had fallen on him. He would continue to remove the topsoil for his quarry work. More trees would collapse, their roots having been weakened. No one would be able to point fingers at him ever.

The death knell which the church bell tolled that day still rings in my ears. I, who had hitherto responded to that ringing as a business opportunity, had been ordered to make a casket for my own family. It sardonically reminded me that the bell would toll for each one of us some day.

I have never been to that cursed wilderness since.

Why should I visit a place where no one waits for me? This coffin shop has become my refuge. My cooking is done in the back porch. There is a small shed in the backyard for my ablutions. Life has taught me that a human being does not need more trappings.

* * *

Whenever he visits, Antappan exhorts, 'Stop living in this blasted coffin shop. Get out of here sometimes.'

Antappan is unaware that I lost the distinction between 'in' and 'out' a long time ago. What differentiates my 'in' and 'out' are the frames of the upright casket. Isn't a coffin similar to the skin which enwraps the human body? When I stand behind the coffin and view the world through its crevices, I am 'in' and the world is 'out'. When I step out from behind it, I re-enter my own world.

Somehow, I prefer standing behind the coffin. I can then see the human beings belonging to the world very clearly. My outward look sweeps past the tailor shop in front and reaches Pundit's watch shop at the end of the street. When I glance through the gaps, I don't see Pundit's face clearly. It is an oblique look that lands there. But the view of the tailor shop is direct. I can see Shari, engaged in her work. She pedals an old Singer machine used by Shashankan in the early days. Shashankan uses a Merritt machine now. The shape of the instrument, with its flaking black paint, reminds me of a rabbit. The rhythmic sound is relentless in its onslaught. The snip-snip of his scissors can be heard next to the cutting table. These two unceasing sounds intrude into my coffin shop. The cloth pieces Shashankan cuts to measure, morph into different shapes due to Shari's hard work.

She had not come to the shop the past two days. I had only seen Shashankan during my regular vigil from behind the coffin. I had no clue whether Shari was ill or something else had caused her absence. But I was sure of one fact. David desisted from visiting me during this time. He knew about her absence.

Now that Shari is back, David's visit inquiring about my well-being is probable. I too have passed this stage of youth, full of passions. But I pretend to be totally unaware about their relationship.

It has its secret pleasure.

Shari is not as beautiful as my Beatrice. But true to the proverb 'the face is the mirror of the heart', the charming purity of her heart shows on her pretty face. Since she is not as intelligent as she is beautiful, she ended up failing spectacularly in her tenth standard. After staying at home for a couple of years, she started learning to stitch. I wonder when Shari and David fell in love. No wonder the oldies snipe, 'Alley cat, silent cat.' There is no external display of passionate love in this case. Only an expert physician of love could have caught the aroma of that burning fever.

David would typically stop his jeep near my shop as if to inquire after my health. But his eyes would be drawn, like a magnet, to the tailor shop. In reply, some frantic glances would flutter in the air and start their journey towards the coffin shop. More than love, those glances would be filled with the feminine fear of being observed. I would smile inwardly at their drama and make myself scarce.

Except for those ardent looks, I have never caught them talking to each other. I have no clue how they communicate. Perhaps their generation has devised a new method for tricking my outdated brain. Maybe they have love's wireless telegraph connecting their thoughts.

I feel sympathy for the love birds who enjoy their trysts in a coffin shop. If I were to use Basheer's words, they should have scouted for a more sensual and beautiful meeting place. Lovers should take flight in a flamboyant world of flowers, butterflies and rainbows. There will never be colour inside a coffin shop. There are only a few handiworks of lace and some pretentious accessories. Love wrapped in lace can claim only an artificial beauty.

Irrespective of decorations, no one would dare wrangle over the cost of a coffin after checking the firmness and grip of the panels. Since death puts an end to all possibilities of a bargain, shopkeepers demand unreasonably high prices for the lace, wicks, flowers, gloves and the rest of the paraphernalia needed for burying the dead. Love should desist from a rendezvous in such callous places.

An external observer can comment as expansively as he likes. Only lovers know the agonies of the heart caused by scalding passion. When love takes hold of your heart, no one stops to consider that the time and place may be unsuitable. Wherever they may be, even if it is a coffin shop, becomes their playground. Lovers will kiss each other seated on a gravestone. Beatrice and I too shared our love inside coffins.

Sometimes, when David sets off on an assignment for Satan Loppo, there is no fixed time for his return. On such days, when I stand behind the coffin, I observe how Shari's worried glances skip their way to my shop. In anticipation of David's arrival, she betrays her feelings. She stays back under the guise of completing some urgent work. She drags her feet at the time of departure, as if iron spheres have been tied to her legs.

Indeed, I am making guesses about the inner workings of ardent lovers. I had never fallen in love before marriage or known the pain of separation from my sweetheart. Before Beatrice, I had not dared to look properly at a woman. Wondering whether any woman would love a coffin maker, I had suffered heart burns. My self-confidence had plummeted to the depths of the seas. I would wither with shyness whenever I faced women, as if I had stepped across a forbidden boundary. Only I am aware of the trauma I underwent when I stood face to face with Beatrice for the first time. For an instance, after seeing her face, as radiant as the sun, I had intensely prayed to the Lord 'to remove that cup from me'*. I was an ignoramus, totally oblivious of the utter sweetness inside that cup which I wished to push afar. Who had known that an angel would become my companion during my life journey, and fill me with blissful love?

---

* Jesus's prayer at Gethsemane

It all seems like a dream.

When your heart is overwhelmed with love, the earth becomes enchantingly lighter. The earth, the wind, and the water start spreading the fragrance of your woman's body. One feels as if all of nature has been channelled into the beloved's body.

In Beatrice's body, in her breath, in her heartbeat, I have known that . . .

I have experienced my own consciousness leaving me while a woman possessed me in entirety. My body would emanate Beatrice's fragrance in those moments. We knew that love never claimed anything or imposed anything. There is no immersion such as love on earth. I have read that like a parched root finding a droplet of water in the soil, love too finds a way to sustain itself.

David and Shari are residents of the skies at present. They are not bound by the rules of earth. I offer my heart in a platter and pray to the Lord that their joyful love knows no impediment. They can expect my full support for the fruition of their passion.

For there is only one thing which can rightfully take the place of love on earth. It is love.

8

A Spurt of Disgust

'The Lord saw how great the wickedness of the human race had become on the earth, and that every inclination of the thoughts of the human heart was only evil all the time. The Lord regretted that he had made human beings on the earth, and his heart was deeply troubled. So, the Lord said, "I will wipe from the face of the earth the human race I have created—and with them the animals, the birds and the creatures that move along the ground—for I regret that I have made them."'

(Genesis 6: 5-7)

When twilight set in, I heard an unfamiliar commotion in the street and got out of the shop to see what it was. The origin of the hullaballoo was Pundit's watch shop. A jeans-clad upstart, whose moustache had hardly started sprouting, was yelling abuses.

'Old geezer! How long do you mean to cling on to this place?'

I assumed it was either Pundit's grandson or great-grandson. It was obvious he had overindulged in liquor, which fortifies the new generation's indolent life.

'Why bother to live when you are so decrepit?' the lad shouted.

Many interested spectators started peeping from hither and thither on hearing the shouting. But I noticed that not a single response emerged from Pundit. Intoxication becomes a license for world-class failures to spout nonsense at anyone! The lad got further provoked by Pundit's obdurate silence.

'Your blasted clocks! I will throw those damned things away today.'

He rushed inside, yelling throatily. I feared that the venerable old life that had seen a hundred years would be harmed. Invading the abode of time, would he throw away the clocks that announced the hour in concurrence? As I stood bewildered, unsure whether to interfere, a ruckus started inside the shop. I then heard a resounding slap. No longer could I sit still.

My hands itched to slap that brat, who being three generations junior to Pundit, had dared to hit him! As I rushed towards the shop, I was greeted with a bewildering sight. The lad, pushed out of the shop, lay sprawled on the wayside. Pundit emerged, his hand raised, ready to rain another blow.

'Get lost, you nincompoop! Why don't you go hit your father instead? He deserves to be beaten up for not raising you decently.'

Having been put in his place, all the pugnacity drained from the boy. Proving true that one tight slap was good enough to awaken the intoxicated, the fellow fled the scene with his tail between his legs! I inwardly saluted Pundit's grit, who even in his old age had taken on a youth.

'Came to question me! That wastrel!'

When Pundit stepped back into his shop, I shrank to the sidelines, pretending to know nothing. Then I heard the undivided support extended to Pundit by all the clocks in the shop. I have now become alert to the hourly united tolling which rises from the 'Shop of Time'.

It was when the resonance of time faded that the echoing bang of an exploding dynamite from a faraway quarry filled the air. That sound is a frequent occurrence too. These blasts rock Aadi Nadu like a sudden roll of thunder. It is a bugle call for the hacking and selling of rocks which stand with their proud chests puffed up to the skies!

A long line of lorries, ruthlessly carrying away the hills, can be seen rushing like frenzied elephants in various directions. The city skyscrapers are founded on rocks gouged from the lungs and hearts of Aadi Nadu's hills. Most of the mines, excavated mercilessly below the ground level, have turned into cavernous hollows. Many impulsive youngsters, tempted by the siren call of the water, have lost their lives in those depths. Wishing to 'drown life in death', some lovers have succeeded by diving into those watery graves.

By annexing neighbouring quarries to his possession, Satan Loppo has built a local kingdom of his own. Initially, he had the ownership of just a hill or two. Mining of rocks wasn't a successful venture back then. It was Loppo who maximized its potential. When the business showed signs of thriving, his adroit brain started slithering across Aadi Nadu like a venomous snake. That was how he started taking possession of those hills that had been left untouched till then. Those rocky terrains had been treated as wastelands, some of which were inhospitable to even a shoot of grass. Paying cheap money to the owners, who did not see anything profitable in keeping those wastelands, Loppo had subjugated each of the hills.

First, he chopped off the greenery. In some places, by mining the topsoil, he captured the rocks hunkering beneath. Each hill got beheaded brutally. The butchered rocks were transformed to gravel and stone in his crusher. Also, through unholy liaisons, Satan Loppo's mining machines started encroaching upon government lands.

If one were to count, there are only two hills that stand free in Aadi Nadu, defying Loppo. One of them belongs to Shari's father Karunan. Though offered an attractive job in Loppo's factory along with a handsome compensation, Karunan did not succumb. It was for the first time that someone in Aadi Nadu stood firm as a rock against such enticements. Hence, that hill escaped slaughter.

Aadi Nadu's hills, inaccessible to the police, were a haven for popular leaders of the people's movements during the Emergency period. Karunan's father, then a teenager, had been a devoted young comrade-in-arms of the fleeing leaders during the period of ban of the communist party. Food, water and secret documents reached the hilltops thanks to him. There were many hideouts within the folds of those rocky hills. These were the *garbhagrihas** concealed by the rocks, invisible to search parties. Many of those exiled patiently waited inside, alert to the heralding song of revolution. Some had price tags on their heads. Karunan remembers many of them visiting his house much later, hailing him affectionately as a 'budding comrade'.

Even today, there are secret passages in that hill known to Karunan alone. They are as special to him as the intimate spaces within one's own household. It is natural that he cannot bear to lose the places where the footprints of his father and stalwart leaders are indelibly imprinted. Though he recognizes that the massive mountains, imprinted with the fierce revolutionary spirit of the past, are being ruthlessly demolished to give way to the treacherous hollows carved out by the nouveau riche, Karunan doesn't sever his connection with the rocks. He believes that a new-age revolution should focus on sustaining nature at her pristine best. In an era when political ideologies are being manipulated for personal gains, it is time to renew outdated slogans.

Karunan's frame leaves no doubt that he was born to grapple with rocks! His body looks as if it was carved from one as well. In that strong, muscular body, there is not an extra ounce of fat. His demeanour epitomizes an aggressive, virile manhood. His bald pate adds to the look. I am reminded of an uncompromising rock whenever I see him.

Karunan has a close relationship with the labourers who undertake risky occupations, and those employed for blasting rocks and operating excavators in quarries actively seek him out. Even Karunan might be unaware of how he has been elevated to the

---

* Sanctum sanctorum of a temple

position of their leader. During the blasts, when exploding shrapnel ends up hurting people, Karunan is among the first to rush to their aid. Sumitra is a living testimony to this fact.

A sharp splinter from an explosion had severed her right foot. When, after she survived her fight with death, no one was ready to marry her, Karunan unhesitatingly invited her into his own life. His father, a true radical, had taught him that bleating out bombastic '*isms*' was not the sign of revolution; a revolutionary's life should exemplify his beliefs. He stood firm on his philosophy that *before setting out to clean up society, one had to clean up his own life*. Whenever I read history, I too feel that every great institution started deteriorating when an unprincipled person tightened his hold over its reins. The deadly seeds of dictatorship would have sprouted in him already. Slowly, the tyrannical tendencies would take root, and grow to devastate the whole land.

It is a great relief to have right-minded people who stand with the truth in such a dastardly world. I have great respect for Karunan, and a special place for him in my heart. Satan Loppo would think twice before provoking Karunan.

Loppo hasn't dared a direct confrontation yet, though he harbours a great dislike for Karunan due to his refusal to sell his hill. Karunan's rock-like physique, his uncompromising attitude and his popularity among the villagers might be factors that held his hand. But I feel apprehensive of Satan Loppo hatching a wicked plot to ensnare Karunan.

The British Sayyip who was the original owner of Loppo's bungalow was a big shot in his time. He was apparently close to Lord Mountbatten during the peak of the Independence struggle. It was said that many viceroys used to clandestinely visit the bungalow for recreation and rest. Some revolutionaries reportedly got to know of Mountbatten's visit and hatched a plot to kill him, but were betrayed by local spies. The skeletons unearthed from Loppo's pool might narrate many more tales. Stories of the times when summer homes were built on hillsides for the foreigners' stay.

The climate is pleasant here. The remnants of those days, when the Sayyips, afraid of the harsh summer, rallied to the hills, are still visible in the vicinity. The iron wheels of an old horse carriage, a historic relic, can be seen near Loppo's bungalow. Aadi Nadu was probably an exception to the practice of white men preferring tea plantations for their summer leisure.

Most of the inhabitants of the village can trace their forefathers to those adventurous migrants who cleared the forests to plant rubber. The first settlers had fought against both wild animals and malaria in their struggle for survival. When the country gained independence, the white men left Aadi Nadu. Following that, many of the villagers moved away to the pleasures of the cities. When they flourished, those who remained got lured to the cities too.

Satan Loppo made his grand entry exactly at this point of time! Some characters are like that: through calculated moves, they ascend the ladder of success to touch the skies. Whether one termed it fate or coincidence, the inexplicable game of *Kalapurusha** was involved in Satan Loppo's case.

Loppo treated safety rules for blasting rocks with utter disregard. The rules caution against filling dynamites in holes beyond a depth of six inches, but Loppo's acolytes couldn't care less. It was profitable to obtain the maximum amount of rock in each attempt. So they dug beyond the permissible limit. When the powerful explosions occurred, not only the rigid rocks, but houses situated far away also trembled. The walls of the houses near the quarries developed deep cracks. Some of them collapsed. The complainants who sought intervention from power centres were left disappointed. The higher-ups sagaciously advised them to sell off their homes if they were apprehensive of the damage due to quarrying.

---

* The Lord of Time or MahaKaal

As the area under mining increased, the wells in the neighbourhood started drying up. Streams and natural water reservoirs started shrinking. Potable water, arriving from far-off places, became costlier than gold. When that became another reason for people to sell their homes and move, almost all the rocky hills came under Loppo's brute force.

When that damned machine arrived to remove the topsoil near my compound, I was still undecided. It was an indication to sell my property at a cheap price and move away. But the tamarind tree crashed, its roots giving away, even before I could make up my mind. Else, I may have built a shack behind the coffin shop and shifted Beatrice and the children there.

Loppo, on acquiring the bungalow, cleaned and widened the pool that the Sayyip had constructed for naked revelries. In that pond where the bodies of beautiful young women had once swum, he constructed a suite that could be lowered into its depths, enabling his debaucheries to spread from the surface to the insides of the water. It must have thrilled him that he could conceal his sinful orgies with a veil of water. The raw arrogance of someone, who at the mere snap of a finger, got all he desired in the water's womb!

However, I know that Loppo cannot fool the world forever. His luxuries have been built over many skeletons. Even if he were to use his muscle power and connections to hide his sins, the dead shall spring anew from every drop of blood and question his autocracy. One day, Loppo's pool of inequity shall dry up to the last drop. The rock bottom shall be seen, and the nefarious secrets of the glass suite shall stand exposed.

As if disrobed amidst a crowd, Satan Loppo shall stand, finding two hands not enough to hide his nakedness! He shall come to realize that the nakedness of the white man is different from that of the native. If I catch hold of him in that helpless state, I shall trap that hideous, naked beast in my coffin and nail the lid tight!

Bereft of breath, I stood behind the coffin meant for Satan Loppo.

Beloved box of mine, you hold all my hopes.
Give flesh and blood to that dream of mine.
Make true its desire.

More than anyone else, I know that it will remain a pipe dream. Mine is a hollow existence, a life that resides amidst coffins like an orphaned corpse. Mulling over the fact that I was a perished soul whose thoughts invariably returned to death, however much I tried to deviate, I felt like spitting hard at my own existence.

'Pthbhuu!'

9

Foreign Relations

'Very truly I tell you, you will weep and mourn while the world rejoices. You will grieve, but your grief will turn to joy. A woman giving birth to a child has pain because her time has come; but when her baby is born, she forgets the anguish because of her joy that a child is born into the world. So, with you: Now is your time of grief, but I will see you again and you will rejoice, and no one will take away your joy. In that day you will no longer ask me anything.'

(John 16: 20-23)

When a jeep unexpectedly screeched to a halt in front of my shop, the chafing sound made me wince.

Occasionally, unfamiliar sounds creep in and scare me witless. As a natural reaction to the sound, I hide behind the coffin and look at the outside world through its crevices. It has become habitual to abstain from gazing openly at the road these days. I need the coffin to mediate between the world and me. The sights are unusual then. Or perhaps, those are the true sights.

I was relieved to observe that it was David in the jeep. But it perplexed me that instead of entering my shop, he marched straight to the tailor shop opposite. That was not normal. He has never ever made a direct approach to the shop where Shari learns tailoring. They have been guarding their love as a relationship in need of a smokescreen. Of course, love often possesses a self-revealing capacity.

I was wondering about David's visit to the tailor shop when it dawned on me that there were other passengers in the jeep. Intriguing me further, Satan Loppo's son, Timothios, stepped out of the vehicle. Soon after Timothios, with his Dravidian colouring and foreign attire, alighted, a madamma followed suit. It was then that I understood.

Satan Loppo's son had arrived from Germany. The woman with him was his German wife. My mind slyly wondered how that milky white-skinned woman could have got attracted to Timothios, who was as dark as Satan Loppo. Like dusky people finding beauty in fairness, could it be that a reverse attraction had happened? Who knew if that was the latest trend in Germany!

Nevertheless, how come they were visiting such a simple shop on the streets of Aadi Nadu? Unable to throw off my suspicion, I stood hovering behind the coffin marked 'S.L.' with chalk. S.L. stands for, you guessed it, Satan Loppo.

Anything connected with Satan Loppo stokes my anxiety. Whether it involved his jeep, his dog or his son's wife . . . The madamma was wearing something akin to trousers, which ended above her knees. That short piece of clothing probably has some strange name unknown to me. It reminded me of the *thorthu* wrapped around the waist by the mentally deranged who loitered around the village. The madamma's upper clothing was a black vest devoid of either collars or sleeves. Her generous breasts swayed visibly within that flimsy dress. Probably tantalized by those luscious temptations, many onlookers were surreptitiously peeking at her.

My mind almost ruptured from the swelling curiosity about what those three were doing in the tailor shop. Shashankan was saying something to them. Typically, excessive gesticulations and facial expressions would accompany his conversations. I could watch everything from my secret hideout. But the box prevented the sounds from reaching me. Though I tried hard, I couldn't decipher Shashankan's body language. Speculating crudely on whether they were discussing further shortening the madamma's knickers, I snickered to myself. That would be a tough task for Shashankan indeed!

Upsetting my cheap fun was the sight of Shari accompanying the trio as they returned from the shop. A shiver caught hold of me, starting from the tip of my toes and slowly crawling upwards. When Shari got into the jeep and sat next to the madamma in the back seat, my heartbeat reached a crescendo, as if my life spirit was escaping. I felt suffocated because I could not fathom the reason for Shari travelling with them.

Meanwhile, David cast a sidelong glance at my shop. But he didn't see me hiding behind the coffin like a ghost. Ghosts are not visible to anyone, but ghosts can see everyone.

If he had seen me, David might have waved at me. But he wouldn't have dared walk into my shop. A coffin shop is obviously not a centre of attraction for alluring foreigners! No tantalizing high tech stuff awaits anybody here. Death is the only entity that has a kinship with coffins. Despite the many changes wrought in other fields over ages, when it comes to coffins, there hasn't been much variation. Though opportunities for travel, availability of food and advances in science have grown by leaps and bounds, the phenomena of birth and death continue unchanged. Death is the eternal truth and eternity has wrapped up its truth inside coffins.

When the jeep moved forward raucously, my mind raced behind, more noisily and speedily. When I couldn't sit still with anxiety, I even contemplated crossing the road and inquiring about the purpose of their visit from Shashankan. Usually, I never visit his shop. Even after so many years, the half-sleeved voile jubbas that he had stitched for me are untorn. Mundu and jubba form my sole garments. Even underclothing has been shorn off my list of necessities. As if I have some place worth visiting! The earth no longer holds any sight or memory to rouse my manhood. It has been ages since I have felt a sexual stirring. My manly part has rusted away like an unused key. Clothes are not a temptation to someone who is limited by a few square inches of earth. Stifling my mind's pressure, I coaxed it against heading to the tailor shop.

It was better to wait for David's arrival.

Every heartbeat bruised me like a thorn thereafter. After an hour or so, when I heard the rumble of the jeep, I retreated behind the coffin and peeped through the gaps again. My existence had become a short drama involving the interior and exterior of a coffin.

I could see that only David and Shari were in the jeep. Shari was in the seat just behind David. It was clearly a well-contrived seating arrangement. To an outsider, they looked like two strangers.

David alighted first. Then he opened the door for Shari.

She got down and cast a furtive look around. Then without acknowledging David, she walked towards the tailor shop.

What a smart one!

I grinned to myself on seeing Shari's artifice. Although they sat in the front and back seats of the jeep, my wicked intelligence concluded that David must have leaned back and kissed her.

After Shari left, David turned to my shop. I heard that familiar call from the front step.

'Uncle!'

The way he addresses me pulls at my heartstrings. I have always had a weakness for endearments in English. I had tried to get my children to call us 'Papa' and 'Mommy'. Beatrice put an end to that plan and decided that the traditional 'Appan' was good enough!

'The call "Appan" has been floating around here for generations. All that love will resurface when our children call you Appan.' I was surprised to listen to Beatrice. When she added that it was her Valiyammachi's* opinion, I had to forego my affinity for English.

---

* Grandmother

The only person who addresses me in English, satisfying my lingering fondness for that language, is David. The rest refer to me typically as 'Indri or Inri'. The shortened versions of 'Hendri' are evocative of the delicious Inri appam cooked on Maundy Thursday. I had not known that the name 'Inri' had stuck to the appam because of the letters I.N.R.I. engraved on the cross of Jesus. Later, I learnt the full form of those letters.

Iesus Nazarenus, Rex Iudaeorum,
Jesus the Nazarene, King of the Jews.

Perhaps due to that name, like Jesus, I have been granted a life in which I always carry a cross. Similar to the fourteen stations in the Way of the Cross, I too have been crawling, falling, stumbling while carrying the heavy burden.

I moved to the shop front, as if to answer the call. The donning of the expression of someone totally unaware of outside happenings was something I had successfully mastered. Appan taught me that the person who knows everything should remain cool, as if he knows nothing. Only a person capable of that can know everything! Because that is the state of the Creator. After creating the whole universe, the Omniscient One hides as if he knows nothing.

I am far from being sagacious as the Lord, and could hardly control my eagerness for the latest news.

David was good enough not to put me in further agony. He revealed everything as soon as he saw me, almost as if reading my thoughts.

'The Muthalali's son and daughter-in-law have arrived from Germany. They are so modish!'

'Oh . . .' I responded.

'Imagine the madamma's whim!'

'What?'

'To dress in a sari and blouse like our local women! I took Shari along to help her wear the sari and to measure her for a blouse.'

'And then?'

'Shari says it was a bit difficult. But they had good fun . . . By the way, I didn't see you when we came to pick her up.'

'I . . . I was at the back.'

Just like pretending ignorance even when you know everything, it is equally important never to lie, even jokingly. Whenever one fibs or acts falsely, the inner radiance reduces remarkably. It is because human beings are surrounded by the darkness wrought by their lies that they are unable to experience their inner light.

Since I was *at the back of the coffin*, I was not telling a lie. David does not know that to see everything unveiled, *one should go beyond the coffin*, does he? I have only told that to Beatrice, my better half. I shall never speak about it to anyone else.

'Shari is lucky. The madamma likes her.' David smiled.

I smiled half-heartedly in reply.

'Madamma insists on a daily visit . . .'

'By whom?'

'Shari! Only then can the madamma learn how to wear a sari.'

I could see that he relished repeating the name 'Shari', like overdosing on a drug. Except for the rhyming beauty in *Shari teaching someone to wear a sari*, I could find nothing attractive about the idea.

'No driving assignments today?' I tried to divert his attention.

'Well, I am supposed to drive the madamma and the Sayyip around today. They will be here for a while.'

'Have they brought German dogs and cows with them again?'

'No one brings cows along with them, Uncle. Those arrive in ships. Time to leave . . . Shall come again soon.'

'Okay.'

I moved back discreetly. Whenever he bids goodbye, I withdraw a bit, a practice I have intentionally trained myself in. David would be seeking Shari's permission for his departure through silent glances. Shari would be answering with her eyes. I shall not allow even my shadow to interfere in their intimate dialogue.

When David left, I took my position behind the coffin again, and stared at the shop opposite.

When I saw Shari's ecstatic face, her inner joy brimming over, I was reminded of Beatrice in her sexually heightened mood. It was obvious that an act of love was gifted to her today. David had been astute enough to make full use of the half-opportunity that had come his way.

If only my Beatrice were alive now . . .!

Remembering a black mole that I had discovered between her two beautiful breasts, a searing pain rose within. A little black mole can sometimes become the greatest loss in the world. I had tracked down that teensiest mark after a most enthralling adventure. I remembered every bit of my Beatrice, including the areas where she had beauty spots. How ecstatic she had been to receive the imprints of my love on those!

As I mourned with my face pressed against the coffin, my nerves stretched taut over memories of the heated kisses which would never get exchanged again.

The church bell tolled, forcing me away from the coldness of the coffin which was receiving my kiss.

It was an announcement of death.

I was sure that someone would come to purchase a coffin today. My shop had not seen much business in the past few days. People preferred to buy caskets from Joppan and Gracy's shop in the western front. For the eight churches in the locality, there were but two coffin shops. Sometimes people went far in search of modern designs in spite of shops near their churches. Some others made sure to visit the traditional shops for their purchases. It was possible that the new owner had arrived for a home built by Joppan.

In order to accommodate the new tenant, Antappan would have to dig up an old mound and throw away the skull and fragments in the Well of Bones.

Which grave would Antappan open today?

10

The Heavenly Box

'So, the Lord God caused the man to fall into a deep sleep; and while he was sleeping, he took one of the man's ribs and then closed up the place with flesh. Then the Lord God made a woman from the rib he had taken out of the man, and he brought her to the man. The man said, "This is now bone of my bones and flesh of my flesh; she shall be called 'woman,' for she was taken out of man." That is why a man leaves his father and mother and is united to his wife, and they become one flesh. Adam and his wife were both naked, and they felt no shame.'

(Genesis 2: 21-25)

It happened finally.

David opened his red-blooded heart to me. I could hear the throbbing of passion in its blue veins.

Like a heart specialist who opens up the chest cavity, as I started examining his core, David blurted out, 'Uncle, I have something important to say.'

Detecting an unusual embarrassment in that prelude, I got a clear picture of the intensity of his sickness. Yet keeping up my innate appearance of a dullard, I asked, 'What's the matter?'

'Uncle, you are not merely an acquaintance to me. I can open my heart to you. See, I need your help.'

'What help can a poor man like me give?'

'At least your moral support. There is nobody else to listen to me.'

It brought to mind the jest of *someone leaning against a man struggling to stand up by himself.* But it was certainly not farcical for David; it was a gut-wrenching matter of life and death. I was right in assuming that the conversation was about the romance with Shari. David presented through his own looking glass what Antappan, from his perspective as a father, considered problematic. Except for the difference in viewpoint, I already knew the facts. Yet I noticed a few changes when David poured out his confession.

With David having opened his heart to me, I could no longer pretend indifference to his relationship with Shari. I have been impleaded as a third party in a sudden turnabout.

This affair was likely to shake up my own existence in times to come. I started experiencing the throes of that dilemma. David's grievances from the right chamber of my heart, and Antappan's peeves from the left, started pecking one another hurtfully.

'Indri, I want to die!' Antappan's fevered remark in the cemetery, as he stared at the darkness on a moonless night, reverberated in my mind.

I was entwined in a phantom thread under an intoxication that loosened my nerves. 'I often wish that too,' I murmured.

'You are hurt by the thought of your dead children. I am hurt by the thought of my living son. If he changes his religion and marries that girl, he will be dead to us, won't he? I shall become unworthy of digging graves in the church's graveyard. How can he ever hope to find a place in this cemetery where my ancestors sleep?'

Depending on the experience of the day, either joy or misery erupts from Antappan when liquor enters his system. His words made it clear that the day had been particularly bitter.

Each human being decides the direction of events using his own internal compass. I felt amused at the thought of a gravedigger worrying about his son missing out on a grave. It was a temporary pit rented for a few years, where the name was displayed under the guardianship of a cross. One had to leave when the next tenant arrived. Yet, look how human beings worried about such a transient pit.

The Lord does not judge a dead man based on what's inscribed on his forehead, does he? *'As long as you did it to the least of my brethren, you did it to me.'* He will judge us according to our deeds.

However, it was my bounden duty to console my bosom friend. I offered a simple solution to his predicament.

'You just have to get the girl baptized, right?'

'David is vehemently opposing any conversion. I think some evil spirit has possessed him.'

The burn caused by Antappan's words, like red-hot metal, is yet to heal.

Now, in the middle of all this, David, who is like a son to me, has approached me with his peeves! How am I supposed to handle him? Until now, I could conveniently pretend to be unaware of anything and act like a dumb fool.

One thing is sure: David and Shari are bound together by a very strong bond. Even if Antappan and Karunan pull from left and right, it will not give way. With the measuring tool of my own ticking heart, I can gauge the depth of the youngsters' love.

Love's black magic is overpowering. In the first stage, two hearts get attracted to each other. In the second stage, attraction alters into recognition. In the third, the lovers experience an indivisible oneness. Even death cannot separate those who reach that stage. David and Shari are on the threshold of the third stage. How did they traverse the two stages of love unnoticed by anyone? When love becomes an end, the means are irrelevant. When a droplet gives up its separate existence and merges with the single entity of water, it is love.

Nobody needs to teach me about love. I have swum across its vastness many times. I take a deep dive the instant I imagine Beatrice and myself in place of Shari and David. Transmuting into the formless state of liquid, I start flowing and spread all over. How can such a person dissuade another from love? The only thing left for me to do was to find out David's plans for his future.

It was then that David threw me into utter panic by revealing that he had shared his love story with Satan Loppo. I stood morbidly still while he naively expressed his confidence in his Muthalali's support for his love. It was an indication of the deep affiliation David had with Satan Loppo, comparable or even finer than what he shared with me.

Whatever be the reason, I find it insufferable when Loppo's breath or shadow falls upon anyone close to me. Apparently Loppo had encouraged David to defy any opposition. He had even bragged that religion hadn't mattered to him when Timothios married the foreign woman.

It sounded true at first, but Loppo had thought it irrelevant to mention that the German woman was a regular church-going Christian. Besides, how was he—living in these hinterlands—supposed to oppose his son who was on foreign soil? Thrilled by the foreigner's wealth, relishing the German luxuries supplied by his son, he was busy being ecstatic in the depths of the water.

However, it is different for simple souls who live with their feet on the ground. Their lives are not as pleasant as the existence inside a secure floating suite.

I felt the stirring of another doubt. What if Loppo, instead of locking horns with Karunan directly, was plotting his fall using David as a pawn? Yes, by sending in his loyal servant as a suicide-warrior, he planned to cut off Karunan from the game. Everyone knew of the recent developments in Aadi Nadu that had instigated Loppo.

Karunan's red blood probably acquired a deeper hue due to his inheritance: Communism. His father, Comrade Damodaran, was a living legend amongst the poor plantation workers. Non-compromising to the core, he would take up arms in his fight for justice. There was a time when the Diwan of Travancore Sir C.P. Ramaswamy Iyer's army went in search of Karunan's father. Their efforts were futile. He hid with other fighters in the secret hideaways inside Aadi Nadu's hills. His parents were humiliated in public when the army didn't find the comrades. Despite such mortification, they did not reveal their son's whereabouts. But the one who hid himself in the hill's womb, hoping for a new dawn, did not stay concealed for long. I have heard some whispers connecting him with the conspiracy to murder C.P.

Whatever be the truth behind that, it is a historical fact that Mani tried to stab C.P., who eventually left Kerala. The fires having been doused, Karunan's father emerged from incarceration, a wreck spewing blood, during the time of the first democratically elected communist government in 1957. Though his bones were broken, he lived solely for the party. Eventually he married and became a good father to four sons. Comrade Damodaran's revolutionary spirit retained its heat even after he was buried under the forlorn rocks of Aadi Nadu. It was this flaming spirit that Karunan obtained as his legacy. If there were a culture of canonizing people as saints in the annals of revolution, Comrade Damodaran would have been hailed as one. He had narrated to his son the incident of A.K. Gopalan[*] visiting his sick bed with the same reverence reserved for a messiah of God!

With the blessings of his father and other Godly messengers, Karunan grew in stature, using the rock as a stepping stone. He maintained a farm by the hillside, which he tried to make into a model establishment. His communist bloodline prevented him from donning the avaricious cloak of a bourgeoise Muthalali. He toiled with his workers, sharing all profits with them, and keeping the minimum for his own sustenance.

---

[*] A stalwart communist leader

Recently, Karunan had taken a popular decision of increasing the wages of his workers. Though the workers were few, they all belonged to a leftist union. The sudden increase in their wages had a ripple effect in the nearby quarries and plantations. It was Satan Loppo, the owner of eighteen quarries, who was the most affected by the vibrations.

Satan Loppo realized soon enough that though it seemed innocuous, the arrow sent forth from Karunan's quiver was deadly upon impact. Reckoning the potential losses, Loppo flatly refused to increase wages. He held fast to the typical bourgeoise argument that he was carrying forward his enterprise despite incurring heavy losses. He took the dictatorial stance that those who did not accept his verdict were welcome to quit.

The gamble went wrong. Posters announcing 'Quarry workers on strike' appeared everywhere. 'Let it be so,' answered Loppo's internal poster.

Though it was an act of obstinacy, when the crusher units shut down, massive losses started accumulating. After a fortnight of the who-will-blink-first game, Loppo accepted defeat before the unity of the organized workers. It was the first surrender of the hitherto unvanquished Muthalali of Aadi Nadu.

Rather than the financial loss, the dent on his image hurt Satan Loppo more. The fact that Karunan, in his humble farm, did not incur much loss from the increased wages, as compared to losses worth lakhs in his own enterprises, was enough to stir his sense of vengeance.

I sombrely reflected that had Karunan been a Christian, Satan Loppo would have already paid me a visit asking for a new coffin. He never fought directly, always preferring a twisted route. An accidental death that never left any trace . . . an unexpected disappearance . . . anything could happen during the reign of dictators. When the corpse lay in front of the communist party office, Loppo would surely arrive with a wreath of red flowers. The savage in him would be salivating at that image.

But when I tried to look at the issue from a different angle, I felt slightly better. Satan Loppo, instead of opting for a direct confrontation, might try to psychologically undermine Karunan. He planned to use David for that purpose. One could surmise that Loppo's honeyed promises to him were meant to cover up that secret. Now, with David opening up his heart to me when matters were so intertwined, I was faced with a dilemma.

An unforeseen development occurred as a result of that 'opening up'. Two hearts hesitating on either shore got the leeway to unite under a single roof. David used his confession to end the covertness associated with his love. Shari and David started speaking openly in my presence. From a state of conversing silently through lovelorn glances, when it became possible to speak face to face, certain new rites developed.

Shashankan used to go home for lunch daily. Shari would be alone in the shop until he returned after his afternoon siesta with his wife. David invited her to my coffin shop during that interval. I did not object to his overture.

Behind the coffins, I placed two wooden crates as seats. No one frequented either the street or my shop during lunch time. To ensure that nobody arrived, I stood at my shop front watching the surroundings like a secret camera. It was my responsibility to warn the lovers well in advance of any potential intrusion. I was enthralled by the fact that not only in ice cream parlours and parks, but in coffin shops too, there was a potential for romance! The world always has something in store for the oddballs, to escalate their madness.

Let them both speak of the feelings overwhelming their hearts. Let them share a piece of fried fish or a snack with each other. Exactly as Beatrice and I had done a long time ago . . .

When they share their love, I will guard the entrance like a cherub appointed by the heavens.

I understand the real duty of Guardian Angels now. It is nothing but the protection of love. Ha! I have become an angel who builds coffins and creates a heaven within it. If so, the box which an angel guards should not be called a death box. It should be christened a heavenly box instead.

'Heavenly Box'. How beautiful it sounds!

The name stuck to my mind, and one fine day I removed the rotting board in front of my shop and scraping the rust away, corrected the words.

Heavenly Boxes for Sale.

I saw the passers-by look up at the truth that I had written, with a new light in their eyes.

The rewriting helped me understand that everything, including heaven and hell, was just a matter of perspective. There was a sparkling insight that 'good' and 'bad' simply involved variations of the inner light.

And the incidents that followed confirmed that it was one's thoughts which turned into reality later.

11

Recognition

'Fear not, O land; be glad and rejoice for the Lord will do great things. Be not afraid, ye beasts of the field: for the pastures of the wilderness do spring, for the tree beareth her fruit, the fig tree and the vine do yield their strength. Be glad then, ye children of Zion, and rejoice in the Lord your God: for he hath given you the former rain moderately, and he will cause to come down for you the rain, the former rain, and the latter rain in the first month. And the floors shall be full of wheat, and the vats shall overflow with wine and oil.'

(Joel 2: 21-24)

I did not know that baptizing the 'Death Box' as the 'Heavenly Box' would usher in harbingers of hope to my shop. Now, not just David, but Shari too had stepped into my circle of friends. I do not remember any woman, apart from Beatrice, entering my coffin shop before. Those who came in search of burial caskets were all men. There was dread glued to most of their faces. If they had the choice, they would have even avoided looking in the direction of the coffin shop, where the fear of death loomed. No wonder the women never ventured near it!

The only exception is Joppan's wife Gracy, who helps him in making coffins. To my knowledge, she is the lone woman in the world who is engaged in that trade. I have seen Gracy at church. That woman brings to mind an expressionless statue. She is neither beautiful nor plain. Her face carries an impassivity that would not fade even with death.

Joppan is a savvy businessman who pays middlemen to strike deals in coffins. His broker, Rappayi, visits houses of mourning on his two-wheeler. The 'ghat-ghat' sound of that vehicle, heard from miles away, is like a portent of the arrival of the God of Death.

'There goes Yama's vehicle,' people mutter.

Rappayi knows how to exploit the vulnerabilities of the grieving. He always carries a photo album with pictures of coffins. The stylized photographs are alluring. The rich place orders for attractive caskets made with costly wood and special accessories, to show off their status. Rappayi adds such photos to his album, and brags about his coffins' opulence to the dead man's relatives. He has a knack for enticing customers.

I typically craft coffins from mango wood. The nature of the wood is pliable and adds to the beauty of the boxes. If people insist on expensive wood, I select teak or rosewood. Appan had worked on the woods of the rubber tree as well as the Devil's tree. The moisture of the Devil's tree is a drawback. Once the water evaporates, the wood starts getting affected deleteriously. Hence, finished caskets of that wood cannot be retained for long. Another tree useful for coffins is the 'Urakka Maram'[*].

Rappayi also has a side business where he arranges for all types of wood. He purchases trees by bulk, converts them into planks and frames in the sawmill, and delivers them to coffin shops. But from my Appan's time, we have never relied on middlemen for our work. We would visit the site of the tree and decide for ourselves whether we wanted it before negotiating the price. It is possible to craft thirty coffins from a decent mango tree. The leftover wooden chips can be

---

[*] Found in mangroves of Kerala

used as fuel. The sack full of detritus and wooden shavings is used to fill up the stoves.

Beatrice's art of stuffing the stove with sawdust was a sight worth watching. As she pummelled the sawdust into the hole of the stove using round clubs, her shapely breasts would sway rhythmically, enchanting me. She would offer sacks of sawdust whittle and chaff to relatives for their use. All such nuances, when one purchased one's own tree, were lost in the dealings with Rappayi. Besides, he charged exorbitantly for his services.

Rappayi would inveigle himself into the homes of mourners and negotiate deals for coffins. His skill at negotiating a hefty commission in his joint business with Joppan was remarkable! Once, when his terms were not met, an angry Rappayi had marched into my shop. He offered to bring in buyers from far off churches if I sold him coffins at a price that was 10 per cent lower than normal. He dangled the bait of special grooves and reapers, used as accessories on the sides of coffins, from a Bangalore company at a cheap rate.

'Indri, don't bother about the price at which I will sell the coffins.' That was Rappayi's condition for the agreement. His malevolent plan was to exploit those made susceptible by their loss, who would not bargain over the price of a coffin. A joint business over coffins! I detested the whole idea of making profit by haggling over death.

'Rappayi, this poor shop does not need any middleman.'

I declined his offer.

'Useless fellow! You are unfit for doing business in this day and age,' Rappayi muttered as he left.

I do not know how to ensnare life and make it bend to my wishes the way Joppan does. His wife, apart from helping him make coffins, runs a business that provides gloves, shoes and even cosmetics for the corpses. Gracy has a ready-made kit for the dead. Sometimes she gets special invitations from Lourdes Hospital situated more than ten kilometres away. She dresses up the corpses lying in their freezer before their final journeys. Probably because of her cohabitation with dead bodies, Gracy's face always has a frosty expression.

I do not have any other enterprises like Joppan and Gracy. I never allowed Beatrice to help me in my work either. I was determined that she and my children would eat the bread that I earned with the sweat of my brow.

Apart from Gracy who has a close connection with coffins, it is only Shari who has dared to enter—with the gentle murmur of a breeze—a place that intimidates even grown men.

She interacted with me as freely as David and started dropping in even in his absence. The refuge they found in my coffin shop was similar to love finding a branch of a green fig tree to rest its tired wings. Shari covered my loneliness with a garment embellished with feathers and frills. It was akin to a beautiful burial cloth woven with pristine feelings.

Shari told me that she had visited Timothios's German wife again. The truth was, it distressed me no end. But I could not disclose my reasons for disliking her journeys to Loppo's residence. My private sorrows should not intrude into Shari and David's lives. Even the most loathed man has friends and relatives who love him sincerely. Both Shari and David now figured in Satan Loppo's list of favourites. I could not severe that attachment with the sharpened edge of my surging hatred. If Loppo was offering to drop an anchor to bring their love ashore, I could not turn my face away in revulsion.

The blouse that Shari stitched had fit the madamma perfectly. She started visiting Loppo's bungalow, even in David's absence, to help the madamma dress.

'Madamma simply loves my stitching,' Shari babbled merrily.

'Good.'

'Muthalali and Timothios said it was good!'

'Hmm.'

'They paid me extra even though I refused. But they insisted . . .'

Shari shyly narrated that the madamma swam in the pool wearing the flimsiest of dresses. I could guess the cause of her obvious embarrassment, having seen films depicting women in swimming costumes. Foreign women wear tight swimwear which conspicuously reveals the shape of their bodies. Apparently the madamma offered Shari a similar swimming dress. Lying that she would fall sick if she swam, Shari evaded the invitation. That was a judicious decision in my opinion. Karunan's daughter should never step out of the bounds of propriety. Our simple, native culture is very different from that of the foreigners.

Though Shari did not participate in the water games, she agreed to the tempting offer of travelling in the suite that reached the depths of the water. Ever since David started speaking of it, she wanted to see the suite. Truth be said, I too have an intense craving to see it. But I desisted from expressing this out of shame. Wishing to see the decadent luxury of my number one foe is a despicable shortcoming. If Shari and David could enjoy the special suite, good for them! Loppo has apparently promised them a trip in it during their honeymoon. For sure, that temptation is hard to resist. Only a fortunate few can celebrate their honeymoon in air and water. How many, including Loppo himself, could partake in such a joy during their honeymoon?

Envy started vexing me, scratching my back with its hind leg. Though I had never seen a water suite before, I started building one in the lake of my imagination. Inside my grand palace-on-water, more majestic than Noah's great ark, I created beauties hitherto unseen. Imagining that Beatrice and I were in the suite submerged in water, I spent an ecstatic night. I found myself making love to Beatrice, as if she were alive. My body burst into flowers and became heavy with fruits. After what seemed like centuries, the closed doors of my senses opened, and when I experienced arousal and ejaculation, I knew that Beatrice had never left my side.

The body is just a medium. Today, I have proof that a truth far beyond us governs the reality of our lives. I yearned to mate with Beatrice in my dreams again. For David and Shari, who were instrumental in my awakening, I felt a deep love.

How lovely would be the first night they spend under the water. They were my children. Let them enjoy their lives dancing, singing and indulging in water games. If Antappan's heart gets broken, I have no recourse but to accept it as an inevitability in the progression of love. When everything comes out into the open, I only wish that my Antappan does not hate me.

* * *

I observed that in David's absence, it was Satan Loppo himself who drove the jeep to drop Shari back when she visited the bungalow to help the madamma.

It pulled at the very roots of my existence.

Since I was afraid of the wild beast inside Satan Loppo, I tried to pry by asking Shari a few absurd questions.

'Why did you travel alone with that man?'

'I requested him not to take the trouble. But Muthalali insisted on dropping me.'

'Did he tell you anything unusual?' I could not restrain myself.

'What do you mean?'

'Anything indecent?'

Shari laughed. 'Muthalali is extremely decent in his behaviour. Never have I noticed a wrong look or word!'

My insides started shaking and heaving as if I was travelling in Satan Loppo's reckless jeep. I could feel the heat and fumes of the feverish engine inside. My understanding of that vile man was at odds with Shari's opinion. The Loppo I knew was a feral beast. He was a devil true to his name.

Even later, the fact that Loppo maintained his respectful distance from Shari and never attempted to muddy the pure waters of that relationship confused me no end. Had I made an error somewhere?

Recollecting past happenings, I even ended up wondering whether I had gone overboard in imagining a satanic figure after mistaking the smell of a cigar. When in a frenzy, everything gets muddled and one is not able to distinguish between right and wrong. I remembered many people gazing at me pitifully as if I was insane. But wasn't that because of my anguish after my wife and children passed away?

Or could it be that I had behaved unpredictably even earlier? Did Beatrice tenderly caress my head, asking me not to get agitated, because she wanted to drive away my frenzied thoughts? Could it be that when Appan took me to Kani vaidyan for the ayurvedic treatments to 'cool my head', it was for something else?

Lord, are you punishing me again by attributing everything to my confounded thoughts?

Causing my confusion to reach a crescendo, Shari came once again to the coffin shop, almost bursting with joy. David was not to be seen; he had left for Coimbatore three days ago for some crusher-related business. It astonished me that Shari exhibited no signs of even missing him.

'Why are you so cheerful today?' I asked.

'I got into the suite today.'

'In the suite?'

'Yes. To use your own words, Uncle, in the ark. The ark which sinks under the water.'

'With whom?' I asked frantically, since David was not around.

'With Muthalali.'

I felt a chill in my very bones.

I stared aghast at Shari. Then, flaring my nostrils, I sniffed, trying to catch a smell.

Could it be that she was covering the bruises caused by Loppo's nails with her sari?

Was there a bluish blood clot on her lips?

'Why are you looking at me like that, Uncle?' Shari asked me warily on observing my changed mood.

'Nothing. I feel that you shouldn't have gone there in David's absence,' I said, struggling to control myself.

'What is the problem? Timothios and Della were there. In fact, they went under the water first. When they returned, they asked me whether I would like to go down too. Since only two people can sit inside the suite at a time, Muthalali offered to go with me.'

I felt a shiver run up my spine. In the privacy of a suite under the water, that depraved beast named Satan Loppo alone with a tender fawn called Shari . . .

'It was astounding, Uncle. So many luxuries . . . like heaven,' Shari gushed. On getting a beautiful girl like Shari alone under the cover of water, definitely the hood of first sin would have reared up in Satan Loppo! I often saw the image of a hooded serpent whenever I brooded about Loppo.

'Muthalali gave me an excellent foreign juice and chocolate. It was wonderful enjoying those while watching the fishes! I could see everything through the glass walls.'

Yes, that was it! I could now see the sequence of events. Loppo must have mixed the juice with a sedative. Shari must have fallen unconscious. Then that bastard must have . . .

'Did you feel odd after drinking the juice?' I asked, my voice trembling.

'Feel what?'

'Dizziness or unease?'

Shari gave a peal of laughter as if I had said something really ridiculous.

'Foreign juice does not cause dizziness, Uncle. It is the local juice which makes people sick.'

I was mortified. How pathetically all my sleuthing efforts were failing! Trying to save face, I asked another question.

'Isn't there a terrible dog in that house?'

'Yes, Hitler. Do you know he adores me? Always wags his tail on seeing me. Hitler is such a darling!'

My devastation was complete. I wondered fearfully about my own mental stability. Had my Appan and Beatrice been tending to my lunacy?

On analysing the events, nothing made much sense and I wondered whether a disease resided within me.

It is said that every madman gets a glimpse of his own insanity at a particular moment. Many try to destroy themselves on gaining that awareness. If it was not insanity but the recognition of it which triggered the final journey, could it be that I had arrived at that juncture? *How come after ages, memories of my Amma came rushing to my mind? Was it true that one remembered the dead when one's own death was imminent?*

12

Amma

'There are those who turn justice into bitterness and cast righteousness to the ground. He who made the Pleiades and Orion, who turns midnight into dawn and darkens day into night, who calls for the waters of the sea and pours them out over the face of the land—the Lord is his name. With a blinding flash he destroys the stronghold and brings the fortified city to ruin. There are those who hate the one who upholds justice in court and detest the one who tells the truth.'

(Amos 5: 7-10)

I was sixteen years old when my Amma died. It was around the time I joined my Appan as his apprentice, having failed the tenth standard examinations twice in a row. Amma could not accept the fact that I had become a coffin maker. She carried a hope, like all mothers do, that I would study well and become a top 'officer'. Perhaps because her wish did not materialize, Amma started experiencing dreams as reality shortly before her death.

When Amma and I were alone in her room, she would insist there was a third person in there. She mentioned that the person was wearing black. When more than one person started visiting Amma, I became afraid of her meetings with the invisible ones. I doubted her sanity, but Appan said that there was nothing amiss. When Appan testified that whatever Amma saw and heard was real, I was befuddled.

'Do you know the uniqueness of truth?' Appan asked.

'No.'

'Truth will reveal itself only to those willing to accept it. My child, it shall never appear before those who are prejudiced against it. Rather than knowing the truth, they are more interested in arguing that they alone are its sole custodians. The "truths" of such people— who arrogantly believe that they exclusively hold ownership over the truth—will always stand against the real truth. Truth shall never grace them with its presence, my son.'

I felt bewildered at Appan's words. For me, the only truth was that my Amma saw sights that were invisible to me.

'Blessed Mother, why are the evil spirits haunting me even when I pray to you all the time?' Amma wailed sporadically.

Amma could see evil spirits.

I was terror struck! I became apprehensive that a group of hideous ghosts had encircled our small hut.

Once Amma leapt abruptly from where she was standing and hollered: 'Look, Satan has reached here after digging up the earth!'

Expecting to see a monster emerge after splitting the earth, I stood with a thudding heart, ready to die.

'Nobody's here! It is just your imagination, Amma.' My attempt at conciliation was as futile as convincing someone of a thing that one was unsure of.

Appan and I alternately guarded Amma during those times. When Appan was in the shop, I would stick around, and vice versa. However, on the evenings when my father was late to return, I was terrified of being alone with Amma. At these time, she would start narrating bizarre stories! When someone narrates an eye-witness account of the triumphal march of Satan's army, won't it scare a sixteen-year-old out of his wits?

Consequently, when twilight arrived, I would light a lamp and seat myself in the verandah. If a ghoul came inquiring after me, at least I could flee! But no ghosts ever came face to face with me. I did not know then that invisible spirits appeared only before those who were nearing death. Amma travelled ceaselessly through the past, the present and the future.

Sometimes when she was in a serene mood, Amma sang in pure melody:

'Kotthachakka thinnangamodam poondappam . . .'
When I relished the jackfruit ripe
A black ant inside my mouth did gripe.
When the ant was tapped into a basket
A chick inside did create a racket.
Sing your song, little chick, little chick.
I too will chirp along, kiyo, kiyo.'

I loved listening to my mother sing that song. Apparently, she would hum the lines as a lullaby when I was a baby. Amma would tease me with the endearment 'her little chick', laughing that I would cry 'kiyo, kiyo' while lying in the cradle.

Amma must have felt happy, else why would she remember and hum that song again?

The only difference was that Amma would repeat 'kiyo, kiyo' endlessly, as I did as a child. Her travel through the present was limited. But it was a great relief to me that at those times Amma did not see the evil spirits.

One day, when I was waiting for Appan in the foyer, I heard Amma's delighted cry.

'Indri, finally the Blessed Mother has arrived!'

I raced inside. Amma was ecstatic with joy. On seeing that her face was lit up as if by the afternoon sun, in that twilight hour, I was bemused. It was like obtaining a vision of the Lord himself.

Amma embraced and kissed me warmly.

'The Blessed Mother has arrived, my child! Our Mother has come!'

My Amma died that night. After eating the rice which Appan fed her and drinking the water that I gave her, Amma left peacefully. She fed both Appan and me with a fistful of rice before her departure. Whenever I saw rice afterwards, I couldn't help remember my Amma. I always felt that 'Annam*' stood for 'Amma'. Perhaps that is why 'Anna' is cognate with 'Mother' in some languages. The name of my mother who taught me that truth was also Anna.

When Amma lay smiling in her casket, divine and serene as the Virgin Mary, it felt as if she was sound asleep as usual.

Amma was the greatest love of my life.

Entangled in the experiences I had in my mother's final days and unable to distinguish between reality and fantasy, I too had been adrift awhile.

Of one fact, I am sure. The world that we see is just the outer foil of an ineffable reality. What is hidden is more expansive than what we see. Amma had narrated to me the visions from these depths to which she had travelled. On recognizing that there were sights beyond those proclaimed real, it slowly became possible for me to glimpse them too. It was then that Appan took me to Kani vaidyan, saying, 'We will cool your head down a bit.'

Perhaps Appan and others felt that I had become delusional like my mother. When another person experiences as real that which seems unreal to us, we tend to call it a delusion. My question is why the other person could not think the same way. He lives with his thoughts and dies one day. I live with my thoughts and pass away another day. If both lives are supposed to break like bubbles, why should I stubbornly insist that he should have lived with the same

---

* Food

thoughts as mine? That is why I snigger when I see people fight over religion and politics.

Hey fragile bubbles, where are you heading busily to?

Anyway, when Appan took me to Kani vaidyan, not only did I not resist the treatment, but I also relished it thoroughly. I liked the look of that slim, calm, amusing man. At first glance, I thought Jeevan Mashai of *Arogya Niketanam** had come alive! The vaidyan checked my pulse and deduced my inner and outer states. When he suggested that I stay a week with him, enjoying oil massages and hot baths, I readily agreed.

When I first read *Arogya Niketanam* from the library of Aadi Nadu, Jeevan Mashai was just an imaginary healer in my mind. I thought that the way he diagnosed diseases by checking the pulse was merely a figment of Tarashankar Banerjee's imagination. Was the disease screaming out its name while coursing through the bloodstream that someone could read it with a touch? My mind scoffed at the thought.

Kani vaidyan, however, dispelled my scepticism totally. Many people came from distant places in search of his healing touch. I became acquainted with a chronic patient of backache who had lost hope with allopathy, and an old woman who was suffering from a terminal illness. Kani vaidyan diagnosed both with great accuracy. How magical it was when he read their diseases from their pulse, without the help of any modern devices!

Kani vaidyan was blunt about the diseases that were incurable. Then he would advise methods for lessening the trauma. He was stringent about the patients maintaining the diets he prescribed and would brook no disagreement. For whatever reason, he never asked me to follow any special diet. Perhaps he felt compassion for my young age. Or, he instinctively understood that staying with my

---

* Tarashankar Banerjee's Bangla novel *Arogya Niketan* was translated into Malayalam as *Arogya Niketanam*. Jeevan Mashai is the eponymous healer in the book.

mother who had the habit of seeing visions had made me that way too.

Nobody would believe me if I were to state that seeing visions is an infectious disease.

But it is so.

After one week of the vaidyan's special treatment using dhara*, my ability to see special sights started weakening and eventually stopped. I am not sure if I have ever seen such images again. Whatever one 'sees' seems real to one. That is why the living do not realize that *what they experience as truth is merely a delusion.* We are credulous folks snared in thoughts.

Could it be that the hatred I have for Satan Loppo stems from unreal sights? Dear Lord, could it be an error of my perspective that I look on Loppo as a devil when David and Shari find him angelic? Will I have to baptize him in holy water and christen him as 'Angel Loppo'?

No, no, never!

I bitterly harangued myself.

That stormy night . . . Beatrice weeping bitterly on the cot . . . the noxious smell of Loppo's expensive cigar . . . those were not my flights of fancy.

I wished David and Shari had not provoked a turbulence within me with their new revelations. If the coffin I had stored for Loppo and the retribution I sought were futile, I would be left with no reason for having prolonged my life till now. Waiting for that son of the devil with a casket would turn out to be a humungous stupidity! I would have to design a new foundation for the rest of my existence.

Appan was right in a way. When the enemy stirs trouble, it is better to light a candle and pray to the Lord to soothe the inner turmoil.

I felt like throwing away the burial casket that I had kept aside for Satan Loppo all these years. If a buyer had stepped into my shop

---

* Pouring medicinal oils on the head

at that moment, I might have given him the coffin at a discount. But the two bodies which needed boxes that week did not fit inside Loppo's casket. One was an infant and the other was a gnarled old man of ninety.

When nobody came to purchase the box that symbolized a meaningless vengeance, I even thought of disposing it of. All I had to do was drag the coffin to the backyard and splinter it to bits before setting fire to it.

But I could not bring myself to do that either.

I could not visit Kani vaidyan for a round of cooling medicinal baths since the yellow-haired death—*Pingala kesini,* as mentioned in Jeevan Mashai's story—had long taken him with her. The only other option was to join Mother Gabriel's prayer group and try to find a sense of calm. I would be relieved from the anxieties of these unceasing tests when I prayed for somebody else without any expectations in return.

That was how I decided to participate in the prayer group after ages.

* * *

The next Thursday, after having duly fasted, when I joined the prayer meeting, people gaped at me. None of them had expected me to step into those precincts again. Mother was not flustered on seeing me. When she smiled at me from her wheelchair, like God's main messenger, I was overwhelmed.

I looked up at the Holy Cross as a disciplined member of the congregation. My intention was to see whether drops of blood were dripping from the cross. No, I was now at the place of true sights. I was no longer a petty man hanging on to revenge and did not want to wreak vengeance by murdering anyone. All I needed were a few interludes of serenity.

I remembered that Satan Loppo's wife Philomena, whom we called Philomenamma, used to be an erstwhile member of that prayer group. Her presence had been a matter of great wonder for me. The marriage of Loppo and Philomena was a clear proof that the Lord enjoyed sticking incongruent pieces together. I had often wondered whether it was Loppo's philandering ways which had driven his wife into becoming a deeply religious woman. And what had happened to that Good Samaritan then?

Last year, the woman had become bedridden, forever ending her visits to the church. Her prayers were sent from the confines of her cot. Whenever I recollected that despite her intense imploring, Satan Loppo had never redeemed himself, my trust in the power of prayer would get shaken.

While Philomenamma kept her devotion quiet, Loppo showed off his own inclinations tastelessly. When he brashly took his place in the front row of the church during the Sunday Qurbana, ahead of the children, I felt as if the devil himself was preening and primping. His ostentatious silk jubba and the thick gold rosary around his neck were gaudy enough to be noticed by those in the back row. I used to wonder about the efficacy of prayers chanted while counting those golden rosary beads. Loppo was savouring everyone's attention. How many times my concentration must have faltered when my glance fell on that man who ought to have been in the back row! More than my problem, that posture of his was an impediment to everyone's spiritual sojourn. Nobody dared to murmur a word against him, probably because Loppo's money had sponsored the pillars holding up the church's ceiling.

When Mother Gabriel opened the Box of Appeals and took out a grievance, I reined in my galloping mind and meditated on the Lord's name. As the name of the letter writer was announced, my composure evaporated in a jiffy.

Antappan!

My beloved Antappan had submitted a grievance for our prayerful intervention.

I waited with bated breath to hear what his concern was.

When I heard that his appeal was a prayer for his son to change his mind, I started sweating profusely, as if possessed by an invisible spirit. Among all those in that prayer group, only I knew what was being asked!

Today, I shall be appealing to sever an intimate love knot holding two hearts together.

Lord, have you thrown me into an ordeal where I shed more blood than you did in your sufferings?

As I harshly reprimanded myself for setting out to rejoin the group at an inauspicious time, the benedictions within started seeping away through all the pores of my body.

13

The Heartbeat of Time

'But let him ask in faith, nothing wavering. For he that wavereth is like a wave of the sea driven with the wind and tossed. For let not that man think that he shall receive any thing of the Lord. A double minded man is unstable in all his ways. Let the brother of low degree rejoice in that he is exalted: But the rich, in that he is made low: because as the flower of the grass he shall pass away. For the sun is no sooner risen with a burning heat, but it withereth the grass, and the flower thereof falleth, and the grace of the fashion of it perisheth: so also, shall the rich man fade away in his ways.'

(Epistle of James 1: 6-11)

When I made my way back after a full day of fasting and prayer, hunger started gnawing at my soul. An obsessive desire for food, hitherto unknown, gripped me. The fragrance of beef cooked in spicy curry, wafting from the small shop near the church, was as seductive as an invitation from sin.

How long had it been since I had eaten some meat, let alone moved out of my shop? I had not even noticed these habits slipping away from my life. Now I felt the craving for not just food but also for some drinks. If Antappan were to invite me to the cemetery, it would be a perfect night to stay among the souls and allow the mind to soar!

I lavishly appeased my hunger with three porottas and beef. The red-hot masala that sanctified the buffalo meat was utterly sumptuous. I remembered my erstwhile Sundays enriched by the delicious sautéed beef cooked by Beatrice.

After the five-thirty morning Qurbana at the church, I used to be a regular visitor at Pranchi's butcher shop where thick chunks of raw and bloody meat were suspended from thin steel rods. After skinning the ox, goat and buffalo, Pranchi would hang their flesh separately upside down. Everybody who attended the Qurbana would invariably visit his shop with the same intensity as following the dictums of the holy church. Whenever he saw me, Pranchi would hand over a kilogram of buffalo meat wrapped in a lush Chembila.

The butcher artistically minced the meat on his bloodied chopping block. Those who had been sufficiently impressed with the sacrificial beast exhibited the preceding day would arrive as customers the next day. Beatrice and the children would await, filled with anticipation, my return with the meat.

How delicious was Beatrice's meat curry! Whatever she touched turned out to be tasty. In those days, my body too became delectable, having been graced by her touch. Now, all these temptations have vanished.

When the hunger pangs were alleviated, the prayer I had to submit to the Lord against David started tormenting me. I tried to console myself that Antappan's entreaty was only for guiding his son down the right path. Though I had been nonplussed for some time, I too eventually sincerely beseeched the Lord. I cast a despondent look at the Madbaha* then, wondering how the Lord would receive that request. Since the One who hung from the cross had His face cast down in death, I didn't receive a clear answer.

---

* Sanctum sanctorum

There was a choir of angels surrounding the One sipping from the Cup of Suffering, imparting strength to Him. How pitiable it is that the Son of God, hanging from the nails of holy suffering, has to take on Himself the vexations of mankind too! What if the Lord decides that to clear the briars and stones from David's path, it was necessary to detach Shari's life from his?

I felt mortified, like a sinner, since I had prayed to cleave them apart. It was evil to force the Lord, the One who looks deep inside our hearts, into narrow squares of human judgement.

Aren't we limiting Him, when we think of the Creator of the sky, stars and the entire universe, as the Lord of an exclusive sect?

In my view, my Appan, who was a humble coffin maker, had more insight about the matter than many erudite theologians. I had once posed a teaser to him:

'Appa, how come Chakkappan and Varky claim that their congregation is the only true one and that only they will ascend to heaven? Why don't we attend their church?'

Appan, smart fellow that he was, started guffawing with the *muzhakkol* raised in his hand. The carpenter's rod was a part of our lineage, handed down over generations. It was seven feet in length and crafted from coconut wood. This family inheritance was destined to reach me eventually.

'Indri, every church and congregation believes they are the select few followers of the Lord. Each will quote a line extracted from the Holy Book to cleverly substantiate their claims. It is amusing that there is just one Lord and one hundred and fifty groups fighting over Him.'

'Who among these are the true believers? On whose side is the Lord, Appa?'

'The Lord's congregation is of Love, my child. It is a congregation of humility and compassion. He accepts you into His fold after examining your heart, regardless of your wealth, status or even sect of church! Even in the throes of agony on the cross, the Compassionate One accepted a mere thief into his paradise. Can anyone tell us the sect of the church to which that little lamb belonged? Christ is not with those who fight over His name. Even if someone does not belong to any congregation, if he is good-hearted, Christ will be with him. Else how can He be the Lord of the entire creation? Indri, remember this: Once someone realizes that the Kingdom of God is within himself, he won't have a reason to pray but for praising the Lord!'

'Are there people like that?'

Appan laughed uproariously. Then he swirled the muzhakkol like a sword. Sometimes, my father's replies would be just laughter! The seeker was left to pick up nuggets of wisdom from that . . . I suddenly remembered that I had never seen my Appan pray to *gain anything*. That would mean that he had inherited the heavens.

I am sure about one fact: The Keepers of the Keys of heaven would not exhibit any signs of possessing them. Appan had told me that they wouldn't be shouting themselves hoarse from churches or delivering speeches from synagogues or constructing places of worship akin to fortresses.

'The Lord of all wealth was born in the manger of poverty, my son! We build gigantic, palace-like churches and let Him hang on the cross, barely covering his nakedness with a rag. But He chooses to be born in hearts that are as humble as the grass-crib inside a cow shed. He asks for compassion and not offerings. Why is it that no one hears what the Gospel proclaims, that *the highest worship is the worship in spirit and truth*?'

* * *

As I walked back to my coffin shop, many vignettes from the past kept flashing in my mind. I hadn't closed the shop when I left for church. Probably a coffin shop is the only place in the world which remains secure in the absence of locks. No police station in the world has recorded any case of a thief stealing a coffin till date. Even thieves are disinterested in the goods of a coffin shop.

I observed that Pundit was hard at work in his watch shop. A long clock had taken possession of the ground in front of him. I recognized the history of that huge time machine in a jiffy. I had seen it undergoing treatment at Pundit's hands just two days before. It was David who had transported it in his jeep and carried it to the watch shop. It was a historical showpiece, belonging to Sayyip's era, lying abandoned in Satan Loppo's bungalow. The foreign daughter-in-law had become fascinated with its antique beauty. The main reason was its German making. The madamma, who loved historical artefacts, wanted to gift it its life back. The time shops of the city failed to bring back its heartbeat. The clock had returned to the Sayyip's bungalow like a corpse.

Loppo, who heeded the saying that dead clocks bring in bad luck, was planning to sell it to the scrap dealer. It was then that David remembered the hundred-and-twelve-year-old Pundit and suggested that they show it to him. Timothios had mockingly wondered what a man in his dotage, in such an obscure corner of the world, would achieve when experts in the city had failed. David had, however, insisted on a last try.

'As if that old gaffer about to conk off will make it work,' Satan Loppo had sarcastically joined force with his son.

'No harm in trying, is there?' David had put in the request.

'Giving life to a dead body in a freezer?'

It was that dead-as-a-nail-clock that Pundit was trying to breathe life into!

'Since it is very old, a lot of its parts are not available nowadays. It does not work on electricity. This is a mechanical clock of yore. Look at these two balls of brass hanging from both sides. When these move up and down, time will start ticking. I can see some holy scripts in German inscribed inside . . . seems like old alphabets. I have no clue what it means.'

'Why not ask the madamma?'

'True. I have copied down the words on that paper. Even if they take the clock, let the words remain with me.'

I looked curiously at the white paper that Pundit extended to me. It looked like a small poem. The alphabets were like those of the English language.

Benutz die Zeit
Die dir gegeben
Denn jede Stunde

It started like this and went on and on. I was not interested in reading more as I was unfamiliar with the words.

I stared at the white man's clock that was part of Satan Loppo's possessions. Its visage seemed to suggest that many memories of an autocratic regime were concealed within. Yet I was sure that Pundit would unveil its secrets and breathe new life into it. *It would be like the Lord God, who created the heavens and earth, breathing into the nostrils of the man formed from the dust.*

In a strange kind of way, I found this cohabitation with clocks immensely exciting.

That night and the next, I noticed that the bulbs in Pundit's shop burnt bright. It meant that the Sayyip's clock had Pundit in its grip, having pushed sleep to the sidelines. Not only Pundit, but the clock held me too in its sway.

I relentlessly observed the old man who, like the Godhead, was utterly engrossed in the Act of Creation. Pundit, with his white beard and moustache, has a resemblance to our Father as depicted in the calendars. If he were to don a cape as the artist visualized, the likeness would be perfect. Like man breathing on the sixth day of creation, would the clock come to life too?

My presumption was not false.

Hidden behind a coffin, I watched Satan Loppo's jeep hurry away with the clock, which was resurrected from death on the third day. Time, climbing David's chariot, was travelling to Satan Loppo's bungalow.

It intrigued me that the madamma, clad in a sari, had herself arrived to take the working clock back. Perhaps it was the passion she felt as a German citizen towards all things German. They were supposed to carry the deep-rooted pride of Aryan blood in their veins.

But time does not differentiate between Germans, Americans or Indians. Recollecting my Appan's words, I felt then that the Lord held a similar view towards various congregations of faith. The Creator would only care if a clock showed the correct time, regardless of the country of its origin.

It is not the problem of time, but that of the clock that it erred occasionally.

Those who vehemently insist that their clocks alone are correct, should first experience stillness, before turning to time and attempting to know it.

14

The Magnifying Glass

'For our struggle is not against flesh and blood, but against the rulers, against the authorities, against the powers of this dark world and against the spiritual forces of evil in the heavenly realms. Therefore, put on the full armor of God, so that when the day of evil comes, you may be able to stand your ground, and after you have done everything, to stand. Stand firm then, with the belt of truth buckled around your waist, with the breastplate of righteousness in place, and with your feet fitted with the readiness that comes from the gospel of peace.'

(Ephesians 6: 12-15)

Meeting Pundit again and rejoining the prayer group stirred many of the dead parts in me back to life. I started enjoying my sojourns to Pundit's time shop. The thought crossed my mind that the school lessons categorizing matter into solid, liquid and gaseous states were applicable for time too. If the coffin shop encompasses the inertia of the solid state, the atmosphere in the time shop has the fluidity of liquid. Without time, no mind exists. That means the human mind can respond only to motion. Then the densely packed inside loses its obstinacy and acquires lightness.

After that, I started examining each clock eagerly. You can read their heartbeat with a touch. I would carry those palpitations back with me from Pundit's shop and hand them over to David and Shari. It is in their lives that the flow of time should abide, not in mine, which is stagnant like a cesspool.

'Pundit is a smart fellow! When everybody gave up, he got that clock working in a mere three days. The madamma is simply thrilled. She might take it to Germany,' David quipped.

'Such a huge clock?' I was astonished.

'As if that is an issue! If they can bring a German cow to this land, what is the problem in taking a clock to Germany?'

True, the rich could transport anything to any place. They could undo the nuts and bolts of heaven and get it reassembled in their front yard.

'That clock strikes the hour in a very melodious rhythm. One o' clock, two o' clock, three o' clock . . . You should listen to it at night. Just imagine a Yakshi, that enchanting female spirit, gracefully walking towards you . . . that is how it feels.'

'Yakshi?'

'Yes, when a Yakshi appears in the movies, there is that special sound effect, right?'

'Did you hear that at night, David?' I asked with interest.

'When I lie in the outhouse, I often hear it chime away. And I wish that a Yakshi would appear . . . a gorgeous Yakshi.'

I observed that Shari cast a piercing look at David then.

'Yakshis drink blood. You know that, don't you?'

'If a beautiful Yakshi drinks a bit of one's blood, it is welcome. Happy end.'

Though David was trying to provoke Shari, I loved that little joke of his. Shari had the looks of an incensed Yakshi then. All that was missing was the enchanting fragrance of the Pala tree and the accompaniment of jingling anklets!

When I met Pundit the next time, I told him about the clock's impending voyage to Germany.

'The clock you repaired is all set to migrate to Germany.'

'Germany, the land of Hitler and Nazis,' Pundit spoke suddenly, as if meandering through some memories. 'When the Second World War was in full swing, any news concerning Hitler was invaluable. There was a stage when it felt like he would capture the whole world. The Germans are an intelligent lot. Have you read *Mein Kampf*? Even Hitler's harshest critic might reluctantly praise him while reading certain portions. He was both intelligent and crafty. If only humans used their brains for good, this world would have been a better place. But Hendri, the world can never be sated with beauty alone.'

'What do you mean?'

'When beauty is created, its opposite is also created simultaneously. When heaven was built, hell would also have been finalized. That is the Maya of creation. There can never be a world filled with just goodness. It has never been there. And neither will such a world ever be. Perhaps I can tell you a historical truth connected with Netaji and Hitler unknown to others . . . Something I have experienced myself.'

'What is it?' I asked, gaping.

'Not now. When the time is ripe, I shall reveal it to you. It has to be in the right place and in the right ambience.'

Having said that, Pundit unearthed an old gramophone from the nook of his shop and opened it. He effortlessly crossed over from the world of Hitler and Netaji to the world of musical instruments.

'I have two precious possessions with me: one is this gramophone, and another, a pendant watch made in Germany. Both survived the bonfires meant for foreign goods during the Swadeshi movement.'

Pundit showed me the pendant watch which hung from his waist, beneath his long shirt.

'I have never worn a watch on my wrist. But time has always been beating next to my body. Did you know that the fingerprints of both Hitler and Netaji are on this pendant watch?'

I couldn't believe my ears! Imagine the staggering historical value of that watch if Hitler and Netaji had touched it!

Nobody in Aadi Nadu, including me, were aware that Pundit was in possession of such a time machine. I had always felt that there was something quite mysterious about Pundit. And now, the old warhorse was being extraordinarily friendly and revealing secrets!

Meanwhile, Pundit started giving life to the gramophone by attaching the lever to the small hole on its side, and slowly rotating it.

'It is only the strength of my hand that shall now make this gramophone sing. To be precise, it is a technique of converting human effort into sound and music, with no help of electricity!'

The gramophone record was rotating very quickly. When the needle was lowered on the groove, it started singing.

'Shinkaravelane . . .' The sweet, intoxicating voice of Pattamal dripped into my ears. It was pristine in its purity. I had heard that song in my childhood. Now, after a long time, I was listening to it again. It was hard to believe that the melodious, crystal-clear notes were being rendered from a gramophone made many decades ago.

Pundit was nodding his head to the song.

HIS MASTER'S VOICE. One could see the world-famous emblem on the gramophone inscribed with those words.

The song reached a mesmerizing crescendo. Pundit stood captivated.

I watched Pundit as he wound up the gramophone to ensure that the song went on uninterrupted.

'Hendri, shall I tell what you are busy thinking of?' he asked me.

I did not have an answer to that. I was gobsmacked when Pundit disclosed it to me.

'You want to gaze through the magnifying glass . . . my monocle.'

My mind had vacillated while listening to the song and had dragged me to the magnifying glass. I was eager to discover the astounding sights he saw through that monocle.

'Go ahead.'

Pundit extended his monocle to me encouragingly.

When I closed my right eye and fixed the monocle on the left, I felt everything going misty. Pundit slipped away from my view.

'That happens when the power increases. It magnifies and shows you only the miniature things. If you gaze at the 'big' things, as we know them, through a magnifying glass, they will appear weird. The universe of the minuscule is quite different from ours, Hendri.'

'What do you mean?'

'If you cannot see the dead, that does not mean that they don't exist. It just means that our eyes are not capable of seeing them in their subtle manifestations. Our eyes can see only those things which reflect light. Souls do not reflect light. Hence, our eyes cannot see them. Hendri, if our eyes gain that capability, we can see the dead.'

'But the body disintegrates after death.'

'A fan not working does not imply that the electricity which traversed through it has vanished, does it? It just means that the fan has lost the ability to let the electricity go through it. Even if the body decays, the life force that once flowed through it shall remain. Like an implement that responds to electric force experiences its presence, a medium which responds to life force can also experience it . . . It is energy after all.'

Lord! I was shocked to the core.

What should I do to catch a glimpse of my Beatrice and children again? What instrument was there to help me?

Pundit responded, as if reading my thoughts.

'Everything is possible. There is nothing impossible in this world. Knowing what the sun, earth, planets, vehicles, trees *really are*, an ordinary person can go berserk! Time is also an extremely subtle concept. I went crazy pondering over it. I am sure you have your own eccentricities. That is why . . . that is the sole reason why I am going to tell you certain things undisclosed to anyone before.'

'After sacrificing my entire youth in the fire of revolution, if I haven't frozen to death on seeing the present state of affairs, it is only because of time! I knew Gandhiji and Nehru closely; I have personally interacted with Subhas Chandra Bose, and was part of his Indian National Army. I have known starvation, and have endured torture in jails. My marriage happened very late and I have a family of many children and grandchildren, almost innumerable. Much later, I came to recognize my own self: that I am a prisoner of time like everybody else. Hendri, the body is a *mantrika petti*, a magic box. A magnifying glass is needed to see what is inside.'

Lord, Pundit's words tantalized me! Wasn't my Appan endlessly discussing the same thing? The words he had used were '*shinkara petti*: *an alluring box'*.

'The Creation befools even the most brilliant among us. Such a large body grows from a miniscule seed; it develops eyes for seeing, ears for hearing and nose for breathing. The heart beats regularly and ensures the pumping of blood to all cells. The brain acquires intelligence. From a seeming emptiness, hard bones and teeth take form! Millions of veins and nerves work with clockwork precision to control everything. And yet, we live ignoring all these marvels, squabbling over the pettiest of things. A brilliant man who lives like that is simply an idiot, isn't he? What is the mathematics behind the body? Tell me, what is the calculation behind the births and deaths of billions of living things? Unable to understand the way things are, we attempt to find out and fail miserably. We live and die, bursting like mere bubbles. *Yet the man who experiences the secret while he is alive is far ahead of the richest and the most powerful person on this earth.*'

'Who . . . who would know that secret?' I asked timidly.

'Ha ha!' Pundit burst into laughter. 'Every one of us can experience it. But one needs to be trained to gaze through a magnifying glass for that. Hendri, those who desist from doing so and disparage the truth will never get to know the secret. While wearing this monocle, what you saw was so different! Though I was here, you couldn't see me. We see the world as it is, because our five senses work within a restricted band of frequencies. Creatures with more powerful senses see a different world. They hear sounds unheard by us and catch smells we cannot. What is the truth then?'

I was dumbfounded listening to what Pundit revealed. Those were things I had never before heard of. They were diametrically opposed to the notions I had maintained about the universe. In those moments, Pundit was taking me to a place beyond the laws of force of this physical world.

'If there are microorganisms inside our bones that cannot be seen even with a magnifying glass, for them the small fissures in the bones would appear monstrously large, like doors to a fortress. Everything around would seem like citadels and cities. The spaces inside the atoms would be like open lands. Those creatures never realize that they are living inside the bones of a human being. See, we humans are like those microorganisms. Living inside the bones of a gigantic creature, we presume that whatever we see *is the only reality*. The sun, the moon, the solar system, are all like the electrons and protons inside a single atom in that creature's body. When the creature beckons with its finger, we are thrown off balance. We refer to it as an earthquake. If that creature moves its leg, we experience a cyclone. Neither do we see the creature nor recognize that we are living inside it. The spaces within the atoms making up that creature is our sole universe. What we discover by sitting inside that space and shooting rockets is akin to microorganisms sitting inside our bones and conducting experiments. Listen, for an ant living in Aadi Nadu, America might be an unknown land which is situated light years away. Humans can reach there, but an ant, caught up in *its own time-space,* cannot hope to do that. Hendri, similar Americas exist for humans, where we can never reach. The only way to reach those places is by gaining control over time.'

'Control over time?'

Pundit laughed.

'If an ant climbs a man-made airplane, even it can reach America, can't it? Likewise, if a human being boards an airplane belonging to a sublime intelligence, he too can reach such Americas.'

Lord, I felt lightheaded and giddy!

Seeing my bemused state, Pundit elaborated. 'I am still continuing my experiments with time. I can vouch for one fact. *There is no such thing called death*. Even if it exists, it is neither the beginning nor the end. *Death is just a continuum*.'

By informing me, the maker of caskets for the dead, that there was no death, Pundit has pushed me into a quagmire of confusion. How am I supposed to view a coffin then?

Everything inside me was smashed to smithereens.

15

Organs

'When he had finished speaking, he said to Simon, "Put out into deep water, and let down the nets for a catch." Simon answered, "Master, we've worked hard all night and haven't caught anything. But because you say so, I will let down the nets." When they had done so, they caught such a large number of fish that their nets began to break. So, they signaled their partners in the other boat to come and help them, and they came and filled both boats so full that they began to sink. When Simon Peter saw this, he fell at Jesus' knees and said, "Go away from me, Lord; I am a sinful man."'

(Luke 5: 4-8)

For a few days afterwards, I wasn't sure whether I was dead or alive. Pundit had hammered inside me the idea that there was no difference between the living and the dead. While I pondered deeply over it, David and Shari continued to visit my shop as usual. Unsure whether they were alive or not, I stared at them intently.

'What is the matter, Uncle? Something is amiss.' When David, the lifeless, spoke thus, the dead me responded passively, 'No, nothing.'

'I have also noticed some changes in Uncle,' Shari joined forces with David.

I did not deign to give a logical reply. Considering everybody in my acquaintance, including my staunch enemy Satan Loppo, as one of the 'living dead', I had started experiencing a twinge of truth. *If this was the world of the dead, in which world was Beatrice and my children residing?* How could I remove the screen separating them from me?

It was during that time, when I was caught in a vortex of my thoughts, that an unexpected stroke of luck favoured the coffin shop. The opposition party decided to conduct a mock 'mass burial' as a symbolic protest against the government, and started ordering coffins from all the coffin shops around. Thousands of affordable caskets were in demand. I ended up making fifty-eight coffins from inexpensive wood in one week.

'Reduce the price a bit, considering the noble purpose behind it,' Shekharan, the body and soul of the opposition party, adjured.

'I've reduced it to the maximum,' I argued.

It was the first time that someone was haggling over the price of coffins with me. The way they went about bargaining for the caskets to bury the ruling party was laughable. How the politicians hankered after power! I never saw any difference between the party in power and the opposition. In their unending zeal to serve the public, they indulged in fights and murders, and manufactured martyrs. How sincere they were in that effort! Justifying that I too should exhibit some sincerity, I had fun negotiating the price of the coffins. Since quite a windfall came my way, I felt a grudging respect for the opposition. For a few days, I toiled continuously from dawn to dusk.

That week, every nook and corner of Kerala overflowed with coffins. The village office, panchayat office, municipalities and secretariat were inundated with burial caskets carried in processions.

The opposition party created many parodies of a requiem for the ruling party.

Power shall fall one day, remember, oh Chief!
Your lifetime's deeds shall also tumble, just as life!

The mass burials were amusing. For those who buried, and those who were buried, it was merely political travesty in a new mode. Both parties conveniently chose to forget that the people were indifferent to their shows, accustomed as they were to the sight of each government resurrecting alternatively every five years, even after being buried inside a coffin hammered in with nails. On public platforms, when they swore on the names of their mothers that they stood with the common man, one felt like laughing in pity.

I could not meet Pundit that week due to my heavy workload.

The week after, having attended church on Thursday, I entered Pundit's shop again. Time seemed to be scampering like a toddler inside the four walls of that place. Since Pundit's previous discourse about time and the universe was indelibly imprinted on my mind, I could no longer view the shop as a normal trading place. There was a deep secret stored inside the shop unknown to the ordinary inhabitants of Aadi Nadu. Indeed, David and Shari should have celebrated their love inside the time shop. For lovers, a dynamic environment replete with the 'tick-tock' sound was more conducive than the morbid silence of a coffin shop. There was no needle turning the wheel of time inside my shop, since I neither wore a watch nor kept a clock.

'Perhaps a new watch can turn someone's time around,' Pundit remarked succinctly.

I could not help staring at my naked wrist where time had never thrummed its beats. Perhaps the lack of a watch to usher in good times was the reason behind my still and silent life. For a place bereft of heartbeats, coffins were the most suitable.

'I want a watch.'

Though a time keeper was the last thing needed for a man who had never followed the clock in his life, I spoke unwittingly, as if someone had driven me to say it.

My forlorn, meaningless life has nothing that depends on a needle's rotations. If I want to keep track of my quotidian life, I can depend on the church bells, which toll thrice a day. Whenever the bells ring, I trace a cross on my forehead and murmur out of habit, 'By the sign of the Sacred Cross.' Apart from reminding me that it is morning, afternoon and evening, the bells never harangue me about any time-bound tasks. The only emergency which might occur in my life is the sudden demand for a coffin. Whenever the bells chimed a death, I had to work on the finishing touches of a half-complete casket.

I usually keep a stock of coffins ranging from a length of five and a quarter foot to six and a quarter foot. Any coffin below and above those dimensions are made fresh, based on demand. The muzhakkol is capable of measuring any human being in the world, and anyone might need its service at any time. In the olden days, people used threads to measure the corpses.

If a person is denoted by 'height' when he is alive, it modifies to 'length' when he is dead. For those who have metamorphosed into 'length', I grab a half-complete casket and ready it as though decorating a new house: I apply putty and follow it up with paint and polish. It is the homecoming of a new owner. My 'Heavenly Box' shop is always ready for their service.

No wonder that I had never thought about owning a watch, hardly ever bothering about the precision of time. Then, why had I demanded one from Pundit now?

Pundit smiled at my request.

'Those who can cross the time barrier are not affected by good or bad times.'

On hearing his words, for some unknown reason, the symbols of addition, subtraction, division and multiplication from my tenth-standard mathematics text book started swirling inside me. How these symbols ever worked on numbers, I could never fathom then or now. All I could figure was that Pundit, like my Appan, had uttered something mysterious.

'I have set in motion many watches and clocks in all these years. All of them always moved time forward. But now I am wondering about something else.'

'What?'

'I want to move time backwards. If "forward" means clockwise, "backward", going anticlockwise, is also possible. In my life, I haven't made anything like that! I want to make an Anti-Clock.'

Anti-Clock!

I was hearing about such a thing for the first time.

Pundit elaborated that the needles should move in the anti-clockwise direction to become an Anti-Clock. He added that his Anti-Clock would have twenty-four numbers etched in it unlike the twelve in normal clocks. One could jump straight from morning to night and from twilight to the heat of the afternoon.

How thrilling it would be! I became impatient to see the Anti-Clock that Pundit had sculpted with his words. Would it transport me from the present to the past? To the time that I had spent with Beatrice and my children? Unwinding my heart's rhythm backwards and beyond, would it usher me to the moment of my birth? And what, after crossing that moment? Who, or what would I be then? Brooding thus, I started to become nervous about the Anti-Clock.

'I shall be busy with the task from tomorrow,' Pundit said, 'See, if I were to buy a Chinese watch and change its polarity, I can do it easily enough. But I am not aiming at that. I want a complete, mechanical clock. A time-factory which shall crush time into seconds, minutes and hours! Like the olden-day clocks, it should work exclusively on human energy. Won't be an easy job to craft it to the perfection that I desire. I have no idea if I am up to the task in the twilight of my life. But if I cannot do it now, it shall never be done.'

I felt doubtful whether a man aged one hundred and twelve could fully involve himself in making an Anti-Clock. It was a strenuous task, from what I could fathom. The pallets, pinions, springs and wheels that make time race in reverse, should work perfectly in tandem. While I was tangled in these anxious thoughts, Pundit went about his job with peerless attention.

* * *

I found myself obsessing about the Anti-Clock thereafter. When David and Shari visited my shop, I told them about it. My eagerness infected them like an epidemic. Both of them believed that Pundit, who had given life to the old German clock, could easily give birth to an Anti-Clock.

David told me that the old German clock, resurrected from eternal death by Pundit, reigned in all elegance and pomp in Satan Loppo's foyer. Shari endorsed that view, having seen it during her frequent visits to the bungalow. Loppo's foreign daughter-in-law had finalized the spot for the clock and ceremoniously placed it there. She had apparently insisted on Shari's presence at the consecration.

The madamma was always seeking Shari's help for everything. Due to Shari's expert training, the foreign woman had mastered the art of wearing the sari.

On hearing all that, I felt incensed at Satan Loppo's demonic, despotic rule. In the native soil of Aadi Nadu, it was Loppo who most intimately interacted with foreign goods.

German-made suite
German cows
German dog
German daughter-in-law
Now, a German clock.

I feel that all those German artefacts are creating a distinct image of Satan Loppo. It reminds us that the distance from an unquestioned centre of power to becoming a tyrant is very short. A breed of acolytes, indifferent to the justice and injustice of Satan Loppo's actions, is being raised to back him unconditionally. I have enough reason to believe that a Hitler, ready to murder his opponents, possesses Satan Loppo.

However, it troubles me that Shari and David relish their intimacy with Loppo's household. I know that even the dreams of their future are tinted a German hue. I wondered wildly whether Shari would leave the shores of Aadi Nadu with David and move to Germany, owing to her extraordinary closeness to the madamma. Apparently, she was asked of her willingness to immigrate to Germany! It is obvious that though it was a facetious query, a seed of desire has been planted inside Shari. She disclosed her willingness to migrate with David. What is impossible in this flexible world if intensely desired and acted upon?

I could not fathom what could have brought Shari and the foreign woman so close, so fast.

'Past life connection, probably.' That was Shari's answer.

She spends most of her days in the bungalow. Shashankan does not object as he is remunerated handsomely. Shari, full of exuberance, believes that Loppo and his daughter-in-law will give flight to her dreams.

But life is not an embroidered handkerchief on which we can stitch anything that we desire.

It was amid all this that Pundit entered with his Anti-Clock, befuddling me even more.

* * *

I am as obsessed with the Anti-Clock as Shari is about Germany. Thinking of my limbs as needles of the Anti-Clock taking me into a time past, I, who had hitherto limited myself to the coffin shop, started venturing into Pundit's shop intermittently. It was as if new transformations were happening inside me, someone who usually watched the world from behind coffins. Even the thoughts of killing Satan Loppo seemed to have left me.

What, what was happening to my life?

Pundit, wearing the monocle, was engrossed in creating the Anti-Clock. Whenever I reached his shop, he would turn his head and look at me. It was a scary sight. One eye would be fixed on the past and the other, on the present. Maybe it was the net result of plus and minus that created an impassivity in him.

I could not decipher the potpourri on Pundit's worktable. Many miniature organs made of metal, clock wheels, some springs . . .

'These have to be fitted with great precision. If one changes its place, all is lost. Then time cannot be captured again. If one tiny bit rolls away, it's a lost case. Taming the clock wheel and spring is as good as holding the ocean in the palm of your hand. While winding the spring, if it slips, the ratchet wheel can spin back with the lightning speed of the Sudarshan Chakra. Woe befalls anything in its path.'

Pundit showed me the deep scars on his face and forefinger. The Sudarshan Chakra had caused those nasty wounds. Then he pointed at the internal organs of the clock.

'Look at the most important part of the time machine: the escape wheel. This fellow works like a dam, stopping time, and slowly channelling it to the hour hand and the minute hand. It gets the energy required for the work from the swinging pendulum. In short, the oscillations to the past and the future determine the present.'

Intoxicated, I craved to caress the pieces. Wondering how the scattered bits of non-living things could give birth to an Anti-Clock which moved time back, I stood impatiently, staring awhile.

But despite the passage of many days and weeks, there was no significant progress.

After a while, with a rush of disappointment, I muttered that an old man like Pundit could hardly make an Anti-Clock with the limited raw material available to him.

Again, I cowered like a ghost behind the coffins left untouched by time.

16

Changes

'The kingdom of heaven is like a man who sowed good seed in his field. But while everyone was sleeping, his enemy came and sowed weeds among the wheat, and went away. When the wheat sprouted and formed heads, then the weeds also appeared. The owner's servants came to him and said, "Sir, didn't you sow good seed in your field? Where then did the weeds come from?" "An enemy did this," he replied. The servants asked him, "Do you want us to go and pull them up?"'

(Matthew 13: 24-28)

'One's time can change for better or worse in a day, Uncle.'

'Why do you say that?'

'Joppan is in bad shape. Heard that he is admitted to Jubilee Hospital . . .'

'What happened to him?'

'He had been suffering from a chronic headache for a while. They discovered rather late that it was a tumour. Time to lay down the cards, I guess. The coffin shop has been shut for the last few days. All the customers will now throng your shop. One person's misfortune creates a fortune for another.'

'That's ungodly! I don't want to profit from another's pain,' I snubbed David.

Insisting that even if a sick man was one's sworn enemy, one shouldn't speak ill of him, Shari too lent support to my view.

At times David impulsively grabs the 'sword of words' and twirls it around recklessly. Inadvertently, someone ends up hurt. Probably because Shari endorsed my opinion, David justified himself with a correction.

'I didn't mean anything wicked. Death entraps people irrespective of place or time, doesn't it?'

I recollected that when I returned from the prayer session last Thursday, Joppan's house was devoid of light. Not only light, the revolutionary songs, always blaring from his shop, were absent too.

Joppan had an entire collection of the theatre songs of the Kerala People's Art's Club*. He also had all the cassettes of Sambhasivan's storytelling performances. In the way the church and temples broadcast devotional songs through loudspeakers, Joppan aired 'red' songs that electrified his shop and neighbourhood.

Whenever he worked, Joppan sang along with the record player. It was an effortless rendering, as natural as a bodily function. When he sang '*Chillu medayil irunnenne kalleriyalle*' (Don't throw stones at me from your glass palaces), he would be fitting the planks with hinges. When he sang '*Ponnarival ambiliyil kanneriyunnole*' (You who threw glances at the golden sickle-moon), he would be engraving a Mar Thoma Cross on the top lid of the coffin. During the Qurbana, I would notice the gospel song emanating from the church '*Swargathil vazhum njangal than thatha*' (Our Father who rules o'er heaven), getting enmeshed with '*Marivillin thenmalare*' (Honey flower springing from the wondrous rainbow). Both songs would merge into each other, losing their distinct identities.

---

* KPAC: Famous for their communist songs and theatre performances

Whenever I walked by listening to the songs, my glance invariably fell on Joppan's tiled house. He had converted the front room into his coffin shop. I observed with some envy the coffins—far finer than mine—that Joppan displayed. Gracy's accessories for the dead could also be seen dangling there. That provided Joppan's coffin shop the added attraction of a fancy store. Gracy earned an additional income as that business worked well. Especially so when she got calls from Jubilee Hospital. She would proceed to the hospital with her accessories to beautify the dead. Not only would she earn money from the sale of those embellishments, but also be paid handsomely by the grateful relatives for her services.

* * *

If Shari was displeased with David's insensitive words regarding Joppan, there was another solid reason behind it. Shari's father, Karunan, and Joppan had been the best of friends since their school days. Joppan's family had transplanted to Aadi Nadu decades earlier. Many families were forced to cut off their roots when their homes featured in the survey list of the Neyyar dam project which predicted the flooding of their locations. The painful exodus happened many years before my birth, in the mid-fifties. Considering the water level in the dam, all families residing within five chain lengths of it were forcibly evacuated. The area consequently came to be known as *Anjuchangala:* five chains.

Joppan's father was among those who had tearfully given up their beloved homelands where their forefathers slept, for the sake of the dam, and migrated to Aadi Nadu. The prosperous agriculturists were suddenly faced with bitter penury. My Appan had taken in Joppan's father as a helper in his coffin shop because my mother's family had been his neighbours. However, the helper soon turned competitor and established his own shop in front of the church. If things had not turned out that way, ours would have been the only coffin shop in the village. We would not have been forced to compete over coffins or endure poverty while growing up.

The generation that included Joppan and I was born after the Neyyar dam was built. By then, owing to the taming of the wild river, both the history and geography of the area had undergone changes. The Kanis, the original tribal inhabitants of those lands, were forced into exile deep in the forests. Led by their Mooppan*, they had been at the forefront of cooperation during the early days of the dam's construction.

They had transported long bamboo reeds from the forests for the survey, to be used as flags and marking poles. It is a blot in history that the same tribals became homeless when water filled the dam that they had helped to build. The tribals were illiterate and helpless, and were unable to negotiate for their rights. Their huts were primitive: settlements made of bamboo, grass thatch and fixtures of clay. Yet, most of them had enough fertile land to earn a living. The document issued by the village officer—the Kani patta—was not sufficient proof of their ownership. The truth was that most of them did not have an inkling about the disastrous future that awaited them once the dam was built.

When the construction of the dam was finished, and the shutters were down, the water level started rising. At midnight, when their homes got inundated, many woke up startled and fled screaming. People escaped to the hills without even a change of clothes. The water flooded the lush farms after swamping Vallikuunu, Clavermala and Ramakothi. The deluge swallowed the huts of those unfortunate people, along with their cattle and pets. Like insignificant ants, the Kanis were forcibly dispersed to the deep forests. Those who survived wandered in a lost manner around shores and forests, and had to start building their fragile settlements from scratch. In a matter of

---

* Clan leader

moments, men who lived like kings were transformed into beggars. There was no one to speak for them or wipe their tears.

When the Neyyar dam project began in 1951, Kanyakumari was part of Travancore. The left canal of the dam, Edathukarakkanal, was meant to bring water till Kanyakumari. In 1956, when the states were reorganized on the basis of language, Kanyakumari became a part of Tamil Nadu and the left canal was stopped at Kaliyikkavila. The right canal, Valathukarakkanal, still makes the lands of Neyyattinkara and Vellayani fertile through its multiple channels.

It is a cruel joke of history that while the water nourishes these lands, there are many families on the other side whose lives have been upturned.

* * *

I too have a relationship, akin to that of an umbilical cord, with the land where the Neyyar dam is situated. My Appan, who lived in Aadi Nadu, had married my Amma, who lived in the lowlands of Pallikkunnu. When I was a kid, he used to point out the place where my mother's home had been located. It was Appan who told me the stories of those lands.

My Appan and Antappan's father would frequently visit the area, intrigued by the ongoing dam construction. Having diverted the strong flow of the Neyyar river, the mammoth structure came up on the side where her flow was less intense. There were innumerable tents for the Tamilian engineers, supervisors and the hundreds of workers who thronged the site. When half the dam was complete, they diverted the river back to the structure, letting her flow through the shutters. When the remaining half was finished, and both parts met each other, Neyyar river exhibited her ferocious power.

I remember so clearly how my Appan narrated the thrill they felt on seeing the reservoir filling up with the waters, and their experience of walking across the dam for the first time. There are many households buried under those vast, flowing waters even today.

Many died pathetically in mishaps related to the dam construction. The orphaned souls of those who died while hauling stones, and those of the women labourers who died after eating contaminated tapioca, must be still wandering around those precincts.

In the generation that came soon after, it was Karunan and Joppan's friendship that gathered strength. Enchanted by leftist ideology and its revolutionary leaders, Karunan even ended up with a left-leaning gait. By virtue of association, Joppan developed a leftist inclination. During their school days, both friends would play truant and take off on trips, keeping everyone in the dark about their activities. Karunan was always alert to the political discourses organized at the Putharikandam compound and would inform Joppan accordingly. He would also make it a point to attend any event—irrespective of the hardships involved—where E.M.S. Namboodiripad spoke. The added attractions were Sambasivan's speech dramas and K.S. George's songs that would invariably follow EMS's fiery speech. On many occasions, they cycled more than twenty kilometres to listen to Sambasivan. Karunan and Joppan could repeat verbatim the lines from the famed performer's masterpieces such as 'Irupatham Nootandu', 'Vyasanum Marxum' and 'Aneesiya', having listened to them multiple times.

Karunan's obsessive devotion to politics was a trait that he had inherited from his father. For Joppan, an orthodox Christian, communism seemed something like Satan worship. Apprehensive about his father's reaction, his excursions with Karunan were furtive in nature. With the passage of time, Joppan's proclivity towards leftist ideology morphed into a rebellion against the church. He stopped attending even the Holy Qurbana on Sundays. However, Gracy, who became his life partner, was a faithful believer. With her impassive face, where no traces of either joy or sorrow were ever displayed, Gracy attended church religiously on Sabbath days.

Though he led the life of an atheist, Joppan dared not turn his face away from his family's coffin business. Appan had made him into a proficient worker at a young age. On Karunan's advice, though,

Joppan tried to set up an association for coffin makers. It failed to yield results. It was not an easy task to unite the scattered members.

And so, Joppan sang alongside K.S. George, listening to songs evocative of olden days.

> *'Vilakku marame, vilakku marame . . . '*
> *'Where have I arrived from?*
> *Where am I headed?*
> *Hey street lamp, hey street lamp,*
> *Do you carry some light?'*

* * *

I felt that Joppan's existential dilemma was still the same. From what David had narrated, the chances of Joppan becoming active again seemed remote. Though he was my professional rival, I was miserable to hear about Joppan's terminal illness. Of course, it is nature's law that living beings grow old and eventually die. Quoting the injustice meted out to me, how many times have I lashed out against the Lord about the law being selectively implemented! I am yet to be enlightened on the ways of the Lord's justice.

Instead, something unexpected happened.

After the holiday on Sunday, Shari came to meet me in a pensive mood.

'Acchan and I went to see Joppan Uncle yesterday.'

'How is he now?'

'He's in a very bad shape.'

'That is sad.'

'On seeing Acchan, Joppan Uncle laughingly sang that old song . . . *Irumeyyanengilum nammalotta . . . Though we are two bodies, our hearts are one; And through one opening do we . . .'*

I did not know whether to laugh or cry at that disclosure. As I stood silent, Shari continued, 'The doctor asked us to notify his immediate relatives. Considering the chances of infection, few should visit him. Joppan Uncle's only brother is in the army and is posted in Assam. We have informed him. He might come by the weekend.'

Joppan was not my relative—distant or near—to warrant a visit to his death-bed. Neither was there a friendship between us necessitating a formal visit. I disliked visiting those whose deaths were imminent. It was then that Shari spoke.

'When he was asked whom he wished to see, he mentioned a name.'

'Whose?'

'Yours.'

I was dumbstruck.

'Are you sure?'

'Yes, he expressed the wish to see you. Please go and meet him, Uncle.'

'But why? We are not that attached.'

'Well, I don't know anything about it.'

Though Shari persisted, I was not convinced about the need for that visit. I can't bear being in uncomfortable environments. Typically, I stay in my shop so I can avoid meeting people.

But that evening, when Pundit repeated the request, I felt a sense of disquiet.

'It is a man's death wish. You should not refuse.'

'But I . . .'

'Nature's law mandates that those who are present today will vanish tomorrow. Don't hold on to grudges against anyone. A person may pass away at an unexpected moment. What is the use of regretting later? You should go and see him.'

When Pundit too compelled me, I had no recourse but to take a decision.

I ruminated on the reason behind Joppan's request, considering that the coffin was the only common factor between us. There was nobody to carry on his business after his death. Since his coffin shop's roots were in my family, could it be that he wanted to discuss its sale? Concluding that it was a futile exercise to speculate, I prepared for that journey.

Wearing an old voile shirt stitched by Shashankan and a faded mundu, I walked past the Church of St. Anthony and reached the bus stop. It was right next to Joppan's shop, which was shut. The bus seemed like a strange contraption which I had not seen in many years. I doubted whether I could board it and reach Jubilee Hospital. I imitated others and managed to climb in. Watching closely what they did, I bought a ticket and somehow reached the hospital.

When I reached his side, Joppan was lying half-dead on a cot, in a desolate room with green curtains. He was barely conscious. It was evident that his life was hanging by a thread. Gracy stood impassively by his side. Not in the least had she expected my presence in that situation. It was unlikely that she knew about Joppan's wish to see me. A green mask covered Joppan's nose, possibly to prevent infection.

On seeing me, Joppan's face showed weak signs of recognition. Turning his head, he spoke to Gracy in a feeble voice.

'Can you leave us alone for a while?'

Like me, it was obvious that Gracy was ignorant about the reason. Yet, she quickly moved out of the room to the foyer outside. Seeing me hesitant and timid, Joppan spoke again.

'Bolt the door first. Then come and sit on this stool near me.'

On hearing that, I grew more uneasy. Throwing the reluctant visitor into more turmoil, Joppan's words again reached my ears.

'There is a secret I want to share only with you. Won't you bolt that door please?'

Realizing that it was the minimum justice I could do to him, I shut the door, bolted it and took my seat by his side.

A warning arose within, wagging an ominous forefinger, at the number of secrets that had been recently seeking my home address.

17

The Secret

'Now learn this lesson from the fig tree: As soon as its twigs get tender and its leaves come out, you know that summer is near. Even so, when you see these things happening, you know that it is near, right at the door. Truly I tell you, this generation will certainly not pass away until all these things have happened. Heaven and earth will pass away, but my words will never pass away. "But about that day or hour no one knows, not even the angels in heaven, nor the Son, but only the Father. Be on guard. Be alert. You do not know when that time will come."'

(Mark 13: 28-33)

I soon realized that being shut in a room with someone whom death has tagged is an extremely harrowing experience. The legs of my stool seemed incapable of handling my wobbling mind. Since I hadn't ever thought about it, let alone prepared for that strange situation, I almost choked over Joppan's next move. As his bleary eyes fell on me, I hastily looked away, unable to face that gaze. Like a person whose sin had doubled by undertaking a false confession, a guilty feeling welled up within me.

'We were both rivals, weren't we?' Joppan asked, 'Continuing the clash of the previous generation, we competed to sell coffins in this small village.'

Though he spoke the truth, it was not a matter of concern for me. I had no particular response to that observation.

'I have heard my father say that the biggest competition was when smallpox killed many in Aadi Nadu. The moment someone walked away with a coffin, another would arrive! A time when any number you made would still be insufficient. It was horrible to compete over death, wasn't it?'

Yes, there was a rank vulgarity in being competitive over death. I was familiar with the story of that disaster which happened in my Valiyappan's time. Death had tightened its grip on Aadi Nadu. The disease considered neither religion nor caste when it came to choosing its victims. Valiyappan had gone bone-weary making coffins day and night. Whatever numbers he churned out turned to be insufficient. There was only one hospital, far away at Airanivattom, which had facilities for the treatment of smallpox. The other hospitals refused to accept patients. Even the Hindus were forced to buy coffins to bury their dead, since nobody was available for cremating the corpses.

While immersed in selling caskets without the final touches, the craftsman himself was taken away by the henchmen of death who came marching in. Valiyappan did not even have the fortune of lying inside a decent coffin.

The competition over caskets that occurred during the epidemic loomed between Joppan and me. If Joppan had an aggressive competitive streak in him, it was one-sided, since I never had any.

Joppan's style of work is different from the archaic style I follow. I use the traditional chisel and mallet method even now. Joppan is an expert in using a cutter driven by electricity. The son of the man whom my Appan trained in making coffins is way ahead of me as a modern-day worker. Except for me, the rest of the coffin makers of the new generation have sharpened their skills to suit modern trends. With the chisel and mallet, one can barely make the necessary structures for two coffins in one day. Those who use electric cutters can easily make them for twelve or more coffins, with the ease of slicing through a cake. But I have never felt the need to create innumerable coffins, stacking them atop one another, in a single day.

Joppan's approach has been different from mine. Proportionate to the arrival of newfangled hospitals in every nook and corner of the land, are the death rates, which are growing manifold. Liver cirrhosis and oral cancer have started catching patients young, sending them to an early death. Purportedly, people die more from the side effects of the drugs they ingest than from the diseases themselves. Joppan has maximized his business opportunities by hiring middlemen who actively operate in the hospitals. And now, this man, in whose body disease has sown its seeds, lies in wait for the harvest season.

'Once I leave, there won't be any competition.' Joppan's words jolted me from my reverie.

'Who knows who shall leave first?'

'Oh, there is no doubt about that. But some matters are uncertain . . .'

I stared at Joppan, unable to make sense of his words.

'Indri, I called you to unload a burden off my chest before I die. A secret I have been carrying for long . . .'

'Secret?'

'Yes, something related to Gracy.'

Intrigue built up and ran amok inside me as I wondered about the secret that Joppan was going to share, that too with a stranger, about his own wife.

'Have you paid attention to Gracy's face? It is never pleasant . . . always washed-out and listless.'

Yes, I had observed it. 'Washed-out and listless' were not the appropriate words; 'stony silence' would have been a better description of her facial expression. *Complete silence*! I shuddered for a moment, thinking about those words. But what was the relevance of Gracy's silence in our conversation?

The explanation, when it came, left me shaken.

'You must be wondering why I am speaking about such things . . . Indri, you are the reason behind Gracy's wan face!'

'Me?'

'Not that it was intentional on your part. Even I never knew until she muttered one night, deep in her sleep . . .'

'What?'

'It was soon after our wedding. Gracy muttered your name and embraced me in her sleep. Not once but many times. There was so much desire in her . . . any husband would have been gravely provoked. Lying close to her, I needled information from her sleepy mind like a thief. When I shook her awake, she continued in that same dreamlike state for some moments. As soon as Gracy realized that it was me who had called her, she was aghast. Her demeanour was that of the guilty! The discomfiture betrayed her. Finally, as though caught red-handed, she was forced to confess everything to me. It was about her obsession since adolescence, which she never disclosed to anyone, but kept repressed within herself. She was a simple village girl who couldn't do anything about her desire. Since the families were not friendly with each other, the idea of proposing a marriage became intimidating. After your marriage, Indri, Gracy dried up; all the fire in her was doused. Nobody can predict how certain things affect people. It was an intense feeling of loss which she buried deep inside her that made her impassive. I have never seen her attracted to anything in life. There are some women like that: their minds are like boxes that are locked up forever. Inside those boxes are their dreams, which have died an untimely death. *Indri, I now feel that the cemetery is basically a graveyard of human desires.*'

I stood speechless, unable to accept Joppan's words, as if listening to an unlikely fairy tale. Having exhausted much of his life energy in narrating this story, Joppan's fatigue heightened.

'One should have simply shrugged it off as a petty matter, the infatuation of a teenage girl. But Gracy is no ordinary woman, Indri.

She never wanted to conceive a child from me. That is why I never became a father. I have never seen a smile on her face. She cooks for me, helps me in my work, sleeps with me . . . But in this life, she was never with me. Gracy was always with you, Indri!'

Both my body and mind started burning in agitation due to the man's uncontrolled, garrulous outpouring. I am not heroic enough to have enticed any woman. Never in my life have I been capable of attracting anybody based on my looks, money, or any other reason. But my Beatrice had loved me with her heart and soul. What was the need for Joppan to shamelessly reveal Gracy's youthful infatuation at this juncture? I did not wish to listen any further.

'I had to tell you about it before death took me away. That was the reason I asked to see you. Never tell Gracy that I disclosed it to you. Even if she is burning inside, she will not display any emotion, such is her nature. She reminds me of a formidable mountain at times. But that is just the exterior! Inside her is a heat which can melt rocks; I realized this ever since I got to know of her secret passion for you. My Gracy is a naïve woman. And I am her failed husband who could never make her happy . . .'

Joppan's words got muddled as he laboured to breath. Seeing him gasp, I intervened.

'Please don't speak much . . .'

'No, I shall not. In life there are certain things which one should speak about at the opportune time . . . or one will never get that chance again. It could be the trivial thoughts of a man about to die, but listen, is there a need for two coffin shops in Aadi Nadu?'

'What do you mean?'

Hardly had I asked him that than Joppan's health deteriorated rapidly. His expression changed as if he had seen the Angel of Death, resembling a red fire, holding the scroll of human fates. He suddenly clutched my right hand. The grip grew tighter, hurting me. Seeing Joppan's state, I extricated my hand and hurried towards the door to open it. Gracy's glance fell on my distressed face as she moved towards Joppan. As if she felt the scalding heat of the red fire, she rushed towards the cot.

'What happened?'

Even as Joppan tried to gesticulate, his eyes left the earth and rolled frantically up towards the sky. In that journey, from the dust used for creating man to the sky confining all creation, he must have seen the rams and yearling lambs awaiting the voice of the supreme judge.

Gracy gave me a piercing look before shouting: 'You . . . what did you do to him?'

The look in her eyes, like the snapping of a taut wire, terrified me.

What sin had I committed to deserve that accusatory look? I was invited to that place only to end up getting humiliated. Why is my fate such that I always face mortification?

The next moment, Gracy rang the room bell and the nurse on duty came running. Though a horde of nurses and a doctor rushed inside the room, Joppan had already joined the flock in the sky, not waiting for anyone. I was afraid that Gracy would burst into tears when the doctor forcibly closed Joppan's eyes.

As Gracy stood like a stolid mountain, coldly taking in her husband's death, I thought I heard a blast from one of Satan Loppo's quarries afar. The splinters from the shattered rocks lodged straight in my heart. As I stood debilitated, having witnessed death in close proximity, Gracy overcame her frigidness and briskly took charge.

18

The Ghost

"'Do not judge, and you will not be judged. Do not condemn, and you will not be condemned. Forgive, and you will be forgiven. Give, and it will be given to you. A good measure, pressed down, shaken together and running over, will be poured into your lap. For with the measure you use, it will be measured to you." He also told them this parable: "Can the blind lead the blind? Will they not both fall into a pit? The student is not above the teacher, but everyone who is fully trained will be like their teacher. Why do you look at the speck of sawdust in your brother's eye and pay no attention to the plank in your own eye?"'

(Luke 6: 37-42)

Death is nothing, but nothingness.

The pit waiting for death is the same too. By digging deeper and deeper into the fullness of the earth, an emptiness is created. And when you bury the one who has attained emptiness by death, in the void of the earth, he becomes part of the eternal emptiness. Now, Joppan too joins it. *Not carrying any secrets with him, having overburdened my heavy heart . . .*

Though most of Joppan's relatives live in Aadi Nadu and neighbouring villages, his brother works in the army and is posted in Assam. Owing to his insistence on attending the funeral, it did not take place the next day. Joppan's dead body was kept in the morgue at Jubilee Hospital.

Meanwhile, there was another storm brewing. One faction vociferously protested against burying an apostate, who had turned his face away from God, in the cemetery. Why should a renegade, who had never attended the Sunday Qurbana or accepted the Sacraments, sleep in the church's graveyard, they asked.

Gracy had never expected such a backlash. She herself was a devout Christian who followed every rite and ritual of the holy church. The opposing faction argued that it did not entail her husband's right to salvation! Although Father Gabriel, in his typical conciliatory style, tried to calm tempers, the recalcitrant faction did not relent. In an urgent church meeting, different opinions fought for supremacy. The scales tilted towards those who wanted to deny Joppan a place in the cemetery. When the factions continued to lock horns, Father Gabriel suggested a compromise: '*Who are you to judge your neighbour?* Whether you bury him here or not, his soul will reach its destined place. However, one should avoid disrespecting a dead body. Taking into consideration that the majority is against the idea, I suggest that at least some space may be given at the back of the cemetery.'

I appreciated that Father Gabriel tactfully abstained from mentioning the words '*pauper's grave*'. Let good befall the one carrying the holy name of the Arch Angel! A silence ensued after Father Gabriel's proposal. It was soon breached by a voice.

'Yes, what right do we have to judge another?'

It astonished me no end that the inspired view was put forth by Satan Loppo. The concession he made was opposed to his core nature. The tide turned in Joppan's favour when Satan Loppo came out in support of Father Gabriel, with all accepting it as the common decision.

What befuddled me was something else. Knowing that Joppan was Karunan's intimate friend, and his stance had always been against the church, why did Satan Loppo favour him? Why didn't he extend his animosity towards Karunan to Joppan?

I couldn't find an answer to the conundrum, even though I mulled over it the whole night. It was solved by Shari the next day.

'It was I who requested Muthalali to support Joppan Uncle's case. He listened to me. What a good heart he has!'

Good heart? What kind words!

Lord, you are again darting those words at me, from the bow named Satan Loppo. But I shall sidestep, and avoid them. I cannot accept goodness ascribed to Satan Loppo.

Joppan lay freezing in wintry conditions for three days until his brother arrived from Assam. When it was time to bring his corpse home, some relatives set off with new clothes and accessories to the hospital. Gracy was usually assigned the task of dressing the female corpses in the mortuary. She was kept away from the dead bodies of men, due to the inevitability of encountering male nakedness.

In Joppan's case, too, the hospital insisted on the same. But Gracy took the initiative and spoke up.

'I shall get him ready.'

'No, it will not be good for you in your present state of mind, Gracy.'

Dismissing all discouragement by both the hospital authorities and her relatives, Gracy headed to the morgue with the accessories. I offered a helping hand in shifting Joppan's body from the rack. Many men and women lay impatiently on the upper and lower shelves of the morgue, waiting for their funerals. I felt pity for them.

Seeing the one who had spoken his final words to me frozen, I raged against death's infallibility. What had happened to the heat of his body and the words he had shared with me? As I stood wondering what it was that had dissociated itself from Joppan, Gracy harshly made it clear that she wanted nobody in the vicinity. She wanted to get Joppan ready all by herself.

Wiping clean the naked body, she clothed it with a new attire. Adorning the body with gloves, socks and an elegant wig, Gracy beautified her husband to a level that no other corpse in Aadi Nadu had ever been. When she emerged from the room with the bridegroom-like body, Gracy cast a pointed look at me. Truth be told, like an arrow piercing me, my vision split apart.

I observed that not a single tear drop gathered in Gracy's eyes when the funeral procession reached the church or when Joppan was being lowered into the pit after the rites. Even when she kissed him for the last time before the coffin lid was shut, Gracy remained placid. I heard two women tittering about her noticeable coldness.

'What sort of a woman is she? Her husband lies dead in front of her and she has no feelings. Terrible!'

My thoughts were exactly the same. I could never believe Joppan's words about this obviously unfeeling woman ever having nurtured a passion for me! From the time I had seen her, her face seemed as if carved from dark wax. Not a muscle moved on that face, expressing emotions.

I stood waiting until each person retreated, having thrown a fistful of earth on the coffin. The ritual—which emphasized that *all are from dust and to dust all return*—was meant more for the living than the dead, though very few realized it. The blessed palm fronds of Palm Sunday are burnt to ashes on the Ash Wednesday of the coming year and a Sign of Cross is made on the foreheads of devotees. The ash indicates the impermanence of the human body.

I stood there until I felt I shouldn't any longer.

'A grave is like a hungry stomach,' Antappan quipped, 'And my task is filling its tummy by shovelling mud!'

I silently wished Joppan eternal rest and moved away as Antappan started his work. Since I could not afford to brood on Joppan's words, I discarded them in that graveyard before my return.

My mind had been squeezed by turmoil for the past three days; I badly needed to relax.

My feet stopped moving on reaching Pundit's watch shop.

'So, the funeral got over, eh?' Pundit asked on seeing me.

'Yes.'

'The universe has decided the exact time when each person's clock stops. It just takes a moment for that. Come inside,' Pundit invited me.

'Even if all the clocks stop, everlasting time shall remain. The same happens when the body stops; the soul remains eternally. Ignoramuses like us spend our lives planning and calculating. We stubbornly insist on changing the world. And what has become of the world after all our combined efforts? It has grown more sordid every day. Hendri, the world will move at its own pace. That realization truly sunk inside me when Netaji passed away. If we hadn't lost him then, the future of India would have been different. I believe that two separate nations called India and Pakistan would not have been formed. But I lost all hope with Netaji's demise. I, who was ready to wrestle with the fates, accepted defeat on bent knees after that event. Rather than trying to change the world, it is when we change ourselves that real transformation occurs. I have continued on that path till today. Now I have just one more assignment to complete. To construct an Anti-Clock. I am deeply engrossed in that task.'

Joppan's death, Gracy's impassivity and Pundit's words started making everything feel ambiguous. I did not feel like responding to anything. Perhaps I need not wait long for the needles of my clock to go still. All the stress and strains would soon render the springs and wheels inside me defunct.

While making my way to the coffin shop, I was pondering on the utter ease with which humans shrugged off their relationship with the mortal world.

Each death is a phenomenon that affects a select few for a limited time. The rest who throng around are mere spectators. They come to sympathize but death never touches even a hair on their bodies. If I die, there might be a gathering of a few indifferent onlookers. It would hardly make a difference to anyone in this world; so much the better.

At night, I was busy meditating on such thoughts when Antappan arrived.

'Come, let's go.'

'Where?'

'To our usual spot. Joppan's wife gave me some money.'

'Why did you take money from that poor woman?'

'I refused but she insisted. Listen, if someone says that she will feel sad if I refuse, what can I do? Anyway, I really need a drink tonight. I fought with him again.'

'With David?'

'He will drive me to my grave, I swear. I am going to drink myself senseless tonight.'

It was beneficial to accept Antappan's invitation, to wipe clean everything. Closing the shop door, I left to celebrate Joppan's death. Since it was the first night after the new moon, darkness was observing us surreptitiously with owl's eyes. We walked silently and reached the ghastly silence of the graveyard. A few birds fluttered on perceiving our presence. Suddenly I remembered my meeting with Joppan at the hospital. He was struggling to tell me something when he lost consciousness and went away on his journey. The last image imprinted in his eyes was mine!

I have heard that souls wander around the mortal world for an indefinite period, hovering around because of their unfulfilled desires. Those who are close to them are able to see them. If so, would Joppan's soul be wandering around nearby? Would he appear before me to whisper what he could not reveal?

When Antappan uncorked the liquor bottle which was tucked away at his waist, I caught a flash of light nearby. On realizing that it was gleaming near the place where Joppan was buried, a fiery breeze seemed to ensconce me. My throat went dry, and I touched Antappan, speechless with terror.

'What is the matter?'

As Antappan started speaking, I covered his mouth frantically and pointed.

Making out someone's presence in that darkness, Antappan froze for a moment too.

'Come.' He clutched my hand.

With an ineffable dread twisting my insides, I accompanied him. As we edged closer, the ghostly presence became clearer, and realizing that it was not my imagination, my heart started beating uncontrollably. Antappan shone his pen torch as we reached the destination. I blanched with shock at the figure I saw in the bright light.

Gracy was sitting on the bare ground near Joppan's grave.

Her reddened eyes were flowing with tears.

There were furrows of anguish on her face.

It was a sight that revealed to me the real Gracy; what I had seen of her till now was her ghost. The realization that Gracy's impassivity was a mere mask for her intense suffering scalded me, and burnt my innards.

19

Anti-Clock

'Consider Assyria, once a cedar in Lebanon, with beautiful branches overshadowing the forest; it towered on high, its top above the thick foliage. The waters nourished it, deep springs made it grow tall; their streams flowed all around its base and sent their channels to all the trees of the field. So, it towered higher than all the trees of the field; its boughs increased, and its branches grew long, spreading because of abundant waters. All the birds of the sky nested in its boughs, all the animals of the wild gave birth under its branches; all the great nations lived in its shade.'

(Ezekiel 31: 3-6)

Since the events in the cemetery on the night of Joppan's burial affected me deeply, I did not pay much attention to Pundit or the Anti-Clock for the next few days. I did not even feel like stepping out of the coffin shop. As I slipped inexorably back into an exhausted state of solitariness, an unexpected guest made an appearance in the shop. Pundit's visit surprised me no end as it was most unusual. His hair was splayed like a tree caught in a storm. Yet his face was radiant with soul light.

I was flustered as I did not have a decent seat in the shop to offer Pundit. There was a stool, as ancient as Pundit himself, but I had hardly paid any attention to it till then. If someone ever sat on it, it would teeter like a hardcore drunk.

Seated on the old stool, which I hastily dusted, Pundit glanced at the treasures I had stored in my little shop. As he looked at the half-finished and the completed coffins strewn around, I came to realize the sheer penury of my surroundings.

Spiders had taken over the corners of the room, demarcating areas with their cobwebs, where they reigned supreme. The cracked cement floor was covered with years' worth of grime. Wooden planks and blocks lay scattered all over. Boxes of death were stacked horizontally on the rack while some stood leaning against the wall. Angle plates of iron for fixing the casket corners, nails of half an inch, three quarters inch, one and a quarter inch meant for impaling, iron hinges for the joints, many variety of chisels, mallets, smoothing planes . . . *I was a cross breed made of the mishmash of all that.*

As Pundit's eyes did a circumambulation, by running over me and the flurry around, he stopped interestedly at a one-and-a-half-feet-long top lid hanging from a nail on the wall.

'Well, just look at that tiny casket lid!' he exclaimed.

'That was my first model when I trained with my Appan. A moulded groove was used to beautify it all over. I just preserved it as a keepsake . . .' I replied quietly.

'Ha ha! Exactly like keeping the photograph of one's first Qurbana, right?'

It was a tiny top lid, hardly half an inch in thickness. Some use coffins that are ten inches in height, including both the bottom portion and the top lid. I prefer making my bottom casket ten inches high and the top lid two and half inches. That gives it an allure! For burly men or those with oversized tummies, special coffins, thirteen inches high, are crafted. The coffin I have made for Satan Loppo is such a gigantic one. Certainly, Pundit's sharp eyes have observed it.

After languidly observing my shop and satisfying himself, Pundit spoke: 'It will get completed very soon.'

'What?' I asked, nonplussed.

'The Anti-Clock.'

My soul praised the Lord as if listening about the holy resurrection. I was filled with the thrill of becoming a witness to a miracle that I had once relegated to the sidelines as impossible.

'Anti-Clocks, however, usher in bad luck.'

Pundit's words extinguished my enthusiasm instantaneously.

'Whenever an Anti-Clock is made, the backward motion of time will shake up the universe! Earthquake, flood, cyclone, pandemic . . . any disaster can be triggered.'

I felt like laughing after listening to that naïve augury. How many Anti-Clocks would have been made in the world till now! A few clock wheels turning a few thin needles backwards . . . the rusty machine was going to tamper with which system in the universe? Though his name was Pundit, and he was a freedom fighter, he sounded rather credulous.

'You don't believe me, do you?' Pundit asked, as if he had directly absorbed my deriding thoughts.

'No, I was wondering whether someone made an Anti-Clock that unleashed the tempest in my life, uprooting the tree and destroying my home. Pundit, you should leave the Anti-Clock alone.'

'Let us forget the uprooting of your tree for a while! If you concentrate on the needles of the clock, you'll notice something: even when the three needles move, their central point remains still. Every movement is based on that stillness. The stirring of stasis— that is time. When the forward motion is reversed abruptly, there can be serious ramifications. There will be an upheaval similar to a forward moving vehicle being suddenly pulled backwards. But I have started on the journey and cannot stop midway.'

Pundit was silent for some time. I wondered whether it was the deep silence dawning in the tranquil centre of the clock needles.

'I became aware of it later . . . after I started the work.'

'What?'

'That we are actually travelling back in time! It is extremely intriguing. My Anti-Clock will be unique in looks and design. It shall work like the human eye. Like a glance on either side, it will usher in the past and the future. We can reach both whenever we desire. If you still your eyes, you can enjoy the calm of the time's centre. When the eyes become immobile, all thoughts cease. When the mind ceases to think, what meaning does the word 'human' have? What is the relevance of time then?'

If Pundit's contemplations were running so haphazardly during the making of the Anti-Clock, what tribulations were in store on its completion?

While speaking, Pundit looked at the shaky stool on which he was seated and smiled.

'Can't you fix this one?'

My destitution, which couldn't offer him better seating, filled me with shame.

'I never had an opportunity to invite anyone to my coffin shop . . . I will take care from now on.'

'No, let the stool remain wobbly. There is a time for everything. *A time to plant, and a time to pluck that which is planted . . . a time to love and a time to hate . . . a time to break and a time to build . . .* Let the stool continue in this state.'

Pundit's eyes started traversing through the coffins in my shop again. The ones which stood leaning against the walls, the ones lying on the ground—each symbolized a desolate human being. His look gathered each one of them and finally impaled me.

'Every box has the same colour.'

'Yes, that's how it stays until the polishing is done. It then becomes attractive, and worthy of a caress!'

'Attractive coffin indeed. Truly, a man needs only such a small home for himself.'

'Hmm.'

'We live in far smaller houses, don't we? In tiny bodies? *The body is the home of the soul.*'

Pundit was bubbling with laughter even when he left my shop.

I stayed perplexed by his words all day long. What had he meant by all those metaphors involving Anti-Clocks and bodies?

Then with a jolt, I remembered my Appan's riddle.

'Petti, petti, nalla shinkara petti
Petti thurakumbol kayam manakkum.'
'Box, the box, so very alluring
An asafoetida smell on opening.'

What was the link between my Appan's shinkara petti and Pundit's hint about the body?

What was the dwelling place? Who dwelt inside it?

I stood hapless, unable to either accept or discard the wisdom Pundit had acquired in the one hundred and twelve years of his life.

* * *

The next day, when David arrived, I shared the latest news about the Anti-Clock with him. He was enthused at the impending completion.

The new generation is impetuous in nature. They tend to be hot-blooded in their responses, not leaving an iota of space for a reconsideration. The net results are short lived! I did not elaborate on the natural disasters that are supposed to shadow the Anti-Clock. Anyway, I was yet to fully understand what Pundit meant.

But soon, certain 'climatic changes' came to pass, pointing to the truth of Pundit's prophecy. The possibility of the occurrence of an earthquake became visible shortly afterwards.

It transpired in the following manner: David impulsively revealed whatever he had heard about the Anti-Clock to Satan Loppo and his daughter-in-law. I could not blame David since I had not forbidden him from speaking about it. Satan Loppo's greed got the better of him when he heard about a clock which moved time backwards. He wished to acquire it by any means. It was his lusty nature to possess anything rare. The German woman's curiosity was also piqued. On hearing that the old man who had rectified the giant clock was making an Anti-Clock with twenty-four time zones, she was fascinated.

'Quote any price. I need that clock,' Satan Loppo instructed David. 'If he needs any advance payment, we can give him. Talk to Pundit immediately.'

David sought my advice before meeting Pundit.

Suffice it to say that I was dismayed on hearing this.

What was wrong with these people? Just because a man decided to make a clock to turn time back, why should they covet his creation? Let time rotate left or right, what was the need to interfere with its flow?

I had never thought that David would share the news with Satan Loppo or that it would lead to such a furore. I wasn't sure how Pundit would react to the situation.

'What is there to debate about so much, Uncle? Muthalali will pay a hefty amount for the gadget. Pundit can enjoy the rest of his days in peace,' David grinned.

It sounded appealing when he said it that way. David inquired whether I would accompany him to Pundit's place. He was eager to make me a middleman, as he knew of my closeness to Pundit.

'Why should I come? You go ahead, David.'

'No, you should come with me.'

'But I will not utter a word.'

'That is all right. I shall make the sales pitch.'

We started off to bid for a price for the time that moved anti-clockwise. If fate decreed that the Anti-Clock should keep time inside Satan Loppo's bungalow, who would dare to stop it?

When we reached the watch shop, Pundit was immersed in fine-tuning the clock. The clockwork, looking like a skeleton, hung from the bars of the window.

On seeing me, Pundit became very spirited.

'It is very likely that its heart will begin beating today!'

My heart began to beat fast, like that of the newly created Anti-Clock.

David revealed the purpose of his visit and elaborated on Satan Loppo's interest in the Anti-Clock. He tempted Pundit with the huge amount of money he could gain out of the deal.

'You might not get a chance like this again.'

I felt that David was committing the sin of leading an innocent astray. As per the Holy Bible, such a sin would be punished by the tying of a millstone around the perpetrator's neck and drowning him in the depths of the sea!

Pundit heard out David patiently. Then he answered with composure: 'The Anti-Clock is not for sale. No one can purchase it by paying money.'

'Muthalali really desires it.'

'The Tathagata has spoken about desire being the cause of unhappiness. What can I do about it?' Pundit smiled.

'Please reconsider your decision.'

'This clock is the epitome of all my considerations.'

I felt soothing rain clouds descending in the valley of my heart. Pundit's words were the condensation of my heart's desire. Pundit had silenced David with his pithy words!

However, the thought of how Satan Loppo, the uncrowned king of Aadi Nadu, would react to Pundit's refusal made me apprehensive. I was scared that Loppo would pursue the filthiest way to seize the object of his desire.

My fear turned out to be true.

'The old buffoon dares to show so much arrogance, eh? Let him finish his Anti-Clock first. Then I will decide what to do about it!' Satan Loppo threw a fit.

When David narrated Loppo's response, I shuddered amongst the coffins, thinking about the Anti-Clock which could unleash thunder and lightning. It was better for Pundit to leave the clock unfinished if those disasters were about to make an advent.

Time, please don't portend evil tidings by turning backwards!

20

New Paths

'If some of the branches have been broken off, and you, though a wild olive shoot, have been grafted in among the others and now share in the nourishing sap from the olive root, do not consider yourself to be superior to those other branches. If you do, consider this: You do not support the root, but the root supports you. You will say then, "Branches were broken off so that I could be grafted in." Granted. But they were broken off because of unbelief, and you stand by faith. Do not be arrogant, but tremble. For if God did not spare the natural branches, he will not spare you either.'

(Romans 11: 17-21)

Though I prayed to time not to augur bad times, indications of change reached me in multiple ways. Many acquaintances started walking into my life uninvited. First Pundit, then Joppan, and now Karunan himself came to my shop.

I never expected Shari's father to visit my coffin shop. Except for the razor-sharp look beneath his joined brows dimming a bit, Karunan remained his rock-like self. The probability of a casual encounter between us being zero, his visit was definitely not for bargaining over a coffin.

On seeing her father, Shari crossed the road and made her way into my shop.

'You go on with your work, dear. We have to discuss a bit of politics,' Karunan gently informed her. Hearing that, Shari went back to the tailor shop.

After making small talk about my business, Karunan started discussing the recently deceased Joppan.

'We were one soul in two bodies. There was no secret which was not known to the other. That is why I did not participate in his funeral. I did not have the strength to see him buried.'

I stared at him, mulling over why Karunan was disclosing this to me. Though he looked tough and hardy, his soft heart was revealed by his moist eyes.

'You know, he risked his life and saved me from drowning in the school pond. Our friendship started then. We loved travelling together. The places we visited! At first, we went for small trips. Sometimes we would cross the Neyyar and venture into the forests of Uttaramkadu where tigers and leopards roam. Or we would visit Manjappara or Oruvappara. We would cycle through Koottapu, Aarukani and Amburi. Or we would take a detour to Kanchiyoor via Pantha. Once we both sneaked away to the land of EMS. I wagered at school that I would meet E.M.S. Namboodiripad and touch him. But when we ended up at his place, we received an affectionate rebuke instead. The first thing he did was to communicate to our parents via his comrades back home that we were both safe. Special instructions were issued to them that our parents should not berate us when we returned. We, however, fulfilled our desire to visit Punnapra and Vayalar.* Those were our pilgrimage spots. After touring every place together, that scoundrel left me behind this time.'

---

* Places of communist uprising against the Diwan of Travancore C.P. Ramaswamy Iyer in 1946

I was familiar with most of the stories Karunan reminisced about. Especially about the emotional bond that Karunan's family had with EMS. When EMS and Gauriamma* had arrived for the inauguration of the Neyyar dam, they had made it a point to visit Karunan's father. The governors of Kerala and Tamil Nadu were present on the dais. EMS, the chief minister of the first communist government, had a good grasp of the disaster which had befallen the people of Neyyar region. He must have remembered the tragic stories of people like my Valiyappan and Joppan, who were forced into exile, leaving behind their homelands and farmsteads for the construction of that dam. The memories of those homes which had got flooded when the shutters of the dam became operational must have haunted him too. There were no political parties or organizations to raise their voices for those traumatized people then.

EMS honoured that weak and hapless lot during the inaugural function: 'I find myself speechless on this dais. The Neyyar overflows with the tears of many families.'

The Neyyar, originating from Agastyarkoodam and merging within herself the majestic waters of Kallar, Valliyar and Mullayar, truly was the river of tears. When a school was established for the education of the children of the engineers and other officers of the dam, Karunan's father led the communist protests. They demanded that the sons of the soil be allowed to study there too. When the dissent became contentious, the management put forward a compromise solution, that the children of the landlords would be admitted. But the party workers did not relent until the common man's children were given admission. Children from Kuttapoo and Aarukani joined the school, wanting to taste the mid-day meal made from American wheat flour. Many old-timers still fondly reminisce about the delightful taste of the uppumavu, served on the giant Vattayila.†

---

* Leading communist party leader
† Macaranga Nicobarica, the giant leaves are used as plates

Karunan's recollections about Joppan were dragging me into the past too.

'Indri, I came for a special purpose. Joppan entrusted me with a task concerning you before he left.'

'I met Joppan . . . In fact we were talking when he . . .'

'I am sure that he must have spoken to you about Gracy.'

On hearing the name 'Gracy' I again felt my muscles stiffen. What I had witnessed in the cemetery on the night of Joppan's death had shocked me to the core. I could never imagine a woman reaching the graveyard at night without a vestige of fear. That too near the pauper's grave! It was a neglected space meant for those who had committed suicide and the ones who had abnegated their souls while alive. Who knew whether they were even cast out from the world of souls? Gracy, who had come all alone to that godforsaken place ridden with wild needle flowers and corpse stinkers, was no ordinary woman for sure!

As my thoughts unravelled, Karunan's voice jolted me back.

'Gracy was his greatest sorrow. Sometimes he wished that he would die so that Gracy could have the life she desired. If the wish is intense, it is likely to come true, isn't it? How many times he must have told me that there should be only one coffin shop in Aadi Nadu!'

I remembered that Joppan had been speaking about it before he died. Those were the last words of a living man. Rather, his life breath had been strangled by those words.

'Indri, why don't you invite Gracy into your life? I have not spoken to her yet. I wanted to discuss this with you first.'

The question startled me. Marital life is not a machine where one faulty piece can easily be replaced by another. Neither my body nor my mind could handle such a change. It was sheer stupidity to forge something against the natural order.

'I know it is not proper to discuss such an issue so soon after Joppan's funeral. Yet I thought I should talk to you directly. Who knows about the vagaries of human life? You know that I am active in the action council formed against the illegal stone quarrying. I have received many life threats from various quarters.'

I have heard about the seeds of a new uprising sown by Karunan and a group of spirited youngsters. It was a revolt against the intemperate destruction of the environment by drilling holes in the hills. The illegal quarrying and the overspeeding tipper-lorries have become a ubiquitous sight in Aadi Nadu. The lorries carrying the mined minerals had killed many innocent pedestrians, leading to public outrage. Satan Loppo had shrewdly intervened to smother the fires of the first few upheavals. It was he who took the lead in getting that road constructed.

It had been an age-old demand that a proper tarred road be built for the people living in the folds of the hills. When someone fell sick, he had to be carried on another's back for many kilometres to reach the nearest hospital. The alternative was to transport him in a makeshift bamboo cradle carried by four men. Many had lost their lives due to the inordinate delay in getting medical help. The only solution to keep such deaths at bay and to ensure the progress of the area was to build a road.

Satan Loppo procured permission from the higher-ups and persuaded those with land to donate for the road. His effort was advertised as an act of benevolence towards the poor. But Satan Loppo surreptitiously also purchased many properties, including the rocky hills. No one realized that Loppo was getting a road built in order to transport the minerals from his quarries. It was much later, when the number of tipper-lorries multiplied manifold, that the likes of Karunan became aware of the insidious harm to nature caused by the mining activities.

Recently, some action council members stopped the outgoing lorries that were cruising without legal permits, leading to a major scuffle. There was a movement against Satan Loppo's crusher unit, which was harming the surroundings. But the mining lobby was deadly. It took recourse to all the tricks of the trade to consolidate its position—throwing money around, influencing politicians and threatening the opposition. When he said that 'a sword was hanging over his life', Karunan was right.

Meanwhile, Karunan failed to apprehend another secret. The secret that his own daughter had shifted loyalty to the enemy camp! Loppo, in his interactions with Shari, never displayed his malice towards Karunan. He had even argued for Joppan in the church committee at her insistence. It was typical of a tyrant to display a poker face, befooling even his closest aides. Unexpectedly, such a dictator would execute his vile plan, affecting all and sundry.

I could not reveal to Karunan any of my surmises.

'Let me leave now. I shall come back to see you. Think about what I told you regarding Gracy. We all need someone to take care of us,' Karunan said.

I wished to scream that I couldn't add another chapter to my Book of Life. It was by holding on to the beloved memories of Beatrice and my children that I existed. To see anyone else step into our sacred space was anathema to me. I had every right to be selfish about those who had passed away, didn't I?

Even after Karunan left, his words left me bleeding. Many interwoven thoughts kept rising within me. I remembered my Appan, my beloved Amma and her maternal home, which had been inundated by the dam waters. An inner calling stirred, beckoning me towards the Neyyar, to tread on past paths. It was an unfamiliar urge. Wanting to walk across the dam and the anicuts where my Appan had once taken me, my hand in his, I started my sojourn in that direction.

* * *

I reached the shores of the Neyyar from where Pallikkunnu was visible. Clavarmala and Ramathikonam loomed ahead exhaustedly. It was summer and the dry rivulets had shrivelled up. The storage capacity of the reservoir had been seriously affected by the sediments brought in by the river. I have heard that this was due to the lack of enough check dams in Kallar and Mullayar before the water flowed into the main dam.

I noticed a crocodile pop its head out from the water. Their numbers seemed to have increased in that area. The species, introduced by the authorities to intimidate the forest loggers, had multiplied uncontrollably. They had started attacking both humans and domestic animals, maiming a few and drowning quite a number more. There is a tribal grandmother called Valli, whose hand was chomped away by a crocodile.

Even after the crocodiles were set free into the waters, the species called timber thieves continue to thrive. The forest guards, with their simple torches, are not of much use. Pythons and crocodiles encroach into the yards of the householders and sneak away with their fowls at night. Even to swallow the fishes, crocodiles, lacking tongues, need to come to the shorelines. They lay eggs on the sandy shores. The number would be around sixty. When the baby crocodiles crawl out of the shells, they resemble chameleons. The mother crocodiles guard them against eagles during the day and owls during the nights. These creatures can be very aggressive during that period.

When I reached the third anicut, my feet stilled. My Appan, a native of Aadi Nadu, had married my mother hailing from the river valley. There was a rivulet running over the sandy stretches. Even now, like a tragic memory, I could see the muddy layers that my Appan had pointed out to me.

'This was the house where your mother ran around as a child . . .'

The remnants of the house where the footprints of my mother were present now lay covered by silt and sediments, destroyed and submerged under water. My eyes became moist as I tried to imagine her house from that vague formation. How many people must have returned similarly, to lament over their farms and homes that they had been forced to leave behind? Appan had told me about those whose homes had turned into their watery graves overnight, since they had never received any warning about the sudden surging of the dam waters. Their cattle perished, the ropes around their necks proving to be their nooses. Among those who scrambled up the hills, petrified of the swelling waters, was a tribal man called Thevan. He had carried my exhausted mother on his shoulders.

Those who had managed to salvage their lives by building homes on the hillside were again being confronted by a new problem. Their houses would be flattened during the widening of the roads. In spite of paying the land dues, they had no documents verifying their ownership. The mutual trust among the people and their belief in the ways of nature were sufficient only in the foregone days.

On contemplating that development granted luxury to a few and intense suffering to others, I felt enraged. I wished ardently for a sincere leader who would rehabilitate the poor and ensure a proper livelihood for them.

For a whole day, I gave myself up to the Neyyar river, which carried both tears and grief within her. Inside my mind, I reserved a prayer for those souls orphaned like me. Many unseen souls made their soothing presence felt during those moments. I returned extremely late from the land of my forebearers.

Night had fallen when I reached Aadi Nadu. When I crossed Joppan's house that night, Karunan's words about Gracy stirred turbulent ripples in me again. How could a lonely woman like her continue with the coffin shop? Since coffin-making was not taught at coaching centres, how could she hire an experienced worker?

* * *

A fortnight later, proving all my doubts wrong, Joppan's shop opened again. The songs came floating from a distance. Joppan's cassette player was at work again!

'Thalaykku meethe shoonyakasham . . .'

'Above my head an empty sky, and beneath me a desert;
I am a hornbill meditating away, would you quench my thirst?'

When I climbed down the church steps, I could hear the rhythmic sound of the mallet hitting the chisel. I concluded that Gracy had appointed a new worker. A needless curiosity pulled me towards the shop. I walked up to it, trying to catch a glimpse of the newcomer, but could not see anyone. Though my mind endeavoured to take me inside the shop, I hesitated due to the indignity of that act. Yet, I could not contain myself. Apart from Joppan, who had died as a coffin maker, who else was proficient in the skill in Aadi Nadu? Since curiosity had taken possession of me, first my mind and then my body crossed the shop's threshold.

I was flabbergasted to see the person working in the midst of the sawdust and lacquer. Gracy was engrossed in the carpentry, clothed in Joppan's lungi and shirt. Seeing me, she panicked, and rolled down the lungi, which had been tucked up conveniently above her knees.

'I . . . I was just trying it out.'

My eyes fell on the new casket on the ground, shining with lacquer. On the top lid was a gorgeously carved Mar Thoma Cross, which clearly showed Gracy's immense skills. It was a testimony that the Goddess of Art could manifest on a coffin too. It was the sole proof needed to confirm that the shop did not need a new worker.

What I acknowledged then happened in due course. Gracy became the first female coffin maker that I saw in my life. Perhaps, Aadi Nadu had produced the world's first woman coffin maker.

She renamed the shop to keep alive the memory of the departed soul: Joppan Memorial Coffin Shop.

Here was my new competitor! How prescient Joppan had been when he had posed that question to me about Aadi Nadu's need for two coffin shops. Till his last breath, he had expected a 'No'. But my mind announced clearly, 'Yes, most definitely yes!' If Gracy was destined to earn her bread from making coffins, so it shall be.

When the next death happened in the parish of St. Anthony, I suggested to the people who came to my shop that they go to Gracy instead.

'I do not have any finished coffin. There is a shop near the church—Joppan Memorial Coffin Shop. You will get one there.'

My mind filled with joy as I could at least support a lonely woman from afar. After all, she had wasted precious years of her life desiring a benighted man like me. Let her be indebted to me for a coffin!

That day, Aadi Nadu witnessed the sale of the first coffin crafted by Gracy's hands.

21

War Time

'Remember those earlier days after you had received the light, when you endured in a great conflict full of suffering. Sometimes you were publicly exposed to insult and persecution; at other times you stood side by side with those who were so treated. You suffered along with those in prison and joyfully accepted the confiscation of your property, because you knew that you yourselves had better and lasting possessions. So do not throw away your confidence; it will be richly rewarded. You need to persevere so that when you have done the will of God, you will receive what he has promised.'

(Hebrews 10: 32-36)

Though Pundit had announced that the Anti-Clock was on the verge of completion, I did not hear about it for a few days. Joppan, Gracy and their issues had shoved me into a different world. Yet, whenever I remembered Pundit and the Anti-Clock, an alarming pressure built up inside. A voice from hell whispered from within that Satan Loppo would adopt any means to steal the Anti-Clock from Pundit.

I recollected that whenever Loppo had eyed anything that belonged to others, they ended up under his control. Whether it was a stone quarry, a woman's beauty or the village authority, they all met with the same fate. The flagrant abuse of the Ninth and Tenth Holy Commandments was his very creed. I was sure that he was simply biding his time, waiting for the Anti-Clock to be completed. The moment Pundit breathed life into the time machine, Satan Loppo would step into the arena like a deadly warrior and seize it for himself.

Meanwhile, I feared that Karunan's move against the stone quarries was leading to a volatile situation. Since Satan Loppo stood to lose the most, it was apparent that he would be plotting retribution against the leader of the action council.

David seemed to be consciously avoiding the topic of the Anti-Clock. Consequently, I did not receive much information about the latest developments in Loppo's bungalow. Shari's wilful silence on the topic made me wonder whether it was a pact between them. I worried whether they would shift loyalty to Loppo altogether and stop befriending me.

However, life had safely locked away some treasure troves that would open exclusively for me. Holding the keys to them, Pundit dropped in one night.

'I need to go somewhere. Will you come with me?'

'Travel? Where?'

'Venture inside the forests, let's say. A byroad from Agastyarkoodam.'

As if lost in a maze, I gazed bewildered at Pundit. On a sudden impulse, I had visited the shores of Neyyar hardly a fortnight earlier. Here was another invitation, almost as a serendipitous continuation of the journey.

'Don't worry about whether this old man will be able to make it! My aged body has more strength than yours.'

Seeing his exuberance, I felt sure that Pundit had some plan up his sleeve. It intrigued me that he spoke only of the trip and did not mention anything about the Anti-Clock.

'What happened to turning time back?' I asked.

'It is not the time to answer that. By the way, we will start before dawn.'

Pundit went away without divulging anything else, keeping the mystery intact. My state of mind was that of a rusty latch, which obdurately refused to either open or shut.

The next day, before Aadi Nadu woke up, Pundit and I started on our journey. We trundled forward in a truck, which wound its way down the valley, slicing through the darkness, following the course of Neyyar's flow. I deboarded with Pundit and followed the path he walked. When morning dawned, I realized that we were walking through a dense forest. Resting awhile, we quenched our thirst by drinking from the river and moved ahead. As Pundit said, I was the one more easily exhausted.

After a while, by the side of the wild river, we sighted some stone steps. Moving further ahead, I saw something incredible: a dilapidated building, its roof caved in! The walls were made of stone. The windows and door were in a state of decay.

I was amazed at the sight of a building that sprang up all of a sudden deep inside the forest.

'I have returned to this place after eighty years,' Pundit spoke. 'In my hot-blooded youth, I had come here alone. A Sayyip was residing here then.'

We were close to the ruins by then.

'The Sayyip preferred a solitary existence in the middle of the forest. He got this house constructed and generated his own electricity.'

'Electricity? In this forest?'

'Look at those wires . . . you can see the check dam nearby.'

Pundit took me closer to the rushing river. It was probably a tributary of either the Kallar or the Mullayar. I could see the remains of stone steps here and there. There was a huge iron wheel lying in their midst. It brought to mind the giant wheel from the legend that was stuck in the mud.

'The Sayyip generated electricity by making this reaction wheel move from the force of water. The wheel was brought from abroad. Several strong men carried it all the way and set it up here. It is all rusted now. I could never understand why that foreigner wanted to leave his homeland and settle down in the midst of a jungle here. I was his guest for a few days. Back then, I was eager to travel to foreign shores too. That desire intensified after being in the Sayyip's company. After many journeys, many searches, many jobs, do you know where I ended up? It might sound strange: as a foot soldier in the British Army. My story, undisclosed to anyone till now, begins there.'

The mists surrounding the enigmatic man called Pundit were clearing up before me. I felt that the all-controlling wheel of time, which had been stuck in the mud till that moment, had now started to turn. Listening intently to Pundit's words, I tried to decipher his past.

'Most people think that my shop, Pundit's Watch Works, was named after Nehru. They are wrong. I had a beloved friend in whose memory I named my shop. He was a Kashmiri, and we became close buddies during the height of the Second World War. When the Allied forces decided to fight the formidable Axis powers, my regiment ended up fighting in the frontiers of Burma. The first field of defence happens to be the troop of foot soldiers. The guns and cannons first spit fire at their chests.

'In that war, where the Allied forces of America, Britain and France fought against the Axis powers of Germany, Italy and Japan, I was among the luckless stepping into the battlefield, since I belonged to the British Army. There was a smart fellow belonging to the Kashmiri Pandit clan who was my compatriot, and I referred to him as 'Pundit'. Hailing from the northern and southern extremities of India, we became dear friends quickly. If you were to ask me how Pundit and I ended up in the British Army, I would say that it was to pave way for future events! There is an extraordinary camaraderie forged between those who fight calamities together. You become one unit physically and mentally. But the friendship between us was destined to be short-lived.

'Pundit was among those who laid down their lives in the Burma war. The sorrowful son of Kashmir wanted to return to his motherland and lead a good life. But he breathed his last with his head in my lap. I cannot tell you how I overcame that moment . . . The ineffable pain which blinds you when someone so beloved lies dead on your lap! As I sat there, unwilling to leave him without a decent funeral, enemy soldiers surrounded me. Along with tens of thousands of others, I ended up as a prisoner of war in a Sumatran jail.

'Life became unspeakably hellish. I felt that Pundit had been lucky to escape that wretched existence. Never did I hope to breathe the air of my motherland again. When most of my fellow soldiers succumbed to the infernal ordeal, I expected to be next in line. But history switched overnight! One day, a messenger of God arrived to visit us. We had lost all track of time by then. It was Subhas Chandra Bose! He had decided to become friends with the enemy of his enemy. He persuaded us that it was far nobler to shed blood for one's country than to die fighting for the British. His speech was so forceful that we all became his ardent fans.

'Since Hitler was Britain's enemy, Netaji had first met him in Germany before visiting us in Sumatra. We took an oath that we would risk our lives to fight by his side. We agreed that it was far better to die fighting for one's country than languishing in jail. When the Indian National Army decided to join forces with Japan and fight the allies, I was one of its three thousand soldiers.

'Our onslaught was aggressive, and we made major inroads into enemy territory. But the Allies used bombs and trapped us in the forests. Some of us were stranded in the dense forests between Thailand and Burma. We couldn't move forward as the bridges and roads were destroyed. As they knew about Netaji's presence, the enemies intensified their attack. British India's greatest wish was to capture the braveheart Subhas Chandra Bose.

'In the terrible bomb attack, bodies of animals and men were blown to bits. Yet, we withstood with fierce resilience. We gunned down the bomber planes. They cut away all external sources of food and aid. Many nameless soldiers who fought for India's freedom died a martyr's death that day! But there is no mention of their great sacrifice in the history of the freedom struggle. Only those like me, who were part of that battle, know about it.

'It was on one such occasion that I ended up saving Netaji's life! He would have been blown to bits in a barrage of bombs otherwise. I remember how he hugged me when I risked my life for him. Netaji gave me his pendant watch as a loving gift. I have kept it close to my body all these years as if it is another organ of mine . . . It is a German-made pendant watch, the one given to Netaji by Hitler with the wish, *"May your time become right."'*

I watched as Pundit retrieved the pendant watch which he cherished like his own life and gazed at it emotionally. Awed by its historical value, I gently touched it. My finger sensed a palpitation.

'Hendri, today I know that nature's judgement can be more fatal than any man-made war. All our hopes were extinguished when Japan lost the war. The Allies overran Burma. Obviously, their aim was the fearless fighter Subhas Chandra Bose. He was their nightmare: the royal Bengal tiger. Their army started scouring every inch of Burma. But Netaji preferred to fight face to face than to stay in hiding. Everybody wanted him to see the Indian flag flying high in Delhi after we secured our independence. It was decided that Netaji should get away in the Japanese bomber plane rather than be captured. That was the last I ever saw of my leader. After Netaji, our colonel, and a few Japanese soldiers left in that flight, rumours ran amok.

'Netaji had planned to reach Russia and strike a strategic deal with Stalin. But I heard that Russia did not side with him. If it had, I am sure India's history would have been different. The devastating news that reached us afterwards was about Netaji's demise in an air crash in Thailand. I was distraught and burst into tears. We prayed on our knees that the news should turn out to be false. But the aircraft had been a faulty one, battered in many war sorties . . . so the crash might have occurred after all.

'It was only after many years that I heard most of the news. In the battle that followed Netaji's departure, most of the soldiers lost their lives. Those who were wounded, including me, were made prisoners of war yet again.

'When there was no news about me for years on end, my relatives presumed that I had met my end too, like Netaji. By the time I emerged from the prison, the Indian flag was fluttering above Red Fort. Life in prison had sapped my vitality. Those who passionately shout opinions from a safe distance can blabber on and on about anything! They haven't faced war or life head on. I, for one, am confident that war is futile. Even the freedom we so proudly talk about is not forever.

'If you examine closely, history is a journey from one form of slavery to another. It is a never-ending saga of wars, conquests, subjugations . . . Neither the conquerors nor the rulers ever enjoy true freedom ever. Every struggle for freedom will lead to newer forms of slavery until human beings realize that the ultimate freedom rests within themselves.

'When I emerged from prison, I heard many tales. Some said that Netaji had died in a Siberian jail. Others vouched that they had seen him in China and Persia. News was rife that he lived as a sanyasi called Gumnaami Baba in Uttar Pradesh. Some tried to trap Netaji between fantasy and history, wanting to reap some benefit out of the chaos. I am not concerned about truths and falsehoods any more. Of one fact I am sure. My Netaji is not dead. *He lives forever in my heart.*'

Pundit held the pendant watch next to his heart and closed his eyes reverentially.

'Gandhiji's ahimsa was very powerful indeed. But India's freedom owes itself to the fierce fighting spirits of those like Netaji too. What's happened to all those strong tenets of ahimsa nowadays? The fickle world where nothing is everlasting has shown me that it is inane to be overly passionate about anything. What happened to Russia which turned her face away from Netaji's request? What happened to communism? What happened to Russia's dominance in world affairs?

'Netaji was never inclined towards fascism. He desired unity and secularism. Today, some people blatantly misuse Netaji's name to justify fascism! Whether it is right or wrong, in my perspective, there has never been a revolutionary leader like Subhas Chandra Bose in history.'

I heard the loud sound of the river crashing against the rocks. It seemed like an everlasting flow of history.

'My journey started from here. I felt as if I owed a debt to this place . . . and I have repaid it now by revisiting it. The return to one's origins remains a favourite caprice for many. This pendant watch wasn't with me then. I have never parted from it right from the moment it came into my possession. It kept beating, warmed by my body heat. It shall continue to do so until I die. But before my end, I must complete the clock which will move anticlockwise from the present to the past. I want to turn time back to recover the soul of India that Netaji and the rest of us dreamt about. On the needles of the Anti-Clock, I shall inscribe that the stinking innards of today's politics shall be purified! Let my Anti-Clock become instrumental in cleansing the sores of communalism and corruption infesting the body of the nation. Let the race of those who play divide and rule get annihilated. That would be my curse on all sinful souls, sworn on the Anti-Clock. Generations to come shall witness how it works. If whatever I proclaim is true, the Anti-Clock shall come to life by itself!'

Since Pundit repeated 'Anti-Clock' many times, I started concentrating on that term. I yearned to go back to the past and be with my Beatrice and children again. I also wanted to see those responsible for my jeremiads undergo annihilation. In that moment I felt strongly that Satan Loppo was the representative of all those despicable souls whom Pundit had heartily cursed. A tyrant who hoped to crush time mercilessly under his feet. If the fate of all such oppressors was to blaze momentarily before dying down, would I get to celebrate my victory over him and free my poor country?

Shocking me with his percipience, Pundit spoke.

'Hendri, the enemy whom you wish to destroy is just a symbol. The one who becomes a despot by draining the lifeblood of the poor and needy gets exhilarated with power. By espousing lies repeatedly for his survival, he claims to be as honest as Satyavan. He sneakily murders those who voice dissent, accusing them of sedition. *When blindness and avarice become the signs of authority, we are no longer speaking of a man, but a system gone to rot.* History needs an Anti-Clock to wreak vengeance on such a person . . . Then those who proffer fealty shall turn against the tyrant. Falsehood propped up on stilts obtain but short-lived victory. It shall ultimately lead one to destruction. History teaches us that only truth is eternal. *Satyameva Jayate.*'

22

Osthippura: The Store House of the Sacramental Bread

'As for you, watchtower of the flock, stronghold of Daughter Zion, the former dominion will be restored to you; kingship will come to Daughter Jerusalem. Why do you now cry aloud—have you no king? Has your ruler perished, that pain seizes you like that of a woman in labour? Writhe in agony, Daughter Zion, like a woman in labour, for now you must leave the city to camp in the open field. You will go to Babylon; there you will be rescued. There the Lord will redeem you out of the hand of your enemies.'

(Micah 4: 8-10)

'We are nearly fourteen kilometres inside the forest. It will not be possible to go back to Aadi Nadu today. Tonight, we might have to stay among these stone ruins. It is evident that elephants have run amok in these places. We are likely to be at risk too. Some carnivore might end up feasting on our aged flesh! Are you feeling scared?' Pundit teased.

'No.'

'Good. What should we two be afraid of anyway? Is there anyone on the face of earth worrying about us or waiting for us? Who cares if we pass away? Our feet tread a common ground. Did you know that special experiences await people like us who have nobody waiting for them?'

'What experiences?'

'One has to undergo an experience to appreciate it. You cannot understand by merely listening about it. Those who vouch for something, merely after hearing or reading about it, are either foolish believers who have renounced their brains or hardy fanatics blinded by antagonism. But the one who undergoes an experience neither needs proof nor cares to furnish any.'

That night, using a huge log, we created a blazing bonfire near the river, next to the stone steps. It was Pundit who discovered the fallen tree.

'This one will burn bright.'

Pundit kindled a fire with dried leaves and twigs. The head of the tree, which once stood majestic, caught fire. Tongues of flame leapt up, washing the surroundings in a fiery light. It was accompanied by an exhilarating fragrance of frankincense. It was a Kunthirikkam tree. We lay down like two animals new to the forest, listening to the lullabies of the wild river, and protected by the fire. I had spent a night in the forests in my youth, when I had accompanied Antappan and friends on a tour to Agasthyarkoodam. That night too we had lit a fire.

But this journey was unique in many respects. I felt that the Sayyip who had led a solitary life in the depths of the forest might still be residing in those stone remains. His indelible imprints were there in some things we found in the area. Rusting vessels, remnants of some sort of a thermometer, metal hooks of chains, parts of instruments seemingly used for experiments . . .

What had that unknown white man been searching for, all by himself? What divine gift had solitude bestowed him with, apart from material riches?

All night, I pondered on the eccentricities of mankind. I could hardly understand what inner calling had prompted the man, born in a foreign land, to live and die in a remote forest all alone. He had felt it was right and was convinced about it. The war that Pundit spoke about had occurred due to the convictions of certain people. Each conviction stood by itself, at a distance from another. Similar to Pundit, I was holding on to my worldview, convinced that it was my reality and my universe. Everybody was walking around with 'his own truth', which often contradicted with that of another!

Leaving behind the decrepit stone steps, Pundit and I started on our journey home the next morning. I gazed at every bit of the green forest to my heart's content, knowing I would never return. Making our way through the windswept trees and crossing the Neyyar, we caught a vehicle and started towards Aadi Nadu. By the time I reached there, some divine credence had taken possession of me.

Pundit gazed up at the steps ascending to the Church of St. Anthony. They were beckoning the souls as though to the portals of heaven. The sounds of work tools arose from Joppan Memorial Coffin Shop situated opposite. The cassette player was blaring out Sambhasivan's dramatic performance 'Twentieth century'. A female coffin maker was hard at work inside.

Without a word, Pundit made his way up the steps. To follow faithfully was my only duty at present. The huge entrance door of the church was invitingly open. I expected Pundit to enter the church after ages, but he abstained. He made his way to the old structure near the graveyard, behind the church. The building, with its outer structure constructed of wooden bars, was more than a century old. On its ancient walls were fading pictures of peacocks and doves. They were living testimony to the symbols of Hinduism thriving in early Christian worship places.

'In my childhood, this was the church where we participated in the Holy Qurbana. Aadi Nadu's first church. The bigger churches came afterwards,' Pundit reminisced.

It was hard to believe that the simple room, bereft of any ostentation, had once functioned as a church. Ever since I could remember, it was just another ancient building. In my case, the Sacraments, including baptism, confirmation and marriage, had been solemnized in the new church. This small building with a tiled roof, covered with wooden planks, was referred to as Osthippura—the storehouse of the sacramental bread. The Osthi appam aka the altar bread used for the Holy Qurbana was prepared here.

When we were studying in the church school, after the classes, we would race to the Osthippura. We would stand clutching the wooden bars, watching Sacristan Anthrayos, whom we called Kapyar, fashion the fair, delicate, delectable appam from wheat flour. The appam that he made first would be large and thin. Then he would use a round mould to prepare many small Osthi appams from the mother bread. The fringes that remained after the separation of the Osthi appams would be distributed among the salivating children. The race from the school to the Osthippura was for that treat! While my friends typically heckled and rushed forward for the tasty tidbits, I would languish at the back. Like the fate of those who could never push themselves forward, I was deprived of the Osthi appam.

But one day Kapyar's attention was drawn to the one left perpetually behind.

'Come here, boy,' he insisted and placed the white appams on my palm. 'Nature will never allow someone to be permanently left behind. She will propel you forward one day.'

That was how I tasted the Osthi appam before the Qurbana was over. It melted on my tongue and merged with my flesh and bones.

Kapyar was young then. Later, when he grew old and could not actively participate in the church events, his son took over as Sacristan. However, despite his fragility, Kapyar never relinquished the holy task of making Osthi appams. He saw the divine body of Christ in the small, white appams. His only wish was to continue making the sacramental bread until he breathed his last. The church granted him his wish, sensing his sincerity and devotion. When his limbs grew weak, instead of stopping his journey to the Osthippura,

Kapyar stopped going home from his workplace. He stayed inside the Osthippura.

'The graveyard is next door! No trouble in carrying me over such a short distance,' Kapyar joked often.

When we reached the place, Kapyar was happily preparing Osthi appams, forgetting all his infirmities. He grinned broadly on seeing Pundit.

'It has been such a long time since I saw you,' he spoke.

Kapyar offered the fringes, evading the wounds of the circular cuts, to Pundit. He received it with the same reverence shown during the acceptance of the holy altar bread. He broke off a bit and offered it to me. As I tasted the appam, childhood memories came rushing back.

'I feel like I have participated in the Qurbana of the old church again,' smiled Pundit. 'This is the real place of worship.'

Kapyar placed his hand on his heart. 'How many people realize what Jesus Christ meant when he said that *the Kingdom of God is within you?*'

'Does it mean that there's no need to visit the church? How can a Sacristan say that?' I asked.

'For those who worship the God within themselves, an old store house of communion bread, or one's own home, or even the whole world, is a place of worship. The All-Pervasive necessarily has to be present everywhere. If he doesn't exist in the netherworlds, how can he be omnipresent? That is limiting God to certain places! This old Osthippura is my church. The humble bread that I bake here in this ancient place, without any pretensions, is sanctified as Christ's blessed body in the church next door. That means Christ is born here, isn't he? This place is the holy crib.'

I felt a flame of terror licking inside me. *Lord, are you inside the devil too? By exhorting 'love your enemies', what was the secret that you left unuttered?*

The spirituality which finds God in a fiend like Satan Loppo is unpalatable to me. I am not sturdy enough to scale those pinnacles.

It was then that I noticed a gigantic stone jar in a corner of the room. It was pitch dark in colouring and wide enough to hide a few men in its belly! There was intricate work on its handles. I caressed its smoothness; it felt like a baby's skin. It had been crafted by a talented sculptor centuries ago. Such massive urns were hard to find these days. I felt it gazed back at me, like a primordial man formed from nothingness.

Observing me staring fascinated at the urn, Kapyar interjected softly: 'That container used to hold water when this place was a church. It quenched the thirst of devotees and was also used as the holy Hannan water for expiatory purposes. We used to refer to it as the "stone water jar of Cana". In remembrance of the stone jars whose water was converted to wine by Jesus during the wedding at Cana in Galilee, every devotee would take a sip from it. Now, the stone jar lies desolate. The chlorinated water brought from Aruvikkara is used for all the holy rites.'

I peeped inside and saw that darkness had filled the dry jar. It resembled men bereft of souls: utterly empty.

When we stepped out of the Osthippura, Pundit said, 'I feel the blissful purity of my First Communion again. A limpidness without any taint. I would like to believe that the Kapyar has offered me the blessed sacramental bread. Hendri, it is imagination that sanctifies an object. To fulfil the promise of the Son of Man, the bread and wine transform into the holy body and blood. For the pure at heart, it really is His divine body. Not only are they rejuvenated, but they are also touched by its symbolism. Do you know why the Kapyar prefers to stay in the Osthippura?'

'Why?'

'There is a sacred burial place inside this building. The holy figurine of the Lord that we carry around on Good Friday, when we enact the Way of the Cross, is stored inside the Osthippura.'

It was inside a crypt in the Osthippura that the full-body statue of the dead Christ, with its heart-rending face, was buried. Once a year, the vault was opened and the figurine retrieved. It was clothed again and sprayed with perfume.

I remembered the Good Fridays when my mother and I circumambulated the church on our knees. We used to make our way amid the many devotees carrying huge stones on their heads, sharing the Passion of the Lord. After the mournful journey, the figurine of the Lord would be placed near the door of the church so that the devotees could proffer kisses. In my childhood, Appan would haul me on to his shoulders and say, 'Give a kiss to our beloved Lord.' Those kisses were evocative of a divine scent.

Kapyar Anthony was staying in the Osthippura along with that mesmerizing fragrance.

* * *

Leaving the church premises, we reached the board, Pundit's Watch Works. Staring at it for a few moments, Pundit spoke: 'I named it knowingly. It is announcing to the world that *Pundit's watch continues to work*. The true Pundit runs this universe. His clock is always active. The sun and the moon are his clock's needles.'

I had no response to his sagacious comment.

Pundit rummaged through a drawer and retrieved an old envelope. He thrust few old sepia photographs towards me. Those were the worshipful memories of his hero.

'Look at this. This snap was taken before we parted the last time, when Netaji was about to enter the aeroplane. I was looking on, unaware that it was the last time I would be seeing him . . . In that photograph, Hitler is shaking hands with Netaji. The meeting which laid the groundwork for war. This photo was taken in the submarine with Japanese soldiers . . .'

In the last photograph were two young men who were strikingly handsome. One was Pundit and the other Subhas Chandra Bose.

They were dressed in the old military style—pyjama-like trousers, hat and boots.

'After getting the pendant watch from him, I became bold and dared to ask for a photograph. Netaji acquiesced. I intensely desire to see my beloved Netaji now. It might be possible. The Anti-Clock will take us back in time. Tonight, it will start functioning. I have anointed the time for its initiation. It will be at sharp midnight. Hendri, come over exactly half an hour before that. You are destined to be the sole witness. Not everybody is permitted to travel back in time.'

I understood nothing. I was in a liminal space: time, time travel, the eternal Pundit controlling time . . . all the vignettes were disturbing my connection with reality. My mind foretold that tonight would be pivotal in my life.

I could not sit still after returning to my coffin shop. The gears and springs inside me were working at a furious pace, intensifying the flow of time. I wished that it would turn midnight soon. When the animals and humans slipped off to sleep, I started walking aimlessly and ended up near the church steps. The throbbing sound of the electric cutter was rising from the Joppan Memorial Coffin Shop. I was astonished to think of Gracy working so late. Did the world really need so many coffins? Or was Gracy trying to divert her mind by undertaking such back-breaking work?

I looked with great hope at the Holy Cross, with its hands spread wide, mounted on the church's spire. Slowly, my gaze shifted to the sacramental bread glowing from the skies, silently proclaiming, '*Behold the light of the world.*'

23

The Silent Centre

'When a gentle south wind began to blow, they saw their opportunity; so, they weighed anchor and sailed along the shore of Crete. Before very long, a wind of hurricane force, called the Northeaster, swept down from the island. The ship was caught by the storm and could not head into the wind; so, we gave way to it and were driven along. As we passed to the lee of a small island called Cauda, we were hardly able to make the lifeboat secure, so the men hoisted it aboard.'

(Acts 27: 13-16)

The distance from twilight to midnight seemed interminable today. Though sleep has never been partial towards me, I took special care not to doze off.

Pundit had assumed a superhuman aura in my mind ever since we returned from the forests. It felt as if the war sagas, the Indian freedom struggle, and other international events of import were occurring within my own self. I was quite willing to follow whatever he might command. I had come to realize that the Pundit of Aadi Nadu, the Keeper of Time, was the guardian of many secrets, albeit in the league of those surrounding the disappearance of Subhas Chandra Bose. What I was unable to comprehend was why he would hand over the key to that treasure box to a humble coffin maker. Of one fact I was sure: the Anti-Clock intrigued me tremendously. I felt a rushing eagerness to know whether it would start chomping up time, starting slowly at first, before grinding away at it vigorously.

I shall be witness to all that happens henceforth.

Consequently, I set off for Pundit's shop far ahead of time. It was as if a machine was attached to my legs that responded to my thoughts. When I reached the watch shop, the Anti-Clock was hanging impassively on the wall like an all-knowing embodiment of truth. But its pendulum showed no signs of life. Did that mean that its heart hadn't started beating, or that it had been intentionally stilled?

Pundit beamed on seeing me.

'I was waiting for you.'

Saying that, he reached forward and removed the pendulum from its pivot. Like an arrow meant to penetrate the heart of time, it stayed docile in Pundit's arms.

'This iron rod makes the time move. Now, carefully remove the clock from the nail.'

As I hesitated, Pundit reiterated, 'Remove it and haul it on your shoulders.'

'Where are we going?'

'Where else? To your coffin shop.'

Time, which was at a standstill till now, started flowing rapturously like a waterfall within me. I plucked the clock from the wall and carried it aloft like a divine ark.

'Consider it a cross. The cross of time. But know this: *Without the cross, there is no crown.* The one who renounces everything becomes the owner of everything. Sacrifice equals gain.'

Again, I failed to understand Pundit. Yet, meditating on the Holy Cross carried by the Lord, I crossed the path from Pundit's time shop to my coffin shop.

Shorn of any adornments, my humble casket shop stood waiting for us. On reaching the shop, Pundit asked me to hammer in a nail on the wall. I delved through my collection for a nail that resembled those which had lacerated the Son of Man, and fixed it on the point decided by Pundit.

'Now climb this stool and hang the clock on the wall,' Pundit commanded.

Unable to understand what was happening, I felt alarmed. Yet, following Pundit's instructions, I hung the clock without the pendulum on the wall. It hung lifeless, like the first man shaped from mud.

Pundit climbed the stool and attached the pendulum to the clock. Then he closed his eyes for a moment before gently flicking at it. Soon, the pulsing tick-tock reverberated in my shop.

It was exactly twelve o' clock.

00.00

A perfect moment to initiate time.

The hair on my body stood on end, as if in deference to the Anti-Clock. The sound of the clock triggered a tremor in my body.

The two eyes, painted on either side of the clock's central point, were spellbinding.

'Told you that they hold time clandestinely, didn't I?' Pundit murmured.

I remembered that he'd once mentioned the left and right movement of the pupils as being indicative of the past and future. When I nodded in agreement, Pundit continued.

'Each moment is segued to its preceding and impending ones. Do you know, every moment of time has a stillness within it? Time is nothing but a continuum of stillness. And so is life. Hence, death always accompanies life.'

Death. I have never been afraid of that phenomenon. In this world, which place was as entangled with it as a coffin shop?

'If there was a lack of a time device in this shop, may it end today,' Pundit pronounced.

Hearing those words, an untrammelled joy, till now forcibly kept at an arm's distance, rushed inside me. In my solitary kingdom comprising a singular citizen, the Anti-Clock was a welcome addition. It would usher in a return to origins.

Yet, it was another thought that made me gape with marvel. Why did Pundit ignore the attractive offer made by Satan Loppo only to indulge an indigent man like me? Did he somehow feel that the befitting place for a time device, which augured tempests and deluges, was a coffin shop?

How would Satan Loppo react to this news? Would he rush in with his monstrous dog *and still my time*, entrapping my throat within its deadly fangs? Pundit had proclaimed that time was a continuum of stillness. It meant that if one measured each moment separately, there was no relative significance to it moving forward or backward.

What recompense could I provide when a clock, made after such toil, was being gifted to me? All I had were some coffins trapped in various stages of completion. A coffin is definitely not a holy object to be bestowed as a return gift.

'What should I pay for this clock?' I asked diffidently. Even if my shop and its owner were to be weighed and sold off together, the amount accrued would not suffice!

Pundit smiled on hearing my question.

'What will you pay the sky for the rain? How will you repay the trees for the living breath? Can you put a price on the flowers, sunlight, breeze and fruits? If each of these had bargained for their payment, human arrogance would not exist. The "sophisticated humans" would have been bowing and begging before them! The marauder never realizes that he is relishing what has been donated freely by the silent, majestic donors. *Certain things cannot ever be repaid, Hendri.*'

My gaze assessed the twenty-four markings on the Anti-Clock holding storms and rains in its thrall.

'This clock shall be witness to your life and shop from now on . . . Indeed, this is its only appropriate dwelling.'

My mediocre intelligence could hardly grasp what Pundit was saying.

'The Anti-Clock follows the true rhythm of the universe. Hendri, the moon revolves around the earth, and the earth rotates on its own axis in an anti-clockwise direction. The planets in our solar system, the Milky Way, the galaxies . . . all move likewise. You have been given a clock that moves in conjunction with the rhythm of the universe. It means that now your time is congruent with the movement of the universe! This is the latest Anti-Clock made in the world. Did you know that the Holy Bible gives a hint about the world's first Anti-Clock?'

'Which part of the Bible?'

Though I read the Bible daily and knew most parts by heart, I had never encountered such a story. My curiosity was immense.

'It is the sun dial of Ahaz. You can read about it in the Book of Isaiah in the Old Testament: "*Go and tell Hezekiah, This is what the Lord, the God of your father David, says: I have heard your prayer and seen your tears; I will add fifteen years to your life. And I will deliver you and this city from the hand of the king of Assyria. I will defend this city. This is the Lord's sign to you that the Lord will do what he has promised: I will make the shadow cast by the sun go back the ten steps it has gone down on the stairway of Ahaz." So, the sunlight went back the ten steps it had gone down,*' Pundit quoted. 'That was the first Anti-Clock. The sun shall turn back many steps from your life too, Hendri. May the Anti-Clock reveal its greatness to you very soon.'

Like a Prophet of the Old Testament returning to the past, Pundit got up to leave after casting an affectionate glance at his beloved creation. The names flashed in my mind one by one: *Jonah, Josiah, Elijah* . . . Who was this old man who had revealed an eternal truth that had been clouded till now, and why did he leave me alone with the coffins and the Anti-Clock?

Soon, Pundit retraced his steps, as if on an afterthought.

'All your coffins are black, aren't they? Hendri, when you make my coffin, make sure that it is white in colour. An opposite of the ordinary, like the Anti-Clock.'

As I stood dumbstruck, Pundit laughed, 'One should stand out even after death, right?'

I was stupefied. Never have I made a white casket in my life. Such a need has never arisen. Death, which always loomed dark, has never demanded any colours from me.

For hours after Pundit left, I continued to marvel at his ironic suggestion. Was the Anti-Clock behind that demand too?

Truly, I could sense that a new presence had taken over my home. One that made the stark stillness, dynamic. A vital and animating presence.

The realization that my life was being turned upside down, of course, came much later.

24

The Mantra of Time

'Indeed, wine betrays him; he is arrogant and never at rest. Because he is as greedy as the grave and like death is never satisfied, he gathers to himself all the nations and takes captive all the peoples. Will not all of them taunt him with ridicule and scorn, saying, "Woe to him who piles up stolen goods and makes himself wealthy by extortion. How long must this go on?" Will not your creditors suddenly arise? Will they not wake up and make you tremble? Then you will become their prey. Because you have plundered many nations, the peoples who are left will plunder you.'

(Habakkuk 2: 5-8)

David and Shari came to view the Anti-Clock the very next day, putting to rest all my doubts about them. As they stood rubbing shoulders, their eyes locked on to the Anti-Clock. I wished for a camera to capture that poignant scene. The new generation is entranced by the camera's eyes, aren't they? The new technique for freezing life.

Shari and David were holding hands intimately. If I weren't there, they would have kissed each other and made a love nest in one of the coffins, like Beatrice and me. They had forgotten themselves in the wild enchantment cast by the Anti-Clock.

Yes, the Anti-Clock possesses a sorcerous allure! Many cravings, which clamour against the natural laws of time, are confined within it.

As Pundit said, was it holding cyclones and thunderstorms inside?

Would there be earthquakes and wildfires within it too?

Could it heave humans from their present state, to the skies upward and hell below?

From that day, I started observing my surroundings and its variations.

I observed the birds perched on the Sapota tree behind the shop. The bats which came at night to feed caught my eyes. I watched a sparrow that lost its way inside the shop and hopped around the coffins before flying away. A yellow-and-black-striped cat meowed 'Hendri' from the backyard. When I fed it some food, it purred at me before gulping it down. I spied on a pair of mating mongooses. The male looked around to ensure that no one was around. Besides these, I felt the presence of multiple creatures amidst the coffins which were exploring life in great depth. Some ineffable source of power was attracting them to the coffin shop. Birds, animals and ghosts would be the first to respond to any new source of power in the mortal world. I believed that Pundit had consecrated the establishment of an unknown force in my humble shop.

At least I could not afford to dismiss it as mere superstition. A presence, which could transfigure the dead moments back to life—like Ahaz's sundial—was residing within my premises.

That night, the rhythm of the Anti-Clock's traversal through the past took my sleep hostage. As if practising a new meditation technique, I found myself gazing intermittently at the needles and at their fulcrum. Soon enough, the needles disappeared from view and only the central point remained in utter tranquillity. *Truly, there are points of stillness amid the motion of time.*

I might have been wholly entrapped by the stationary centre as I forgot to shut the shop that day. Throughout the night, the door to the shop was left wide open, seemingly addressing the streets, inviting all and sundry. Probably due to the silence which had solidified inside, not a soul ventured through the open door.

Indeed, at its pinnacle, stillness is a stronger and firmer protection than a stone fortress. Nobody can cross its boundary, and gain access to a person.

In the morning, I was jolted awake by the loud clanging of the newspaper vendor's bicycle bell moving northwards. The song glorifying the Father, the Son and the Holy Spirit flowed from the Church of St. Anthony. It evoked the memory of Kunjonachhan in the movie *Ara Nazhika Neram* where he awaited his death. Today, it was the same.

After a while, the cycle bell trilled non-stop in the southward direction and then rang agitatedly near my open door. Presuming that I had opened the shop early, the man came rushing in.

'Pundit . . . he . . . in front of his shop !' The newspaper vendor was panting for breath.

The time coursing through me gasped, 'My God', before freezing.

I ran frantically towards Pundit's watch shop. Pundit was lying with his face down, on the steps, as if hit by an earthquake. On touching him, my fingers felt the moistness of snow. A coldness crept up my body, as if I had stepped into the central point where time stood still. After hundred and twelve years, life had turned full circle. I was facing a total emptiness, but I remained unfazed.

Death, here I was, touching you yet again. You have gifted me the holy experience of touching the stillness of the time device.

As I stood mystified in the centre of all movements, I caught sight of a parchment Pundit clutched in his right hand. A piece of paper that looked like a will or testament. Loosening it from his grasp, I straightened it.

I had seen those German words in Pundit's watch shop before. A translation in English was scribbled beneath. In that ambience of death, I did not feel like reading further. The need of the hour was to take care of the dead man. The newspaper vendor and I lifted his corpse and laid it on the table where clocks were once repaired. Pundit lay on his own table like a motionless machine that time had discarded.

'Go and inform Pundit's family,' I instructed the vendor curtly.

When he hurried away ringing his cycle bell, Pundit and I were left alone in the house of time. I touched the forehead of the man who had left after sowing the seeds of time inside me. Startled at a sudden movement, I noticed the pendant watch dangling from Pundit's waist. It was still beating. Like a thief, I unchained the watch imprinted with the fingerprints of Hitler and Netaji. There was no need for it to end up with someone ignorant of its historical value.

I gazed at Pundit's serene face. All that he had told me about his Anti-Clock started frothing and roiling within. I felt sure that it would usher in many more inauspicious tidings, demanding heavier payoffs.

As if anything mattered! Only those who wish to live are afraid of death. For those who are ready to die at a moment's notice, going back causes no trepidation. That was what Pundit had told me near the stone ruins of the white man's building, deep in the forest.

I have a debt to repay.

The debt of a white coffin.

Once I pay it back, I won't be held accountable for the Anti-Clock, bought at the cost of a coffin, and the experiences it portended.

I reopened the white paper which I had extricated from Pundit's grasp. It was a copy of the German words inscribed on the ancient German clock. My eyes fell on the blue letters inked on that sheet.

Benutz die Zeit
Die dir gegeben
Denn jade Stunde
Turmt das Leben

Und mit jedem
Pendeschlag
Furtnaher
An das Grab

The translation was written right below. I had no idea how Pundit had managed to decipher it. Could he have approached the madamma? Or did someone else help him? How come he had it in his hands that night?

I struggled with my limited knowledge of English to understand what was written. I was filled with an urge to paste it on the wall of my coffin shop. Those lines were worth reading often.

Make good use of time
that is given,
while each hour
adds to life.
And with each
pendulum swing
you will be closer
to your last
resting place.

With the recognition that every pendulum swing took a man closer to his final resting place, I sought refuge in my workplace to create a white coffin, the first and the last of its kind.

25

The Return Journey

*'To the pure, all things are pure, but to those who are corrupted
and do not believe, nothing is pure. In fact, both their minds and
consciences are corrupted. They claim to know God, but by their
actions they deny him. They are detestable, disobedient and unfit for
doing anything good.'*

(Titus 1: 15-16)

There was unanimity in Aadi Nadu about participating in Pundit's
funeral procession. It was akin to bidding farewell to an adored local
hero. That did not imply that any sort of recognition which was
due to a freedom fighter came searching for Pundit. He had never
demanded it, neither did any chase after him.

While those who had never even scribbled 'Salt Satyagraha' on
their school slates got pensions meant for freedom fighters, Pundit,
who was tortured in jail with lathis and rifle butts, never found his
name on a pensioner's list. After all, a war fought in a faraway jungle
did not count as a struggle for independence, did it?

Pundit stayed away from the hypocrisies and shenanigans while
pursuing a profession he was well versed in. Maybe due to that, not a
single political leader of repute attended his last rites.

The one who strove to correct the nation's time had taken off after giving me backward-moving time!

Pundit lay peacefully inside the white coffin that I had crafted for him. In reality, I had no clue how to make a milky white coffin. Neither did I know of any white wood that could be used for the purpose. I made a frame using the planks carved of a Venthekku*. Covering it with mica, I constructed a pure white bedroom for Pundit. The top and bottom parts of the casket were covered with white satin. I gifted Pundit a beautiful white pillow too. He lay inside the coffin wearing a white jubba, white khadi mundu and white gloves. With white socks on his feet and a white rosary in his hands, it became a pristine white farewell. Pundit deserved a transition which had the colour of purity.

I felt a great sense of relief and satisfaction. This poor coffin maker could give at least some justice to Pundit. Rappayi, the middleman, had tried to get a casket arranged from another shop. The deal involved his commission and bonus money for booze. Pundit's relatives were on the verge of accepting that temptation. However, I approached the family through Antappan and disclosed Pundit's wish.

'White coffin? Never heard of anything like that before. Bound to be expensive,' a jeans-clad youngster commented.

He must have sniffed an ulterior financial motive in my offer.

'I did not ask for money, did I? This is what I owe Pundit,' I answered gruffly.

When a box was offered for free, the apprehension over whether white was a suitable colour for a coffin vanished. Probably thinking that it was a profitable deal to pack off the old man without spending any money, they decided to accept the white casket.

For the first time, death became a delight to the eyes. A beautiful death, where no one shed tears. I even felt a quiver of envy at the perfect departure.

---

* Ben Teak, a deciduous tree, with white wood

Laying a white kerchief on Pundit's face, each relative was dropping his final kiss on it. Though we were not directly related, owing to the deep connection forged between us by the Anti-Clock, I had persuaded Shari to stitch a white kerchief for my use. When I kissed the kerchief on Pundit's face, I observed that many were looking at me bewildered, wondering about our kinship.

While kissing him, I whispered into Pundit's ears, 'Go in peace. I shall keep the Anti-Clock safe.'

The sound of a white dove flying from the graveyard towards the church could be heard at that moment.

After everyone left, I remained with Antappan, who was busy shovelling earth into the newest grave. My Beatrice and children were buried in the same row as Pundit. I stared impassively as the pit filled with mud.

Why had Pundit gifted me the Anti-Clock and not charged even a rupee for his efforts? It was like dangling a precious gem on the grubby wall of my coffin shop.

* * *

I started locking my door whenever I went out because of the Anti-Clock. Ever since it gained entry into my home, it was changing my routine and habits. I started worrying about Satan Loppo's nefarious designs because I knew he had an eye on the clock. Albeit perversely, I could not help wondering whether Loppo's shadow loomed behind Pundit's unexpected demise. Habituated to trouncing anyone who opposed him, he might have decreed death as penalty for a clock. But since Loppo had the bizarre habit of purchasing a coffin for his foe after finishing him, I started doubting my own doubts!

Yet, expecting Satan Loppo to arrive any minute, I found myself watching the street fearfully. Banishing sleep, I stayed awake during nights and guarded my shop as if it hid a treasure chest inside. Indeed,

I found myself contemplating stockpiling weapons to handle Loppo
if he turned up!

But Satan Loppo did not come.

Still gnawed by doubt, I decided to tactfully ask David about it.
I felt he was my sole refuge.

When I shared my fears of Loppo raiding my shop and taking
away the Anti-Clock by force, David started guffawing.

'Uncle, you gravely misunderstand Muthalali. I don't think
he bothers about the clock any more. After all, a gift is something
given willingly by the donor. Muthalali says that it should stay where
Pundit wanted it to. He is so large-hearted! I know him to be a very
decent man.'

David's words dripped with honey. Once again, my deductions,
arrived after much analysis, had been proven wrong. Loppo wasn't
giving me any chance to validate my diabolical portrayals of him.

What a daunting enemy he was! He overpowered not just me but
my perceptions too.

As I meekly went on with my life, another incident happened.

Shari paid a visit to my shop, along with Timothios and his German
wife. They wanted to see the Anti-Clock. As soon as she entered the shop,
the madamma stretched her hand towards me. When the millionaire
white woman extended her hand to the humble coffin maker, I cringed
in inferiority. She caught my hand in hers. Whether it was due to the
coldness of my hand or the warmth of hers, the handshake between
Germany and Aadi Nadu left me with a scorching sensation.

Without exhibiting any peeve towards me, both Timothios and
the white woman gazed unblinkingly at the Anti-Clock and savoured
the finesse of its making. They leisurely strolled around my coffin
shop. Occasionally, they caressed a few coffins. When their fingers
flicked across the vertically placed coffin meant for Satan Loppo, I
felt acutely discomfited.

I brooded that the German coffins might be of a different make
altogether. Hardly had I thought about it, when the madamma

became loquacious about foreign coffins. What she revealed was beyond my wildest expectations. Timothios enthusiastically contributed to the discussion.

Germany had companies which were into coffin manufacturing. They competed with one another using a spree of advertising, showcasing scantily dressed models. It involved displaying the beauty of both the female models and the coffins.

To prove her words, the madamma showed me some advertisements on her mobile phone. They showed foreign models, without any sense of embarrassment, frolicking with the death boxes. One had her right leg atop a coffin, and her back towards us. Her dress was just a waist chain and a few pearls dangling from it. A man could not be blamed if his imagination went wild after catching a glimpse of that luscious temptation. Another woman exposed her bountiful bosom, her hands clutching the sides of a coffin. Each picture made me wonder whether the woman was making love to the coffin. The corpse lying inside would have been turned on by the sight.

What marketing tricks were in vogue in the modern world to increase the sales of coffins!

I was told that certain men, mesmerized by the models, would book coffins that were 'touched by female nakedness' in advance. It sounded similar to the practice of building family graves and reserving chambers for bragging purposes. When Della, Timothios's German wife, told me that her grandfather had pointed out his coffin before his death, I couldn't believe my ears. She was laughing when she narrated the tale of the old man insisting on one advertised by a model called Treesa, who was completely naked while she embraced the coffin. Della's grandfather was buried in the coffin he desired. I could not help chortling at the thought that the old man might have laid peacefully inside, meditating on the naked model who was embracing him. What had he achieved after death? Erection or resurrection?

Della must have noticed my snide grin.

'You can try some of those tricks here,' Della laughed.

I went red on hearing that suggestion. What a sight that would be. Naked beauties showing off their assets inside my coffin shop. Add a tagline to that sight: *Try Hendri's coffins with a legacy of 126 years for travelling to the heavens with gorgeous beauties.*

Wow, that would be terrific indeed!

Timothios interjected that the church was against vulgarity associated with the coffins.

'The church views disrespect to the dead body as a grave sin. The manufacturers refute that coffins are just like cosmetics and ornaments.'

I felt a stab of envy on listening to them. What was there to compare between a poor coffin maker in a mofussil place and the modern coffins costing lakhs of rupees? I knew of certain Chinese-made coffins, costing a few lakhs, purchased by the neighbouring parishes. They were longer than the local ones and it was hard to bury them in the limited space available in the graveyards. The pits required for these Chinese coffins were extra-large. Since concrete chambers were fast replacing manually dug pits, the foreign coffins were not in big demand.

When it was time for them to go back, I noticed that Shari was looking forlorn. She told me sadly that Della would soon return to Germany. Shari was anguished about their bond getting broken, since she had grown very close to the madamma.

I stood motionless in the coffin shop, staring after them as they left. Thinking that I should have gifted the Anti-Clock to Della, I felt a twinge of regret. My eyes darted to the board of the shop that was shut—'Pundit's Watch Works'.

Yes, Pundit's time machine was working fine.

At that moment, I remembered Pundit in his white coffin, bedecked in white, his face pale. When Satan Loppo placed a ring of red roses on his chest, it had resembled a circular drop of blood on Pundit's snow-white body.

26

Prescience

'If I speak in the tongues of men and of angels, but have not love, I am a noisy gong or a clanging cymbal. And if I have prophetic powers, and understand all mysteries and all knowledge, and if I have all faith, so as to remove mountains, but have not love, I am nothing. If I give away all I have, and if I deliver up my body to be burned, but have not love, I gain nothing. Love is patient and kind; love does not envy or boast; it is not arrogant or rude. It does not insist on its own way; it is not irritable or resentful; it does not rejoice at wrongdoing but rejoices with the truth. Love bears all things, believes all things, hopes all things, endures all things. Love never ends.'

(1 Corinthians 13: 1-8)

Maggots.

When Antappan warned that they were hiding in the air, waiting for an opportunity to sneak inside our bodies, I laughed it off as a stupid lie.

'They are all around, trust me! Squirming maggots surround every one of us.'

I couldn't bring myself to believe it. I have never seen any worms except in decayed dead bodies. So how could I take Antappan's words at face value?

But Antappan routed the unbeliever in me with his irrefutable logic.

He was adamant that the maggots were lying in wait for us. Regardless of the highest echelons a man might have enjoyed in the world, he was ultimately meant to be food for squillions of worms. After life leaves the body, the worms riotously run over their kingdom and reign with absolute freedom. They wriggle around their empire without restrictions, reproduce plentifully and consume every bit of you. Your body gets digested in the intestines of the worm and metamorphoses to that of a worm. You end up as a swollen maggot, coloured black or white. Just like the meat of the animals that we consume become part of us, it is obvious that we become part of the bodies of the worms that feed on us.

I was thunderstruck when I realized the truth.

Most of the people around have bodies built by eating chicken, buffalo, goat or pig. A man weighing 75 kilograms is roughly constituted of 25 kilograms chicken, 10 kilograms buffalo and 5 kilograms pig. Probably because of the lack of 'human' inside the body, man does not show much humanity and instead exhibits the characteristics of the animals that he consumes.

If one's food determined one's body and mind, undoubtedly Satan Loppo was made of chicken and swine! What waited for him was nothing but worms. Horrifying, nauseating, black worms.

It was mindboggling that the maggots appeared from nowhere the moment one's life breath renounced the body. They were omnipresent and patiently bid their time. Considering how prone to decay the human body was, the innate desire to indulge and pamper it was shockingly deep. Ruminating thus, I prodded my own body.

Antappan knew more about the utter absurdity of the human body than anyone else. All the beautiful bodies decked up to the hilt before burial were dug out of earth by him in their putrefying forms. He explained to me the difference between opening the family stone graves and those buried under the earth.

Most of the family graves had nine interconnected chambers. There would be three rows of vaults made one on top of another. They would all be linked to an *asthikuzhi:* a bone pit, so to say, a hole in the ground meant for the skeletal remains. All the decayed parts would be shoved into it. Whenever a death occurred in the family, the oldest grave would be opened, and the remains pushed into the bone pit.

Those with family vaults continued to lie chatting and bartering gossip with their dear ones even after death. Antappan said that while the bodies buried in the earth decayed fast, those buried inside stone graves deteriorated slowly, often resembling mummies, the skins shrivelling up and sticking to the bones. Some ancestors reclined regally, wearing sunglasses and new dresses. But on applying the slightest pressure, they crumbled into bits and dropped into the welter of the bone pit. No one knew how friends and foes celebrated their existence without physical bodies in that tangle.

I had witnessed Antappan's unspeakable agony when he dug up his own Appan's grave. The anguish of a son who had to gather up the skeletal remains of his father also affected me that day. Antappan, who exhumed innumerable bodies dispassionately, had been greatly overwhelmed at that moment.

'Indri, I cannot do this,' Antappan had mumbled wearily.

The one who had cohabited with death since his childhood, roguishly playing inside the Well of Bones, that same man couldn't bring himself to look at the remains of his father.

He felt the same pain when he dug up holes for burying babies. How many times he must have rued his fate, of spending life in a place where all lamentations converged?

'Destiny, what else?' Antappan once said, 'If a grave digger does not work, the world would soon start stinking with corpses. The Lord has appointed me for this task, Indri.'

'Yes indeed,' I would console him, 'The Lord created my job too. Where would the dead get to sleep otherwise?'

* * *

On the night of Pundit's burial, Antappan visited my shop to invite me for a get-together.

'What about this new clock?' he asked, staring at the new entrant.

'It is not a clock. Happens to be an Anti-Clock.' I showed him the time machine which contravened the normal direction and explained the way time travelled backwards.

'Backwards to the origin, eh?' Antappan's words were measured. 'Now that can be a painful trip.'

I could not appreciate what he said then. After all, I had no clue about the heart-rending information he would tell me that night.

In the cemetery, Antappan got heavily drunk.

It was evident that something was troubling him deeply. Pundit's death could not have affected him because they were mere acquaintances. If David was the cause of his sorrow, recently he had become tight-lipped about his son. The grief over his father had long been buried inside the casket of his heart.

Though I knew about his application, which had been read out in Mother Gabriel's prayer group, I pretended to know nothing about it. I had no intention of departing from the devotees' pact.

I knew nothing about the cause of Antappan's agitation. He would reveal it slowly, as was his wont.

Soon enough, Antappan said, 'Indri, you are my dearest friend, aren't you?'

'What is there to doubt it?'

'Do friends keep secrets from each other?'

I was dumbfounded. In our adolescence, we had been comfortable with each other's nakedness. But now, I was intentionally hiding what I knew of Shari and David from him. I wondered whether he had inexplicably dug it out from the depths of my heart. He must have known that my coffin shop had become the lovers' hideaway. I had sinned against him as a friend.

My body sweated even in the coolness of the graveyard. I sat there like a corpse, silence enshrouding me.

'I cannot help telling you, Indri,' Antappan sobbed.

'What?'

'You should not lose control.'

'No preface please.'

'Pundit was buried in the third row . . . you must have noticed?'

'Yes, the same row as Beatrice and my kids.'

'That is what I wanted to say . . . if there is another death in Aadi Nadu, I will have to dig up their grave.'

Lord of heaven! A sword, shaped like a crucifix, struck me and split my heart wide open.

And behold, the veil of the temple was torn into two from top to bottom. And the earth was shaken, and the rocks were split.

I relived that Biblical moment again. I was unable to breathe for a few moments.

'My Beatrice, my children,' I wept.

'I know how you feel, Indri. There are certain things which have to be faced.'

'Will I . . . be able to see them?' I asked tremulously.

'See them? Never!' Antappan hastily crossed himself.

The single cross inscribed with four names was fated to vanish soon. Till now, I could visit that place in the belief that my beloved family was sleeping nearby. As soon as Antappan dug up their resting place, that last consolation would disappear.

Where will I light the candles?

Where will I strew the flowers?

Everything about them would be wiped away from my life. The only grave in the world to hold four bodies would soon be destroyed.

I felt utterly debilitated.

Dear Lord, why do you cast on my shoulders experiences that weigh more than your own cross?

In the days that followed, I suffered the scourging that our Lord endured before crucifixion. I fell on my knees and prayed that no more names should be slashed from St. Anthony's parish register. Even Satan Loppo, my eternal enemy, should remain alive forever. I beseeched that the resting place of my beloved family should not be desecrated.

With every backward tick of the Anti-Clock, I felt that my own existence was getting diminished. Every morning I found myself waking to its heartbeat, wondering whether death had struck Aadi Nadu. It was just a matter of time before the news of a death drove a nail through my heart.

Those whom the Lord loves, shall be subjected to excruciating challenges, to make them shine like purified gold.

Why do you love me so much, my Lord?

Why can't you hate me a smidgen at times?

27

All Souls' Day

'But mark this: There will be terrible times in the last days. People will be lovers of themselves, lovers of money, boastful, proud, abusive, disobedient to their parents, ungrateful, unholy, without love, unforgiving, slanderous, without self-control, brutal, not lovers of the good, treacherous, rash, conceited, lovers of pleasure rather than lovers of God— having a form of godliness but denying its power. Have nothing to do with such people.'

(2 Timothy 3: 1-5)

'Lambs of the parish, those who proclaim the greatness of our Lord and King!

'We have gathered in this cemetery to commemorate All Souls' Day. The cross that you see rooted on each grave has a heartbreaking story to tell you. One day, you and I shall sprout in this homestead of crosses that has been nurtured with tears. And when you stand as a cross, with arms spread wide, your life history will narrow down to the two dates of your birth and death. Yet, forgetting that unassailable truth, we are tempted by the lure of the flesh, even when death sneaks upon us.

'Of course, you have the right to question, why the pleasures of the flesh were created, if not to relish them? You are free to conclude that the Lord is a dictator who tempts us with multiple fares, but forbids us from partaking of the feast. Harken then! Like the dress hides the wholeness of a man, ignorance conceals the light within him. *If then the light within you is darkness, how great is that darkness.*

'I appeal to each one of you to take up an adventure. On a rainy night, come and stand in the graveyard all alone and get drenched to your bones. When the realization seeps in that ultimately, each one of us is destined to feel the rain alone in the cemetery, life's illusionary hold on you will weaken. *Seek and you will find.* You will wonder whether you were seeking what was to be sought. The illuminating truth about life, revealed by the candles lit for the dead, shall present itself before you.

'Know that each man is a candle which burns from head to toe, losing its thread and spine before vanishing into nothingness. Close your eyes and visualize yourself as one. The childhoods of most of you have already melted away. Some of you have melted halfway, some three quarters, and some are on the verge of burning away completely. And when the light reaches its origin and merges with it, the signs of physical existence cease wholly.

'When you exhort that life should be celebrated and not repressed, be cautious. In every freedom exists friction, due to the opposing blades of desires. Blood flows when minds clash, and there is fire and smoke when loving relationships are set ablaze.

'And that is why *the poor in spirit are blessed and they are promised the kingdom of heaven.*

'As misunderstood by many, it doesn't mean that the poor people on earth are going to have a splendid feast in the heaven above. The spirit should have a dearth of desires. It is a promise that when your soul lacks desires, it exhibits its self-shining capacity, and enables you to experience the kingdom of God within you. It is not different from what the Buddha spoke *about desires being the cause of misery.*

'If you cannot carry anything from this world along with you, why should you spend your time stealing and hoarding? When the Angel of Death, coloured like red fire, arrives with death's message, any beseeching for an extra moment to get ready shall be turned down. At all times be prepared for death's arrival, as if you have the foresight of the exact hour and second.

'If you sneer that death shall never touch you and only snare others, remember the green leaves strewn at the foot of trees, shaken by a passing breeze. How many green leaves are likely to fall, severed at the stem, when an unexpected storm brews?

'If an ant's life is too insignificant to affect us, how much more inconsequential are our human lives in the entire course of this universe? Or else please tell, what happened to the glories of the kings and emperors who died helplessly at the end of life's great wars? With his hands dangling out of the coffin, didn't the Great Conqueror of the Worlds persuade us that nothing pillaged was being carried along with him; and that wars, bloodsheds and the incapacitation of foes were all cursed and futile?

'He could have left after leading a peaceful life with his dear ones, loving his fellow men. But he was restless and chased after conquests all his life. He murdered everyone who came in his path, anointing him as an inveterate enemy. His end was forlorn, unable to even see the face of his mother. The only realization he carried was the helplessness that nothing belongs to us.

'Yes, all of us have to take off on that journey, renouncing all glories of our status and prestige. Before that, strive to abstain from the illusions of the temporal world and store up for yourselves treasures in the eternal world. Instead of spiting each other, become a trellis supporting one another.

'Realize that the prayer for the departed souls is a preparation for our own journeys. Let us mark this day by truthfully answering the question, "*Have I run a good race?*" Let us raise our eyes to heaven and pray for all those who are dead and alive. In the name of the Father, the Son and the Holy Spirit, Amen.'

When Father Gabriel finished his discourse, I stood rooted like a wooden cross, which was meditating on death, at the spot where Beatrice and my children slept. Typically, the All Souls' Day speech was delivered from the pulpit, but Father Gabriel wanted to have it at the graveyard for a change. He suggested that we should move near the resting places of our dear ones and remember them with love.

Human lives are a flow of unending memories. I was at the earthen mound of my dear ones to join that continuum. But when it hit me that there might not be a cross to commemorate their memories on the forthcoming All Souls' Day, a piercing pain started assaulting me.

Dreary days were awaiting me, where I would be denied even the sole ownership of a grave. My loved ones would soon have to vacate that tenancy. Once the period of residence mentioned in the contract ended, there was no scope to renew it. Next year, on this holy day, another person would stand here with a heavy heart.

Six feet of land in the graveyard would be consigned for me in the future. Would there be a single person weeping for me on All Souls' Day?

Will it be Antappan digging a pit for me?
Will his hands shake? Will he feel a pang in his heart?
Which carpenter shall chisel my coffin?
My box.
My residence.

Dear Lord, I, who have crafted so many coffins, have never spared a thought for my own box till now. As Father Gabriel said, I too have to prepare for my day of departure.

Was there any arithmetic left incomplete in my homework book, needing attention before I left?

Even my feeling of retribution for Satan Loppo has lost its edge, whittled down by harsh realities.

I am a man emptied of everything. Utterly barren.

By far, I am the most qualified to have my name added to the scroll of death. A person who has no one waiting for him, and nothing left to do, is a long-deceased man.

Stumbling over the thoughts that sliced through me, I haggardly looked around. There was a huddle of relatives around each grave. Some graves were crowded, some were not. A few were bereft of any human presence and lay orphaned.

My gaze fell on Satan Loppo, who was standing next to a marble-panelled posh grave. On that ostentatious family grave, many candles were glowing bright. Expensive flowers were arranged all over. I could see Loppo's gleaming silk jubba, sparkling rings and golden rosary from far. All I had brought with me was a small pack of candles costing ten rupees. Would the dead feel ashamed of the stark differences in their world too?

One thing became clear to me: *the cemetery is a village of the dead*, in a way similar to the visible Aadi Nadu. The homes of the rich and poor were clearly differentiated as when they were alive. The class differences which enveloped the community were carried over to the cemetery too. Yes, the cemetery was a village in itself.

In the city, the dead lay in their concrete graves constructed next to one another, akin to people living in flats. The urban cemetery would be a facsimile of the city. The final resting place can only replicate the life that was lived.

Which place is free from discriminations? In the religions that exhort that a single god manifests in everything, in the political movements that envision equal rights for all, in arts, in literature . . . every sector has its own divisions based on economy, caste or other categories.

It was then that I saw Gracy near the wilderness far beyond the chapel. That sight sundered my heart like an animal slaughtered in a butcher shop. Gracy was standing near the lone pauper's grave in the cemetery, cast out and mortified. It was a painful sight not just for me but those around when she pleaded to the heaven for Joppan's soul from the corner of the cemetery overrun by weeds. Even those who had spoken ill of Joppan seemed to be repenting their intransigency.

I railed at my conscience, asking who could stand in judgment over another. Who would be cast aside by the Creator on the Day of Last Judgment? Those who claim to be Men of God, how much did they understand the ways of the Lord's justice?

I wanted to move towards the woman, who was as lonely as me, and console her. Like a human cross, I stood there with an unwavering gaze. Then inexplicably, I felt as if an invisible force was impinging on my body. Something intense, as if it were a revelation from the Lord, was pinning me down. With utter shock, I noticed that Gracy was staring at me. Unable to endure that look, I turned my gaze towards the steeple of the church. Two white doves with red eyes were watching the dead souls.

Someone prodded me and I turned to look.

It was Eron!

Eron was an old man who would appear in the cemetery regularly on All Souls' Day. Nobody had a clue about his whereabouts in the interim. He would continue to stay in the cemetery for a week afterwards, chatting with the souls. Any grave would become his sleeping place. Alms given sufficed for his food, and he often went hungry. After a week's stay in the graveyard, he would vanish from the land of death and return after a year.

Nobody knew where he had sprung from or what language he spoke. He never uttered any word. Everybody in Aadi Nadu referred to him as Eron. He was Aadi Nadu's enigma, whose comings and goings remained mysterious. Why was the itinerant man, who, like a migratory bird arrived and left without warning, standing next to me, touching my arm?

Eron continued to smile gently at me.

I remembered suddenly the whisperings that if Eron touched anyone on All Souls' Day, the person would not survive the next year. A sudden surge of happiness rose in me. Wishing that this would turn out to be true, I congratulated myself and wrung my left hand with my right. Two terrified eyes from the pauper's grave pierced me with more force than before.

From today, I am the man that Eron touched.

28

Harmony

'For the Lord reproves the one he loves, as a father the son in whom he delights. Happy are those who find wisdom, and those who get understanding, for her income is better than silver, and her revenue better than gold. She is more precious than jewels, and nothing you desire can compare with her. Long life is in her right hand; in her left hand are riches and honor. Her ways are ways of pleasantness; and all her paths are peace. She is a tree of life to those who lay hold of her; those who hold her fast are called happy.'

(Proverbs 3: 12-18)

As I moved past the Osthippura during my return journey, Kapyar stood clutching the black wooden bars of the building. His half-blind eyes were surveying the crowd thronging the graves.

'How many souls have descended on earth today?' Kapyar remarked as he saw me, 'My eyes dim when twilight arrives . . . It is all dark afterwards . . . *In the darkness, my eyes begin to see.*'

'How do you see in the dark?'

'The real sights are hidden in the darkness. You must learn to observe,' Kapyar commented. 'By the way, did you pray well, Indri?"

'Yes.'

'Must pray. Light the candles too. Prayer and light make the dead happy. They wish their loved ones would do that for them. Prayer is the strongest memory.'

'Sometimes I wonder . . . What's the use of praying for the dead sitting on earth? No guarantee that it will reach somewhere!' I objected.

'Those dead and those on earth are mutual extensions of one another. The living fail to realize it, but the dead experience it. The eyes of the living are always open outwards. Indri, I can see that some of those walking around will not be alive in the coming year.'

I could not believe what he said. An argument ensued.

'To say that you can see death . . . impossible.'

'Some newcomers shall arrive next year to pray for those who are praying today.'

'Tell me that I will not be alive next year,' I became obstinate.

Kapyar smiled sardonically. 'The secret of death cannot be revealed to the living.'

Bitter disappointment clouded over me. Since Kapyar did not specifically say that I would not die, could it mean that I might? The only prayer in my heart today was for an early death. If Kapyar could see death, he should have seen my future. Yet, without quenching my thirst, Kapyar shambled away to the Osthippura. Perhaps, there were white circles of the holy bread to be made.

I got ready to leave. Meanwhile, Kapyar stopped in his tracks, turned and hailed me.

'Eron has arrived, hasn't he?'

'Yes.'

I felt as if lightning had struck me. Eron had touched my body. Could it really be that I might not be alive when the next All Souls' Day arrived? As I stood stunned, Kapyar spoke again.

'He will come here to eat the remains of the Osthi appam. That is his only food. Some people stuff themselves with food, some eat normally, some eat very little . . . some consume just sunlight. Such people are radiant like the sun.'

I couldn't make any sense out of that statement. Did Kapyar mean that the vagrant Eron, dressed in rags, was radiant as the sun? It was beyond my grasp that a primitive grave dweller could be more evolved than the fashionable lot around. What was so special about that Avadhuta*?

'Every time Eron comes here, he speaks to me in his special language. He asks whether we will be able to see each other again. There are two interpretations to that question. Either he will not be coming the next year or I will not be alive to meet him. Today I have kept aside some Osthi appams for him. I shall not give anyone that portion. Not even you!'

'I wasn't waiting for that.'

Irritated, I moved away. Wondering what the day would usurp from me, I descended the church steps. When I saw Joppan Memorial Coffin Shop, the picture of Gracy standing forlorn in the cemetery flashed before my eyes. Momentarily, I pondered entering the shop. It was unnatural for me to contemplate such a step. Especially when I was yet to digest Karunan's revelations. I hadn't given them much credibility. However, after contemplating on death being such an unexpected affair, I found myself overcoming my inhibitions and moving towards the shop. Gracy was standing at the door, as if expecting my arrival.

'Please sit,' Gracy said, pushing forward an old aluminium chair with dented edges. 'I was preparing some tea.'

Hardly had I sat down when Gracy returned and courteously offered me a glass tumbler of steaming tea.

I found myself desperate for a gulp of the hot liquid. Since Gracy had brought it without even asking, I had to make small talk.

'I saw you praying near Joppan's grave.'

---

* Mystical wanderer

'Can we call a wailing meant for the Lord, a prayer?' Gracy spoke softly, 'If so, my whole life has been nothing but a prayer. I saw you too, drooping by the grave.'

I relished the tea. Inhaling its fragrance and sipping slowly, I reflected that certain people were destined to meet each other late in life. Even after years, my tongue was quick to recognize the delectable taste of home-made tea. Old luscious memories of the palate stirred within. Even the glass tumbler evoked tender memories of touch.

'Eron touched you, didn't he?' Gracy asked suddenly.

'Yes.'

'Wish he hadn't.'

'I thought it was appropriate.'

'Maybe all those stories regarding Eron are cooked up.'

'I pray that they are true,' I got up to leave. 'I am leaving. Just stepped in for a while.'

Out of the blue, Gracy spoke from behind me. 'I know why Joppan called you to the hospital that day.'

I flushed with embarrassment, as if a teacher was boxing my ears for failing in arithmetic! It was my presumption that Gracy was oblivious to the secret that Joppan had shared with me. Karunan too had indicated something to that effect. Otherwise, I would never have dared to visit her place.

Seeing me look mortified, Gracy spoke. 'Forget all that. Nothing matters any more. Perhaps in the youthful days, I might have experienced some infatuation. Who will carry it lifelong?'

'Whew!' I let a voluble sigh of relief escape me.

'If you liked the tea, drop in again some time.'

'Liked it a lot. I shall come, definitely.'

It would be gratifying to receive that glass tumbler with the heart-warming liquid again. I might not have savoured it so much had it been poured into a steel tumbler. Tea takes on various tastes depending on its container.

I walked back to my shop with an elated heart. A song from Joppan's cassette player sang out behind me.

'Chakkarapandalil thenmazha choriyum . . . '
'Prince who rains sweet honey in my heart,
I desire to be the sweetheart in your fantasy . . . '

My feet stilled for a second due to the craving call in that song. I became empty like a glass tumbler which had been washed and left to dry in the sun. Yet, I felt moist tenderness welling up within me.

Writers could write anything they wished! I was wondering why Gracy chose that song when it ended abruptly. I knew that she had stopped it deliberately. Gracy should have let the song play on. As soon as I thought so, my conscience pricked me.

I was dealing with a woman of extraordinary grit. She had purposefully given me an excuse to wriggle out of Karunan's mediations. Although I consoled myself thus, the relief was short-lived. Karunan came to see me that day and poured an ounce of bitter juice into my dried-up glass tumbler.

'Indri, you still have not understood Gracy. She knows how deeply you love Beatrice and your children. A woman who knows the depths of love will be loath to steal it from another. It is not necessary to stay under the same roof to unconditionally love another. *Love lasts even after the body perishes.* Living together or seeing one another are inconsequential for love. These words aren't mine, but Gracy's!' Karunan said quietly.

I was gutted thinking about how a woman, despite feeling such intense love, never expressed a twinge of it, having restrained herself with manifold locks.

Karunan resumed: 'Today, when I went to see her, she was building a coffin for a little girl . . . like she was dressing up her own unborn daughter. That is what I felt. Indri, Gracy's eyes were overflowing.'

A woman was reminding me yet again that love outlasted bodily death. I wished to experience love both in the past and the future. As Father Gabriel had suggested, I yearned to stand in utter solitude in the cemetery, getting drenched in heavy rain, watching the graves and crosses. Gracy, yes, she was the one who hammered that desire deep inside me.

The next day, rain fell, out of the blue, as if to fulfil my wish.

I was busy in my coffin shop then. It was eleven in the night, as I could make out from the left-turning Anti-Clock. I decided that it was isolated enough. I had never ventured to the cemetery at night by myself. I went there only for the occasional drinking rendezvous with Antappan, and I had never thought of facing the cemetery alone. In my last visit, the unexpected sight of Gracy had petrified me. But right now, a new courage was taking hold of me, similar to the inner fortitude of someone approaching death. I had no clue whether it clawed its way up from the depths of hell or climbed down from heaven. Frankly, I couldn't care less.

When someone decides to throw away his soul, neither night nor the darkness are objects of terror. A man, convinced of the proximity of his death, is no different in his brashness.

In accordance with Father Gabriel's sagacious advice, I stepped out on to the street, drenched by the downpour, to undergo the loneliness raining down in the cemetery. No other lamb from Father's flock would have dared it. Only the most intrepid dreamers could access the daunting, promised land.

Wasn't it an indication that not I, but someone else, was directing my actions?

A heavy wind was roaring. Thunder echoed in the distance. Indifferent to my surroundings, I walked towards the home of the damp souls.

I strode through rain-drenched paths, crossed Gracy's coffin shop, crushed underfoot the gravel of the church yard, and made my way to the graves. There was no light in the Osthippura. With his half-blind eyes which could espy souls shut, Kapyar was asleep. I reached the cemetery and unlatched the iron gate.

I observed the burial ground stretched ahead like a deserted empire, seemingly waiting for me.

Were the dead huddled around somewhere, soaked by the rain? Would my Beatrice and children rush to my side? If they did, would I get startled, considering their ghostly spectres?

No, no, there is no trace of fear in me.

Though they are dead, they love me deeply. Everyone here is beloved to someone.

True to what Father Gabriel had said, the cemetery was like a lush field bearing crosses. Beneath each cross lay a human seed eager to sprout, waiting for the Master who would harvest a hundredfold bountiful crop from them.

It struck me suddenly that Eron, who had arrived on All Souls' Day, must be somewhere close. But I couldn't see anyone in that deluge. Had Eron gone away because of the downpour? Maybe, regardless of the rain, he was curled up somewhere.

Making my way towards the cross beneath which Beatrice and my children slept, I touched the Truth affixed vertical and horizontal, its warp and weft woven from Love. As I embraced it, the atmosphere altered suddenly.

I inhaled the enchanting fragrance of frankincense. Loving embraces pressed me close. Four beloved presences wrapped around me and I merged into them, unwilling to let go.

Either I should be with them here, or they should be with me there . . . Dear Lord, extend your protecting hands over us so that we may be together. My lamentation became a prayer.

I do not know how it will come to pass. But nothing is impossible for our Lord.

At that moment, I heard a band playing a melodious hymn. I remembered a divine song played by the St. Anthony's church band many years ago. The utter sweetness of the cymbals, clarinet and drum merged harmoniously. I gazed bewildered, wondering from where the music played in that darkness and heavy rain. Not seeing anyone, I listened keenly to the sweet instrumental music flowing towards me from the land of the souls.

'Appa, Amma . . . ' I screamed, sinking deep into the earth.

Slipping back into the mortal world, I sprawled on the mud, drenched along with my loved ones. I remembered my children, who would snuggle fearfully under the cot on thunderstorm nights. Beatrice and I would lie above them on the cot, and that would be their protection. Like a wooden plank, I stretched myself, so that those lying in the grave wouldn't get wet. Let my children, sleeping under the mounds of earth, be reassured that their father was shielding them from above.

The needles of the rain stabbed me unceasingly. When they splattered mud all over me, I felt the thrill of the last ritual after death: when your loved ones cast a fistful of earth on you.

The rain gathered me in its embrace, reminding me gently that death was the paroxysm of ecstasy.

29

Going Back

'Yet these people slander whatever they do not understand, and the very things they do understand by instinct—as irrational animals do—will destroy them. Woe to them. They have taken the way of Cain; they have rushed for profit into Balaam's error; they have been destroyed in Korah's rebellion. These people are blemishes at your love feasts, eating with you without the slightest qualm—shepherds who feed only themselves. They are clouds without rain, blown along by the wind; autumn trees, without fruit and uprooted—twice dead.'

(Jude: 10-12)

When I woke up, the rain had retreated to its origins in the heaven. Spending an endless rainy night in the company of the dead, the last door and window of my perception closed, and I was bereft of life's heat.

Benita, who arrived to light candles in the graveyard before the early morning Qurbana, saw a cold human form lying on the ground and sped away screaming. I heard much later that she became incontinent at that sight. Waking from my death-like state on hearing that bloodcurdling yell, totally disoriented, I could only see a fleeing figure. I had transformed into a mud-spattered termite hill.

A thousand damp crosses loomed around me, at marked distances from one another. Before another person mistook me for a ghost, I departed with my mud-stained body. Someone could have easily suspected me to be the first man the Lord shaped from clay.

The news that Benita had sighted a spectre in the graveyard spread through Aadi Nadu's narrow alleys. By the time the believers rushed in, I had returned to the coffin shop, like an apparition. Since I was too embarrassed to reveal the truth, the 'ghost in the cemetery' fortuitously became part of the legend of Aadi Nadu. The foundation of the horror story was further fortified when a few who lived near the graveyard swore that they had witnessed ghouls in the vicinity! There was nothing I could do in such a situation.

I did not know whether a tragedy of unknown proportions would take over my life. My erstwhile self seemed to be shedding skins like a serpent. I was a man who had died multiple times in my physical body. I hoped that the cohabitation with the Anti-Clock might pave the way for the resurrection of my soul. After the return from the graveyard, I made a conscious effort to avoid anyone's notice. The fact that someone would recognize the man behind the 'ghost of the cemetery' was reprehensible to me. Deep within me, the conviction that I was moving away from a normal state of mind became stronger.

Watching the Anti-Clock sojourn backwards turned into a paganist ritual. New movements seemed to have taken residence inside my silent shop. I felt that I was not alone and that someone was whispering to me. When the Anti-Clock ticked nearby, like a living object intrinsically linked with the primordial, I slid into a fantasy that I might be able to usher in the past simply by staring at its needles.

My mind, having escaped my body, was exhibiting a circus right in front of me. I found myself watchful of its antics. Not all ruminations could be discarded as drivel. Unless you snag the tail twitching outside the hole, how can you conclude if it is the powerful deity of a golden serpent or not? Surprise! The cohabitation with the Anti-Clock had driven away my terror of snakes too. All the inferiorities that had pulled me back were shrinking their hoods. The audacity to openly challenge the whole world stirred inside me.

But who was there to fight with?

The coffins that were crafted for strangers?

Or the humans fated to recline in them?

I felt emboldened enough to believe I could summon Satan Loppo to my shop if I wished. The Anti-Clock would mesmerize him, and like a sleep walker, he would reach my shop. And like a puppeteer, I would control him by the strings I pulled! However, the circumstances having doused the flares of vengeance inside me, such wishes were not pertinent any more.

Whatever I was experiencing could be verisimilitude . . . Probably, Pundit's prediction of untoward events being connected with the Anti-Clock was the reason behind my perceptions. Yet, how could it be a mere coincidence that Pundit departed immediately after the completion of the Anti-Clock? It could not be a matter of chance that soon afterwards, the grave of my loved ones became endangered.

What was the Anti-Clock planning for me?

What had prompted Pundit to entrust its beating heart to my custody?

Was it true that you could predict the future and talk with invisible beings when you were nearing death?

I had witnessed my mother speak to otherworldly creatures in my childhood. She had told me in delight that my dead grandparents had visited the house. They had apparently advised her to tidy up the unkempt house. My grandparents expatiated that all external and internal actions were mutual reflections, implying that keeping the exterior tidy would lead to inner purity.

Amma, a slatternly housekeeper till then, became fastidious in ensuring that everything was in its place. The kitchen pots, the clothes, even the brooms and mops found specific storage spots. She encouraged us to keep our footwear lined up in a row. Amma exhibited the same scrupulous dedication which Pundit brought to the creation of the Anti-Clock, by carefully linking every tiny bit and piece. The home she left behind had been spotless and serene.

Though I, like a doubting Thomas, was sceptical of my mother's hallucinations, my Appan never denounced even one of her experiences. I could now feel the devastation of traversing through the teetering line that separated truth from falsehood. Wherever a man manages to find a foothold, that becomes his universe of truth, his *satyalokam*. That forms the foundation and the rafters of his existence.

Though I wanted to be enraptured by the visions as my mother, I found myself in a stupor instead. My mind pliable as clayey mud, I was floundering along somehow when Satan Loppo's son Timothios and his German wife again paid me a visit. David and Shari accompanied them. Unable to bear the additional mass of four human beings, both the coffin shop and my mind felt compressed.

I suspected that Shari and David had wilfully kept me in the dark, since neither of them ever hinted at the likelihood of such a visit.

'We are returning to Germany tomorrow. Well, we thought we should pay you a visit, Uncle Hendri.' Timothios smiled.

I wondered why the millionaire residents of the Aryan land wished to fraternize with a humble coffin maker. Except for ordering a couple of local coffins to take along, of what use was I to them? I shall volunteer to lie inside one as a free offer if they purchased two!

'Do not mistake me. Della wishes to take this Anti-Clock along with her.'

Birds that were pecking around *time*, fluttered inside me and took off noisily. I could distinctly hear them flapping their wings. They were like the ones which pecked wheat grains fallen on the road from a lorry, scared off by a monstrous vehicle, which would speed away, raising a cloud of dust in its wake.

It was evident that all four had conspired to assail me. In their previous visit, they had said many cordial words before bidding goodbye. The demand for the Anti-Clock had been nowhere in the picture. Besides, David had assured me that Satan Loppo would never eye my Anti-Clock. And now . . . ?

I aimed a razor-sharp look in David's direction, which embodied all my fearful apprehensions. He looked hurt.

'Muthalali has already given up, you see . . . But Junior Muthalali's missus really pines after it!'

Yes, Pundit's Anti-Clock was enchanting. One could not turn one's spell-bound gaze from it. Not only were there twenty-four markings moving in the anti-clockwise direction, it also contained indicators of thirty-one days of a month. On the months with thirty days, it took a leap across the thirty-first day. In February, it would take a jump across three dates after twenty-eight. Pundit had revealed these tricks exclusively to me. I had even pointed out to David the crescent moon that Pundit had forged at the tip of the needle marking days. The lack of forthrightness on David's part, in spite of knowing everything, displeased me strongly.

The world sets no limits to anyone's desires. But it is dangerous when a human being fails to set a boundary for himself.

'David, you know that I shall never part with it.' I was gruff in my tone.

'Uncle, why show such obstinacy? What is the use of keeping it here? You will gain much on giving it away.'

'Gain what?'

'Junior Muthalali will buy you a fine clock if you wish. Not only that . . . '

Timothios interrupted David in the middle of his speech.

'Look, I am going to offer you an exorbitant amount for this clock. One lakh rupees. Of course, no one pays that much for any clock.'

The price of a clock made by a simple man, from common material, was a lakh of rupees! I wished to call back the soul of Pundit and pay obeisance to it.

The financial bait was highly tempting for a village coffin maker. Even if I toiled all my life, I couldn't hope to make that sort of money.

However, my feet were firmly planted in a small square of my own self-respect. I would be committing a terrible sin if I sold the Anti-Clock that Pundit had gifted me after turning down Satan Loppo's offer. Only I know that the eye of the tornado and the door to the rain are under the captivity of the Anti-Clock.

'Please . . .?' The madamma touched my hand pleadingly.

A woman's mesmerizing touch.

I felt my strength drain away. Her rose-coloured skin was soft and warm. But I had to harden my heart against that entreaty.

'It is not a matter of money. I cannot sell this clock.'

My reply was unequivocal and dignified. A sliver of my vengeance towards Satan Loppo bristled inside me before piercing Timothios. As if hurling a stone at the man who had hurt my little son's forehead, I felt a retaliatory sting of pleasure. I also needed a teeny-weeny victory at times, didn't I?

The madamma whispered something to Timothios. I couldn't decipher the undulations of the German words. In fact, I was expecting Timothios to pick up a fight with me over my intractable stance. Watching the serpent-hood of my own stubbornness rise to strike was astounding. I preferred to attribute it to the strange energy of the Anti-Clock. I kept boosting myself up by reiterating that I was no longer the timid Hendri of yore.

Timothios did not lose his temper as dreaded. Instead, he offered a mind-boggling amount.

'If you think that the price was too less, well listen, here is my final offer. Five lakhs.'

My body shattered under the impact and the bits flew to the ends of the world.

Flabbergasted at the sudden spike in the amount, Shari and David gaped at Timothios. Their hearts were beating five lakh times faster, I ruminated. If they could, they would have accepted the money, which assured a lifetime of luxury, and disappeared from the desolate Aadi Nadu in a jiffy.

A humble clock, costing a few thousands at most, was being valued at five lakh rupees.

Ha, look at the money a rich man was willing to throw after his obsession!

That amount would enable me to reign over Aadi Nadu like another Junior Muthalali for the rest of my life. Was Pundit's clock so impressive?

All of them were sure that I would swallow the bait. No man in his senses would repudiate such an offer. Even as a selfish voice whispered to me that I could easily get another Anti-Clock made after taking the money, the realization struck me. Pundit was revealing the true value of the Anti-Clock through that odd bargaining. I could hear the creator of the Anti-Clock speak from within me:

'Never give it away. *What price will you put on the secret of life and death?*'

It would be suicidal to let go of something that couldn't be outweighed with money. I was unwilling to degrade its greatness. My life should be a testimony to the Anti-Clock's superiority, which was far above money.

At my firm refusal, Timothios's dark face grew embittered. I could sense the filthy blood of Satan Loppo flowing in his veins heat up. His eyebrows corrugated, and his face muscles twitched ominously. With his heavily built body, he could easily fell me with a single blow. David, expecting a skirmish, looked befuddled. He might have to take sides if it happened, either protect me or stand by Timothios.

It was miraculous that things did not turn awry. The German woman took the initiative to sooth her husband.

'It is okay . . . leave it,' she touched his arm.

Shari was staring at me aghast as if she couldn't believe her eyes. What was she wondering about? My utter stupidity in kicking away the hefty amount or my strength of spirit?

None of them knew that the Anti-Clock, which governs my existence, must necessarily remain in my shop. There are others who rightfully wait to experience its powers. If another name gets slashed from the register of St. Anthony's parish, four souls will lose their resting place and look up to my wretched self for refuge. I needed the Anti-Clock with me at that point of time.

I watched as the four visitors, beaten by my absurd intransigence, walked out of the shop. The coffin shop, freed from the temporary suffocation, heaved a sigh of relief.

Then the Anti-Clock chimed the time.

Tim. Tim. Tim. Tim. Tim. Tim. Tim.

The church bells tolled at the same moment.

It was 7 p.m.

I watched impassively as David manoeuvred the jeep through the path, which dimmed and faded out.

It struck me that I had long forgotten the lessons preached by Father Gabriel on All Souls' Day. In the mortal world, I was firmly attached to a silly clock! Yet my conscience came up with a counter argument to my own self-accusation. Someone who had turned down the temptation of five lakhs so glibly had prevailed over the glue of worldly desires, hadn't he? My soul was indebted to the heavens for protecting me from avarice.

Forget five lakhs, even five crores could not tear me away from the Anti-Clock, which was a part of me like my heart and liver. It was both my mind and my conscience. Fleetingly, it dawned on me *that it was truly me.*

The next day, disheartened at not possessing the Anti-Clock, Timothios and his wife left for Germany.

30

The Holy Remains

'I will abandon the House of Israel, walk away from my beloved
people. I will turn over those I most love to those who are her enemies.
She's been, this one I held dear, like a snarling lion in the jungle,
growling and baring her teeth at me—and I can't take it anymore.
Has this one I hold dear become a preening peacock? But isn't she
under attack by vultures?'

(Jeremiah 12: 7-9)

After the departure of the Germans, Shari's vivacity seemed to be in exile. From behind the coffin, I watched her pallid face. It was obvious that she was doing her work without an iota of interest in anything around her. I marvelled at the intimacy that had permeated Shari's relationship with Della. Though they had been friends for barely three weeks, much mourning and weeping had taken place during their parting. A stranger would have even suspected that they were sweethearts. Such intimacies were fast spreading from foreign lands to the local areas nowadays.

When David returned after dropping off Timothios and his wife, the streetlamps were spitting a sickly yellow light. I had seen a sad-looking Shari make her way home sometime before. She had hardly cast a glance towards my shop. She seemed to be floating away, as if she'd forgotten herself. David came in while I was frowning over Shari's state of mind.

Though David was fatigued, he picked up a fight with me.

'Cannot bear to think how callously you turned down five lakhs! Who can make that sort of money, even after toiling for ten lifetimes? I just don't get it, Uncle.'

'Well, when money blinds one's eyes, it's hard to understand things which are greater,' I replied solicitously.

'Life demands pragmatism, does it not? I would really want those lakhs which you turned down,' David bridled at my answer.

'True, life demands many things from us. But that same life might denounce profits of lakhs at times. Circumstances dictate the true value of things.'

'What is the true value of this clock?'

'I am still trying to estimate its value. Perhaps, one day, you too will realize it! Now, what about your plans of migrating to Germany?'

'As if the madamma was serious about it. Pipe dream, what else?'

There was a golden watch, curled like a snake, around David's wrist. I found it intriguing, since David never used one.

'It was the madamma's parting gift for driving her around. She says a driver needs a watch foremost. It is supposedly expensive . . . Unlike you Uncle, I will sell it if I get a buyer.'

It was a premium Seiko brand watch. Pundit would have regaled us with stories of its legacy if he was alive. I knew that David, if he received a good offer, would never hesitate to sell off that top-class watch.

'I am thinking of Chakkapan's relative. That fellow has a weakness for foreign brands.'

David left soon afterwards.

I was relieved about one thing. Since Della was gone, Shari had no more reason to visit Satan Loppo's bungalow.

However, on the very next day, as if mocking my conjectures, Shari climbed into David's jeep and left for the bungalow. What was wrong with the girl? How come she never endured a prick of conscience while misusing her liberty without her family's knowledge? For a moment, like a father, I felt flustered at what was happening beyond Karunan's line of sight.

That afternoon, when Shari came back and dropped in for a visit, I raised my question.

'When nobody is there for you to teach how to drape a sari, why visit that place again?'

'There is someone languishing there unable to don a sari. Philomenamma enjoys my company. Poor woman, she is bedridden.'

'Yes . . . she is a poor thing. An angel caught in hell fire.'

I had no clue that Shari and the Good Samaritan Philomenamma were friends. To be friends with a good soul was a good thing. Speaking or thinking something against that would be against the Lord's will. Why should I worry about Shari's whereabouts anyway? My full focus should be on the death tolls from the church bells.

I attuned my hearing towards the church to ensure that no sound slipped past unnoticed.

* * *

I lived a reclusive life shuffling between the coffins and the Anti-Clock until the church bell started wailing horrendously one day.

Though I was expecting the death knell, my body went up in flames.

My terror grew as if all the bells of the world were ringing together.

A death in the parish was being announced.

A new coffin would be needed, and an old grave would be dug open.

Lord, the blasphemy was imminent . . . The resting place of my loved ones would be defiled soon.

Needled with fears, I madly raced towards the cemetery. I did not even bother to shut the shop. My sole aim was to meet Antappan, and my feet gathered speed. Though Gracy was staring flabbergasted at me from the Joppan Memorial Coffin Shop, I whizzed past her without stopping. Flying up the steps of the church, crossing the Osthippura, I reached the cemetery.

Antappan was readying to dig a pit. He looked at me uneasily.

'Will you be digging up a grave today?' my voice quivered.

'One needs a hole to bury the dead . . . Indri, please go to your shop. Let me finish my work.'

'No, I won't leave. I shall stand right here.' I was blabbering like an insane person.

'Indri, please don't interfere with my job.'

'You are my best friend! Antappa, help me see my loved ones.'

'Never. No one should see that sight. I underwent that damnation when I dug up my Appan's grave. You will suffer more than me.'

'I will handle that suffering. I will handle it . . .' I insisted feverishly. Truly, I was burning with heat. Antappan could sense it better than me.

'I should never have told you about it. If the church authorities get to know, I might lose my job.'

'Nobody will know. Antappa, you dug up your father's grave, didn't you? Let me see them. '

Antappan could not be blamed for doubting my sanity. He had never faced such a predicament before. No one in the parish knew the agony of a grave digger who had dug up his own father's grave. A grave digger's name never appears in any church meeting.

'Indri, you have beautiful memories of your family. When the grave is opened, it will be gruesome. You will not be able to bear the sight of the skulls and splinters of bones,' Antappan pleaded with me.

'I will see their true forms in what remains of them. Please take pity on me.'

I stood firm like a fanatic until Antappan ceded defeat before my obduracy.

He seated me on a tomb. Until he allowed me, I was not supposed to budge an inch. I was duty-bound to obey his command.

I heard the shovel hitting the white sheet of sand spread over Beatrice and the children. My God, they were sleeping beneath it! The specks of sand were simply covering their peaceful and beautiful forms. Soon the earth would shift and I would see them.

With each earth-splitting strike of the shovel, my heart was torn asunder.

Struggling to restrain my heart from bursting, I started reciting the prayer, '*Our Father who art in Heaven, hallowed be thy name.*' Else, blood would have oozed out of my ruptured chest. Unable to chant it for long, my frantic prayers changed to '*My Jesus, My Jesus*', and then shortened to '*Jesus, Jesus*'. There was only the unceasing intonation of the sound at whose door all prayers knock finally.

Was it the continuance of life's sacred sound?

As I wondered in a dazed whether it originated from me or the universe itself, Antappan placed the holy remains wrapped in a white cloth on the tomb.

'My beloved children!' I heard a scream emerge from myself.

As I collapsed, a friendly arm held me tight.

31

Crossroads

'The bows of the warriors are broken, but those who stumbled are armed with strength. Those who were full hire themselves out for food, but those who were hungry are hungry no more. She who was barren has borne seven children, but she who has had many sons, pines away. The Lord brings death and makes alive; he brings down to the grave and raises up. The Lord sends poverty and wealth he humbles, and he exalts. He raises the poor from the dust and lifts the needy from the ash heap; he seats them with princes and has them inherit a throne of honor.'

(1 Samuel 2: 4-8)

The face is the hallmark of any person.
It is the symbol of ownership over the body.
Love stamps her kisses on the face. I need the faces of my loved ones back.

While I was blabbering on, Antappan mercilessly replied that I was demented and started scolding me.

Yes, I was crazy. I loved that craziness! The world has nothing left of my loved ones. But nature was magnanimous enough to safeguard and send back some traces of them.

The foreheads that I have kissed, the cheeks I have caressed, the love that I have held on to closely . . . Now, reminding me that life was all about these, they have alchemized and returned to me.

Why should I abhor those who were once a part of me?

What more shall I renounce from my soulless existence? All these bones were part of their bodies when they lived. Does a man deplore his own bones when he lives? That is why I can't loathe the remains of my beloved. By reading the signs on these, I can recognize each of them.

Why do we open graves, retrieve the holy remains of saints and bury them in specially earmarked crypts? Weren't there stories of the bodily remains of great leaders being brought back to their motherlands centuries after their deaths? These are not just skulls and bones to me. They are holy remains worthy of reverence and worship. I was experiencing the earthly presence of my loved ones again, totally and completely.

I preferred to believe that the Anti-Clock had travelled back in time to bring my family back to me. Pundit's words would never be ineffectual.

Swathing them in a silk cloth, I readied a holy resting place not besmirched by human touch for my loved ones. Many might raise their eyebrows at the mention of a *pure place* inside a coffin shop. I do not care for the erratic beliefs of humans regarding purity and impurity. At least, I shouldn't forget that the laws of nature, and the laws of providence and justice were skewed when it came to my life experiences.

Out of the blue, a feeling of completeness ensconced me. That which had left me, had returned to live with me.

Life, you have been kind enough to fill my goblet of wine yet again.

I love you as much as the seas and beyond the skies.

Enchanted by your golden attractions, I am sipping your spirit over and over.

Now, I will have Beatrice's companionship at night.

I have with me Rosarios, Alphonse and my Roselyn, delicate as a little bird.

That night, we slept with arms around one another on a single mattress, amongst the coffins. The Anti-Clock stood watch over our peaceful repose. Being the proud possessor of invaluable treasures, if I wished, I could crow about my good fortune to the Lord and the whole world. Together, the Anti-Clock and my loved ones had handed me back the past in all its glory.

However, I shall not exhibit the treasury of my joys to anyone. Inside a chest with seven locks, beyond the reach of the world's evil eye, I have safeguarded it. Not even Shari and David, who are likely to drop in unannounced, should get a hint about it.

I hid my secret gain in an obscure corner of the shop. The next day when the lovers traipsed in, I welcomed them cheerfully as if nothing new was in the air.

'Uncle, you seem so jovial today,' Shari commented pertly.

Women must have inherited the art of surmising inner thoughts by reading faces from Eve's time! When the Lord shaped her from Adam's rib, she was busy abducting man's cogitations too. That's why no one can beat a woman when it comes to prying out secrets. Hey man, the woman has been designed in such a way that she can smell out your dalliances even before you reach home!

I turned into a wily Adam and concealed the secret of my delight. Since attack was the best form of defence as far as war strategies went, I questioned David peevishly.

'How long has it been since you have gone home? Don't you feel like seeing your father?'

'Too busy, Uncle. Why go there only for the reprimands?'

David, always at the beck and call of Satan Loppo, had taken residence in the bungalow's annex. He was the devoted charioteer whose vehicle was ready for Loppo night or day. With that role, David had left the other cronies far behind. He bragged that many of Loppo's acolytes were jealous of him. Smart chap! I have no doubt that he will scale the pinnacles of life using the tool of diplomacy.

'Fathers are bound to scold. Once you become one, then you will get to know.'

'Okay, then I shall try to be a father as soon as possible to understand it!'

As he quipped, David's unruly eyes explored Shari's lush body lasciviously. Probably remembering the arduous efforts behind motherhood, Shari blushed like the beloved of Solomon in the Song of Songs. I remembered the metaphors of the luscious pomegranate, intoxicating wine and the lovely bay laurel tree in the Old Testament.

Since I read the Holy Bible daily, I know most portions by heart. Whenever I encounter the awe-inspiring literary penmanship, I deeply regret my own long-buried writing dreams. When I was studying in the tenth standard, Saraswathy teacher used to show my Malayalam answer sheet to other students, saying, 'Look and learn how to write an answer.'

They did learn. Writing proper answers, they scaled various heights of life. But what about me?

It was my futile hope that the gift of language in me was not dead but in slumber, awaiting an appropriate day for its resurrection. Even if one did not copy them down, couldn't lovely expressive words be merged in one's self? Yes, I can feel it in my thoughts and my very breath.

The great book crafted by a coffin maker who engraves words shall one day be completed. In a way, every coffin is a creation written in its own unique language. Every chip of the chisel is a vowel or consonant. How many such compositions have I formed! I belong to the company of those anonymous writers who lack the skill to grab fame.

David encroached into my scholarly musings.

'Uncle, you should look after this girl. I am away for a week.'

'Going where?'

'To Coimbatore with Muthalali. He plans to start a new unit.'

'What's the need for a new one?'

'Folks approached him regarding the port project. They wanted to purchase rocks wholesale. Muthalali was not interested in that offer. Since river sand is scarce, manufactured sand or m-sand will be in high demand for the upcoming port. Muthalali wants to start an m-sand unit. Bet business worth crores will pour in!'

'Aadi Nadu's throat is already parched. Its lungs are cancerous. And now you plan to choke it to death?' I asked wearily.

'As if it is only Muthalali who owns crusher units over here! How can one man change the world, Uncle? What about development?' David became combative.

'The world will change only if it starts with a single person. That is the science behind it.' I was unyielding.

'I am clueless about science and stuff. See, since the locals are against it, everything is top secret. Muthalali has confided only in me,' David preened.

'How come you are his only confidante?' Shari retorted.

'He says that I am his lucky mascot. Why do you think he has a soft corner for us?' David replied.

'So, your plan is to ascend the skies, eh?' Shari asked cheekily.

'Want to bet? I will reach the zenith.' David was in a boisterous mood.

'True, God shall let some people climb the ladders while some are fated to slide down the mouths of the snakes.'

Shari caught the drift of my philosophical mutterings.

'What did you say, Uncle?' she asked sharply.

'Oh, I was just remembering my Appan. When I played snakes and ladders in my childhood, I never understood that I was gambling with life. Every time I became ecstatic on climbing a small ladder, a few serpents were lying in wait to swallow me. One needs luck to evade snakes,' I shrugged.

'If everything depends on luck, what is the necessity of hard work or prayer?' Shari laid a woman's snare for me.

'Prayer is the invitation for luck. So is hard work. Appan said that only a fool waits for luck to drop on to his head.'

'Uncle, I find it difficult to accept that prayer has special powers,' David objected immediately. After all, he was the atheist son of the parish grave digger.

I remembered the advice that a coffin maker, who wasn't a scholar, had given his young son. All I had to do was to change the name 'Hendri' to 'David' in that discourse. The rest of Appan's words would stand the test of time.

'David,' I said, 'Only a fortunate person gets to be a believer. When you pray with faith, it is like channelizing all your energy into a single tube. If it rushes down from the heights, it can light up your life with its electricity! It can make many magical instruments work, which are usually beyond human capacities. It is the same energy that resides inside the believer and the atheist. But the atheist has no reason to focus his energy on it and enhance its powers. Or else he should possess an extraordinary will power. Even that needs the support of destiny.'

'All preachers mix up multiple arguments. If everything is predestined, how can prayer change one's fate, Uncle?' David mocked.

'Ha ha! That is an intelligent question. Suffice it to say that those who are not fated to acquire anything through prayers are given the destiny of being unbelievers. They will argue intelligently and stay away from prayers. What they wish for does not happen either! The "intelligence" we know of is a stupid illusion which drops to zero if one dozes off. But there is another "intelligence" which stays awake even when a person is asleep. A man who experiences that while he is awake is super intelligent. Those were my Appan's observations, by the way.'

My exposition didn't please David much. Let him live peaceably with his own convictions. If everybody gets convinced of the same things, life would be a boring affair. Instead of 'fate', if I had used the word 'experience' David might have acquiesced. No one could denounce experience as false. Every future moment is being shaped by an action leading to the experience.

Shari looked dull at the prospect of spending a week away from David. The weekly forecast for me would be to watch a girl's morose face from behind the coffin. When David tried to bid goodbye, I slipped away to the back porch. Why should I be a nuisance if he felt like kissing Shari in the seclusion of the coffins?

However, I became vexed at the thought of Beatrice and my children witnessing their kiss and hurried back. The couple seemed to be blissful, having celebrated the stolen moments splendidly. When I returned hurriedly, not wanting to overindulge them, Shari's hands were resting in David's. Evidently, they were the type to unhesitatingly step on thorny briars and glass slivers in their exploration of love.

That evening, David, along with Satan Loppo, drove away to Coimbatore in an Innova. The horn blared and the throbbing sound faded into the distance as a plume of dust billowed over Aadi Nadu.

That journey, Lord, that journey should never have happened! How many times must I have beseeched the Lord about obliterating it forever! Whether one called it 'fate' or 'experience', it remained a scalding truth that could kill.

32

The Word

"Behold, I will make you small among the nations; you shall be greatly despised. The pride of your heart has deceived you, you who dwell in the clefts of the rock, whose habitation is high; you who say in your heart, 'Who will bring me down to the ground?' Though you ascend as high as the eagle, and though you set your nest among the stars, from there I will bring you down," says the Lord.'

(Obadiah 1: 2-4)

Most unexpectedly, today I discovered an old leather bag tucked away among the coffins. White fungus had traced a map of Antarctica on its visage. When I opened it carefully, I was both astounded and overjoyed at the find.

There were cinema notices and a total of seven marbles, what we called 'soda-vattu', used in soda bottles. There was an array of curious matchboxes, no longer in circulation. I had picked them up in my childhood from side roads and the areas around the local shops. It was as if a laughing, boisterous childhood had come rushing in from the past to embrace me warmly. The child in me started frolicking over the farms and village paths again.

I could not recollect putting the precious possessions of my boyhood into that bag. My father or mother might have safely preserved their son's innocent fancies. By walking along the edge of that delightful discovery with the help of the Anti-Clock's backward movements, I thought I could return to the past. It was then that another marvellous artefact caught my eye—my Appan's clarinet box.

At a mere touch, a powerful rush of energy jolted me, transforming me into a conduit of electricity. The enchanting band music which I had been privy to, as I lay drenched to the bones in the cemetery, made its pristine presence felt again. Memories of an era when the St. Anthony's church band was active raced into my mind.

I picked up each part of the disassembled clarinet with the same reverence as that for a divine object. Like the ancestral muzhakkol, the clarinet was also my paternal legacy. I tried to assemble it. First, the bell and the lower joint. I affixed to it the upper joint with the barrel and mouthpiece, ensuring that the reed was duly moistened. Ever since my Appan laid it to rest, there had been no other fingerprints on the clarinet.

I wasn't sure whether it would work. Yet, with a sudden hope, bringing it close to my mouth, I blew my life breath into the clarinet's body. As the life-spirit travelled through the ancient mouthpiece, its pulse stirred and responded to my breath. Waking up from its sleep after many years, it emanated a sorrowful tune. How many years had it been since I had heard it? My Appan seemed to have bridged the distance between us through pure sound.

In my childhood, on observing my curiosity, Appan had taught me a few tunes. Digging into that memory, I hesitantly tried to play an old hymn.

'*Davidadmaja Mariame, dhanye thanwangi . . .*
Ninn vritthantham varnippan, njan aprapthan thaan . . .'
Daughter of David, Mary, blessed and full of grace
Unworthy am I of narrating thy story divine . . .

I was utterly dismayed at the results. It was then that I noticed someone peeping through the front door of the shop. Oh, Benjamin! He was the son of Franklin Uncle who used to play in the church band along with my Appan. There was a time when Franklin Uncle's drum and my Appan's clarinet had thrilled Aadi Nadu. The families were remarkably close to each other. Though Benjamin and I were fast friends as children, for some unfathomable reason, he had become cold and distant with time.

Benjamin must have been attracted by the sound of the clarinet. But I felt slighted when he whisked away as soon as I caught him looking. Our fathers having passed away a long time ago, why was he still aloof with me? Failing fantastically in an attempt to play a few more tunes, I returned the clarinet to its box.

Beset by dark clouds of misery, I sat brooding, and then Benjamin unexpectedly returned. Easing the gathering tension, he said sadly, 'Indri, I owe you an apology. It was something my father owed yours.'

'What?'

'Indri, we were like one family, weren't we? Yet what happened? For a silly reason, the relationship broke off. A wicked man's manipulation!'

I remembered that being separated from Franklin Uncle had been a source of life-long misery for my Appan. With the thrill of discovering the missing part of the puzzle, the Anti-Clock chimed, inviting me to the yesteryears. It was akin to a signboard that intermittently ushered me from the present to the pages of the past. Ever since its arrival, the small and large wounds of my past were being slowly uncovered and gently assuaged.

The band of the St. Anthony's church, a favourite in all the Feast Day celebrations near and far, was relegated to a mere memory for many decades. Appan used to grieve that it was a trivial misunderstanding which had torn apart that brilliant team. Franklin Uncle had been the leader of the Gorothy prayer group, which was one amongst the eighteen gospel groups of the church. Every month, each group would meet in the home of a member, along with the parish priest, for prayers and a meal.

Franklin Uncle, who carried out his duties as a group leader sincerely, had been hurt by some dark mutterings, and decided to quit. In the meeting held for selecting a new leader, among varied voices, my Appan had put forth a suggestion: 'It is better for Franklin to continue in the post. The Lord has decided the work for each one of us.'

Appan had meant to highlight that Franklin Uncle's dedicated work was the Lord's mandate. But Samuel, who was seated next to my father, slyly twisted his words.

'He is good only for that.'

Samuel's insinuation was that 'only those having no other work ended up as leaders'. He was notorious for his captious and dishonest ways. Appan corrected him promptly, stressing that nobody could replace Franklin, who considered his duty as the Lord's own work.

Though Appan forgot that private conversation with Samuel, the latter, in a treacherous move, stoked slander and destroyed a friendship. When the venomous gossip was injected in Franklin Uncle's wife by Samuel's wife, the original tête-à-tête acquired spiteful proportions. The accusation was that in the prayer meet, Appan had laughed at Franklin Uncle as a good-for-nothing who simply wasted time as a leader! The news, whispered by one woman to another, reached Franklin Uncle's ears with added embellishments, turning the matter extremely grave. Franklin Uncle, who believed the inanity, started bearing a deep-seated animosity towards my Appan. Since the wily Samuel had extracted a promise from Franklin Uncle that his name should never be quoted, he never sought a clarification from Appan. In Kali Yuga*, falsehood and treachery triumph. The venal machination of a third person succeeded in cleaving apart two intimate friends.

---

* In King Mahabali's Treta Yuga, as per a popular folk song, there was neither falsehood nor treachery.

When Franklin Uncle refused to participate in the church band, Appan got wind of it. Though he tried to reach out, Franklin Uncle eluded that gesture by commenting bluntly, 'But I never complained about anybody.' Appan, aggrieved that Franklin Uncle chose to believe a gossip monger rather than his bosom friend, decided that he would not try to clear his name again. He was determined that until Franklin Uncle realized that he was innocent, he wouldn't play the clarinet. The band of St. Anthony's church broke up because of a malevolent man's intrigue.

What happened later was even more bizarre. Franklin Uncle and family became cosy with Samuel, who had badmouthed him. Appan never revealed the truth about Samuel, though he could have easily done so; he always maintained a dignified silence.

'This is the age of falsehood. But you can never cheat the One who sees it all. No confession can wash away that stain,' Appan said dejectedly. After that incident, apart from attending the Qurbana, he avoided all other church-related activities and focused exclusively on his coffin shop.

After many years, when I evoked a tune through the 'wounds' of the clarinet, here was Benjamin at my doorstep!

'Appan was deeply hurt that his friend doubted him based on some gossip.' I had only one truth to tell Benjamin.

'He did not doubt, someone made him doubt! It took many years for my father to realize his grave error. Samuel revealed his true colours many times. My father regretted that certain knife-like tongues succeeded in cleaving human hearts. It was too late by then. Before an apology could be tendered, your Appan had passed away. Soon after that, my father died too. If I were to ask for forgiveness in the place of my father, would the debt be paid?' Benjamin asked softly.

'Some debts remain outstanding even after death,' I answered.

'Who knows whether both our fathers have started a new band in heaven, Indri? What fun it was when they played the instruments in the olden times,' Benjamin smiled sadly.

Oh God, when Benjamin said that, a heavenly note started flowing through me, turning me into a clarinet. On that rainy night I spent in the cemetery, I had heard the melodious band music played by both our fathers. When death exposed the dishonesty that life concealed, the transient victories of mudslingers changed to shameful defeats.

I felt like embracing Benjamin. We used to sleep on the same mattress when we were kids. Glory to the Anti-Clock hanging on my wall, for giving me back that old friend.

Dear clock, what more are you going to draw out from the past?

When he left the shop, Benjamin looked deeply relieved, as if a heavy stone had been lifted from his heart. Feeling confident that Franklin Uncle's soul would feel the respite of a debt repaid through Benjamin, I picked up the clarinet and blew into it. The stains of tears shed by a maligned, innocent man should no longer remain on that instrument. The clarinet deserved a special place in my possessions, along with Beatrice and my children.

I was happy thinking that Appan's soul must be delighted by the auspicious turn of events. It was then that Shari dropped in and bared her bundle of woes.

'I had a bitter fight with Acchan today,' Shari said.

It was serendipitous that Shari mentioned her father when I was thinking of mine.

'And may I know of Karunan's great fault?' I asked.

'Everything is his fault! He has hardened his stance against Muthalali's crusher unit. His action committee has blocked the roads to Aadi Nadu to prevent the movement of Muthalali's lorries. What's his problem if someone's doing good?' Shari asked angrily.

Ah, that was the way the wind blew! Shari's vociferous protest was against Karunan's opposition to Satan Loppo.

'Shari, your Muthalali is sucking the lifeblood out of Aadi Nadu. Loppo's new crusher unit will smother the last life breath of our village. Karunan and the environmentalists are resisting that looming destruction,' I tried to reason with her.

The razed hills, a part of many folk stories and myths, had been rich with medicinal plants. When Hanuman flew with the mountain from the Himalayas to Lanka, a portion of it is said to have fallen in our village. The rare herbs in our region is attributed to that story. Neelayamari*, Pathimugham† and Kallipala‡, with their healing powers, had long vanished. There were no hillsides left for them to unconditionally thrive in. Now, there was no hill of Hanuman to point out to the next generation.

As far as the eye could see, only monstrous, sky-high heaps of gravel were visible. There were huge crevices where holes had been drilled into the hills. Tipper lorries rushing pell-mell had become a ubiquitous sight. Satan Loppo had recently imported some infernal vehicles to crush the rocks. When those hammered the heads of the hills, the bowels of the earth shook in terror. My coffin shop shuddered as a result of the tremors. Many villagers fell prey to respiratory diseases due to the all-pervasive rock dust choking their lungs. It required just a few seconds to blow up the magnificent statuesque rocks, which nature had taken millions of centuries to sculpt. But can any great science reconstruct even a small rock from the remains?

'Acchan has a hill in his name, right? He brags that old-time leaders hid in its caves. Can't he be happy with that? Now, with his strikes and protests, he is messing up my life! Muthalali is willing to extend support to us, and Acchan is hell-bent on fighting him,' Shari interjected harshly.

If Shari was trying to define life with her minimal womanly dreams, I couldn't blame her for that. I knew that none of my logical arguments could appease that simmering rage. Yet, to cool her down, I said: 'Your father is a good man. Karunan is fighting against those

---

* Indigo
† Indian Redwood
‡ Common milk hedge

who are destroying the inheritance of the next generation. That sort of revolution is the need of the hour.'

An upset Shari left without uttering another word. She was caught between the love for her father and her unflinching loyalty to Satan Loppo. I gloomily reflected on Shari's small dreams.

However, when Shari came to my shop the next day, she was bubbling with excitement. She looked striking in a yellow chiffon sari with green dots, an obvious gift from her lover.

'Uncle, great news!'

'What?'

'Della's letter arrived from Germany. Philomenamma was waiting impatiently for me in the bungalow today.'

'Really?' I replied indifferently, 'what is the big deal about that?'

'It is a big deal, Uncle ! Della has arranged our immigration to Germany. I knew Della's promise would never be false. She likes me so much!'

'Is that true?'

'Yes. When they called Muthalali, he promised to bear all the expenses for our trip. Uncle, you always disbelieved me when I spoke of Muthalali's generosity. Hope you appreciate him now.'

Shari was over the moon when she said that. I could see that she was flapping, in her flight of fantasy, far above all the clouds over earth, towards Germany. It was certain that despite all their efforts, Shari and David would never have been able to raise funds for such a trip. Even if they collected the money, who would have invited them to Germany or offered a place to stay?

The incredible fortune which suddenly stepped into a village girl's life was the sort which one dared not dream of. It was really miraculous! The circumstances which paved the way for Della to visit Aadi Nadu, befriend Shari, and invite her to Germany mandated the amalgamation of many remote probabilities. The icing on the cake was Satan Loppo offering to sponsor their trip. It was natural that Loppo's stature would be much, much higher in Shari and David's eyes than an acquaintance like me with his pointless existence.

To refer to their mentor as 'Satan Loppo' seemed paradoxical now. When her father started revolting against such a man, it was an affront to Shari. But when I ruminated from Karunan's perspective, I felt upset that he was unaware of all these developments. Shari's journey would crush his inner resilience, like a gigantic hammer shattering rock. Maybe that was the secret dart that Satan Loppo had reserved for Karunan.

Love is something which can drive even a girl like Shari to defy her loving parents. Hey love! You do enjoy playing with fire and sword, don't you?

'Philomenamma promised to gift me ornaments for my marriage,' Shari gushed.

'Is that so?'

'Even while lying paralysed, she keeps praying for everybody. She is so saintly!'

'She was an inseparable part of Mother Gabriel's prayer group,' I replied quietly.

'Why did such a fate befall her despite her prayers?'

'Her prayers were not for avoiding such a fate.'

'What did she pray for then?'

'Life is like a 10,000-metre race. Some might feel that they have fallen behind. But the winner is the one who races to the front in the last lap,' I replied.

'Last lap? You mean death?'

'Wise people say that death is not the end. There is a doorway which opens beyond that. One can see the dead as living beings through that opening.'

'Cooked-up story,' Shari scoffed.

'No, it is the truth. Shari, those who die continue to exist.'

'How do you know all this?'

'I know for certain.'

I knew that Beatrice and my children would vouch for me. Since I could not expose the secrets of death, I controlled myself.

'Philomenamma was asking why you don't participate in the prayer groups any more.'

'Oh, I attended last week. I plan to go again.'

'She will be glad to hear that. I will tell her tomorrow.' Shari was pleased.

I gave a non-committal smile. After exchanging pleasantries for a while, Shari got up to leave.

'They will be staying in Coimbatore for a few more days, is that right?' she asked.

'Yes.'

'It must be tough to drive all that way.'

'Not so difficult. I am sure they are used to all that driving,' I consoled her.

Shari's worry did not dissipate.

At that point of time, I had no clue about the hardships awaiting everyone. The Anti-Clock was continuing its cyclical loops, which launched squalls and tempests. The circling of time was like the ceaseless recitation of a mantra, an *Ekajapa*. Constant repetition leads to magical powers.

When magical powers are acquired, anything one wishes for is possible. That's what time does incessantly.

* * *

The day had more in store for me. Without warning, Gracy came to my shop in the evening, and threw me off balance.

'Can you please help?' Gracy asked eagerly.

'What?'

'A top real estate businessman from Vithura has placed an order. He has a photograph of a coffin which Joppan once made, and wants one exactly like that. I won't be able to do it alone. Can you help me?'

I was nonplussed for a moment, contemplating the manifold changes occurring in this world.

Gracy's invitation meant that the competition in the coffin business, a legacy of generations, would draw to an end. Casket-making never involved profound strategies; it demanded prompt action. I couldn't find a single reason to refuse her request. How grand that the real estate businessman from Vithura had piles of money and a craze for a glossy coffin! The photograph in Gracy's hand demonstrated not just the stateliness a coffin could possess, but also its smugness.

I immediately proceeded to Gracy's coffin shop. Since she had readied the basic structure and the accessories, the rest was easy. We worked in harmony to make an enviable coffin, with lovely satin work, attractive embellishments, festoons of roses and gorgeous white doves adorning the top lid. For hours, we were alone in the shop. Gracy handed over the appropriate work implements instinctively and silently, whenever I stretched my hand. She made me hot tea thrice in between.

It was two in the morning when the coffin was finished. Not having laboured so hard in recent times, I was fatigued. Joppan's words rang in my mind: 'Aadi Nadu needs only one coffin shop.' I felt that the words had come true in a different way. It was a warning for human beings to be cautious before wishing for anything. It might materialize out of the blue before you change your mind.

Gracy extended a wadded envelope when I prepared to leave.

'Exactly half of the money given to me.'

I did not have the heart to accept it.

Hey woman, you who carried me in your heart all your life, this portion is for you . . .

'Please keep the full amount with you,' I murmured.

I knew that Gracy would be gazing after me as I turned the corner. So, I did not look back.

33

The Shift

'That day is a day of wrath, a day of trouble and distress, a day of wasteness and desolation, a day of darkness and gloominess, a day of clouds and thick darkness. A day of the trumpet and alarm against the fenced cities, and against the high towers. And I will bring distress upon men, that they shall walk like blind men, because they have sinned against the Lord: and their blood shall be poured out as dust, and their flesh as the dung.'

(Zephaniah 1: 15-17)

As I witnessed the lone street lamp gasp to its death, there was a subsequent dimming of my positive feelings. It appeared that darkness, with its primitive weapon, was out on a hunt. I imagined a terrorist's face to it, one that would attack without leaving a clue as to when, where and how.

Three days after David's departure, Shari stopped coming to the tailor shop. It worried me no end since David had entrusted her in my care. I wondered whether she had fallen ill. Could it be that Karunan, getting a hint of her German journey, had forbidden her from stepping out of the house? Else, there was no reason for her sudden absence.

Usually, I don't visit Shashankan's tailor shop. I never feel the need to chat with him. Occasionally, I would go to him to get some shirts stitched. But he had been chagrined ever since someone convinced him that my coffin shop, right opposite his own shop, was an inauspicious eyesore. Who would want a situation where every outward glance fell on a death box? Shashankan believed that his business hadn't prospered because of mine; else he would have been a textile tycoon by now.

Hence, he maintained a distance from me, and I adhered to it strictly. An unspoken, polite distance from each other is always better than an artificial camaraderie. The mutual understanding that one should not harm even if one does not help, forms the basis of our neighbourhood kinship. There is never any wounding look cast by either side. Because of that, a silence always creeps in between the two of us who've been physically so close to each other for such a long time.

It wasn't easy for me to overcome that pact and approach Shashankan to inquire about Shari. An ill-begotten pride, similar to the one which prevented a person from begging even while dying of hunger, stopped me. My sojourn was through a rampant helplessness where one stretched forth his hand only to withdraw it soon after.

But when a couple of more days passed, I found my resolve slackening.

Letting go of my inhibitions, I crossed the road and reached the tailor shop.

Without any prelude, I asked tactlessly, 'What happened to Shari? Haven't seen her for the past few days.'

Shashankan assessed me from top to toe, as if measuring me for a full body outfit.

I was expecting that.

There was nothing unnatural about him wondering whether something was going on between Shari and me. Love hadn't sought anyone's permission before building a hanging bridge between the tailoring shop and the coffin shop. His look was censorious, but he had the dignity to restrain himself from asking, 'What's your business?'

'No idea. Maybe she's sick,' he replied.

His answer was terse, leaving no opportunity for a further probe. I returned to my refuge, crossing the road.

Outside, a storm was conspiring to surge. A bevy of birds flapped away noisily to the east, croaking a curse of heavy rain over Aadi Nadu.

On entering the shop, the first thing to catch my attention was the Anti-Clock. The minute needle and the hour needle were merging at that point. I had a premonition of an unfortunate event. I struggled to decipher the hallowed secret on the Anti-Clock's mysterious face. As I watched the clock moving its eye from left to right and back, traversing into the past and future alternately, my nervousness rose. The Anti-Clock's trick was to spin off multiples of the observer's feelings. What was happening inside me was nothing but a multiplication of anxieties.

Until David returned two days later, I was beset with acute unease. He came in like a whirlwind, throwing me into turmoil. David's unruly hair looked as if tossed about by a natural disaster. Fraught with tension, his face looked ready to explode. That smouldering look churned my innards.

'What? What's the matter?' I gasped.

Without answering, when David seated himself on the ancient stool with his eyes cast down, I noticed that he was panting heavily. The sight unnerved me.

'For the past few days, Shari hasn't been coming to the shop,' I revealed the worry that had been eating me up.

'Don't expect to see her any more.'

'What do you mean?'

David looked up. I saw the blazing furnace burning within him. That face was new to me.

'I'm going to kill someone!'

The fire burning within David singed me as he uttered these words. How casually had he declared his intention to kill someone, as if he was going to purchase something from the market! Had he fought with Shari? I have heard about murderous rages when lovers fall out. But why would they fight when their German trip was fast approaching?

'What has happened to you?'

'I shall slaughter him!'

'Who?'

'Him, that Satan!' David's explosive reaction was like dynamite shattering rocks in the quarry.

Trembling, I called out the Lord's name!

Just a week before, David had taken Loppo's name with the same reverence as addressing God. Listening to the unceasing showers of his benedictions, even my dream of retribution had gone up in flames. The same David was now talking about killing Loppo. There was definitely something venomous afoot.

'Please tell me the truth!' I begged.

'Before that I have to finish him off.'

'David, please . . . He's powerful and well-connected,' I tried to dissuade him.

'I know his connections, power and weakness! More than anyone, I know how to crush him!' David was unrelenting.

Had it been any other occasion, I would have exulted madly, hooting and hollering with excitement at that statement. I was a lifeless man enduring a mortification worse than death. When someone else set out to vanquish a man I never could, I deserved to know the reason.

'What happened after you left together?'

'It was a ruse. That bastard came back, leaving me behind . . . three days ago.'

Splitting me from head to toe, something sharp sped its way to the skies. If there was a satanic presence in Aadi Nadu three days before, that was the day Shari had gone missing!

Shaking David's shoulders, I shrieked, 'Where is Shari? Tell me!'

As the monsoon rain fell wailing piteously over Aadi Nadu, I remembered my Beatrice. I looked at the Anti-Clock with a blazing fury. Staring unblinkingly at its eye, which moved between the past and the future, I growled, 'Kill both! Him and his damned dog!'

As I ground my teeth with uncontrollable rage, David, who had sown the wind a long time ago, set out to reap the whirlwind. *After ages, truth be spoken, I smelled death in the air.*

34

Revenge

'In the greatness of your majesty, you threw down those who opposed you. You unleashed your burning anger; it consumed them like stubble. By the blast of your nostrils the waters piled up. The surging waters stood up like a wall; the deep waters congealed in the heart of the sea. The enemy boasted, "I will pursue, I will overtake them. I will divide the spoils; I will gorge myself on them. I will draw my sword and my hand will destroy them."'

(Exodus 15: 7-9)

That night, sleep declared a no-show in my residence. My mind's intractable arguments made any chances of reconciliation futile. I lay trapped in a dungeon of despair, worried sick about what David was up to. The very air seemed poisoned by fear, and I felt choked.

David was like a son to me. No, he is my son. I cannot allow any enemy to lie in wait for him.

Yet, he had stormed away after locking me out of his secrets and thrusting me into the depths of confusion. I could hardly blame him.

The way I had responded to the world hadn't been much different. No man who loves his woman can tolerate the slightest aspersion cast on her. The cigar stink that had besieged Beatrice was a secret that I had hidden even from my best friend Antappan; I could empathize with David.

What terrified me more was Pundit's prediction about the interventions of the Anti-Clock. The downfall of every autocrat starts from his close circle. If you analyse history, you will find evidence that nobody in power can befool people forever.

The auguries and contemplations mingled with one another while I awaited David's arrival. I had decided the previous night that the next day, which was a Thursday, I would join Mother Gabriel's prayer group after rigorous fasting. There was a mountainous woe to lay down at the Lord's feet. Never have I submitted a plea in the Box of Appeals. But today, I yearned to pray from the innermost depths of my heart. I wanted to forego even a sip of water while fasting. Then the fire of the stomach—the *Jadaragni*—would, in its upward journey of refinement, purify the body, the mind and the soul in that order.

I started sweeping the nooks and corners of the musty room run amok with cobwebs. Spiders, both small and large, petrified by the demolition of their homes, scattered and fell. Recognizing that someone had unleashed earthquakes and cyclones in their lairs, there ensued a mass exodus. I did not kill the fleeing creatures; just swept them out of the room. Despite my care, some frail spiders ended up with broken legs. Some of them tried to crawl up the walls, but to no avail. I was sure that they were yelling in pain like humans who had fractured their limbs. Since my hearing was not designed to hear those cries, they did not reach me. Suddenly, as if my ears were opening to all the screams around me, a wave of misery enveloped me. Those who had to flee when water filled their shanties overnight, when the Neyyar overflowed, might have been subjected to the same terror.

I could not help remembering the mouse which I had once maimed by severing its tail. At every stage of life, the lack of a tail must have affected it cruelly. A tail provided balance to a small creature, and was not ornamental. I felt sorry for having brutally robbed it of its fluid movement.

If it appears in front of me now, I will apologise sincerely.

'Please, dear mouse, forgive me!'

No sooner did I think that than a 'chil, chil' squeak startled me and a mouse screeched past the coffins.

Lord, it was the same mouse!

Its stub of a tail had swollen a bit. Thick hair fanned around it; nature balancing out the loss in its own way. I have had prior experience that for every problem, nature has its own solution. Unsolicited, how artlessly the holistic intelligence of nature works to protect itself and maintain the balance!

Watching the tailless creature was no joy. Why had it appeared in my sight after the interval of many months? Why didn't I feel like smashing it with a piece of log?

'Sorry,' I murmured, 'Like my son Rosarios said, I hope I did not end up making your children tailless.'

The mouse squealed before vamoosing inside its hole. Perhaps it was a rejoinder to my penitence. But there was undoubtedly a warning in its unexpected appearance. A script containing instructions for my overhaul.

After removing the cobwebs, I felt that the floor, which had accumulated dirt of the past, deserved a cleaning too. Appan used to quip that all inner cleansing began from the exterior. When a *Virat** being sets out to clean the world, the trees would be uprooted, and civilization would be purged. Perhaps cyclones and thunderstorms would be his broom! When I brushed away the cobwebs, except for experiencing a thunderstorm, the spider would never have realized that a man stood beneath, brandishing a broom. If a human being could take on a *Virat* form for a spider, it is possible that many *Virat* forms existed in the universe, unperceived by humans.

---

* Giant proportioned; Hindu concept of vastness of nature

I recollected Pundit telling me about the microscopic creatures living within the bones. Never have I known the millions thriving within my own body. Neither did they know me. Thinking of it, I felt amused.

I may have been mopping the floors of my coffin shop for the very first time after it was built. The sodden, murky floor cleared up slowly. I wondered why I was scrubbing myself clean in that manner. Who was the *Virat* being provoking such inspirations from within me?

I knew it was them—my Beatrice and the children.

The treasured loves of my heart, who have returned from the past to live serenely amidst the darkness of these coffins. Like the midpoint of the eyebrows is for the whole body, that was the meeting place of my strength and the sacred spot of my worship. Unlike Antappan's apprehensions, I haven't felt frightened by their presence; instead, my confidence has rekindled. I could also feel the grace of my late parents embracing me closely.

My shop has an air of expectation, as though something or someone would appear soon.

I knew that it was a ploy of the Anti-Clock.

I started sorting out the disarray in my shop. I stacked the coffins on the wooden shelves, and gathered my work tools into a tool box. While realigning the misplaced tunes of my life by disciplining myself, I worshipfully remembered my ancestors. I picked up the measuring rod, my family heirloom, and touched it to my forehead respectfully. Glory to the muzhakkol which had known the sweat and touch of my forebearers.

Here I am, like a man preparing for death, receiving the last rites, after all my confessions.

I can clearly hear my mind confirming that this was the most crucial day of my life.

As I systematically arranged the scattered work implements, a revelation flashed before me like the edge of a scalpel.

The coffin meant for Satan Loppo shall soon fulfil its purpose.

I tried to shrug off the intuition as if it was a trickery of my mind, but in vain.

'Mind, are you monkeying around with me, tying a chain around my hip? By fasting and praying, when I am coming to terms with myself, relinquishing vengeance and seeking forgiveness, why do you follow me like Satan who sneaks up from behind before attacking? I have no wish to hear about anyone's demise.'

My mind underwent an upheaval, thinking about David who had gone to challenge Satan Loppo. He was strong and shrewd, and brawny enough to trounce any opponent. Having known his Muthalali closely, he could assess every foible adroitly. Would David attempt anything drastic that would allow the giant coffin to finally come into use? I couldn't bear the thought of his life ending up behind bars.

The only way to evade such worries was to focus on work. My dwelling place turned spic and span by the afternoon. I converted my residence into a decent coffin shop, bedecked to welcome a special guest.

Though I had enough stock of coffins of various sizes to satisfy any order, I felt the urge to work. I dedicated myself to finishing a half-complete casket. Till the evening, I abstained from food. I was getting ready for a bath before the prayer session when David came rushing in.

'I have finished him,' he screamed on seeing me.

'Oh God!'

The spear of St. George impaled my heart.

Did I hear him right? Was Satan Loppo dead? Could David finish off a vicious man like Loppo so easily? I stared at David's hands, trying to see the drops of Loppo's blood staining them.

No, there was no blood anywhere.

'David,' I called out with apprehension.

'Yes, I have trapped him well and good. No trace left!'

'What do you mean?'

'He and his damned sinking suite. It will never float again.'

'I don't get you, David!'

'He went to have a whale of a time inside the water! I locked him up proper. He will not rise again.'

Dear Lord, should I cry or laugh? The fortified battlements that I could never conquer lay crumbled before my eyes.

'How . . . how did you manage to do that?' I gawked at him.

'The devil was boozing away in the suite and did not notice when I snapped the connection.'

David knew the functioning of the water suite. It was Satan Loppo himself who had trained David in operating the emergency switch. He knew how to make it non-functional. If so, a ghoul in human form had fallen into the pit which he had dug for others. Instead of an earthly grave, it was a watery grave for him. He deserved it fully.

'He has no clue, Uncle!' David yammered, flush with victory. 'When he tries to get out, nothing will work! He will hysterically try the emergency switch. It will not work . . . Soon, the damned man will suffocate to death. By the time help reaches him, he will be a corpse . . .'

A primitive expression, unseen hitherto, had taken hold of David's face. I still could not make myself believe that such a formidable foe had been vanquished so easily. David had never given me the slightest hint about his plan. It was time to celebrate by squandering all my wealth!

'Uncle, get a coffin ready for him,' David hissed.

'I've been waiting with it for such a long time.'

Having responded unthinkingly, I struggled to put out the fire of my overenthusiasm, and endeavoured to create a smokescreen between us. It was too late in the hour for confessions. When I tried to obfuscate the mention of Satan Loppo's coffin, David turned the topic to an unexpected direction.

'There is one thing I have been wanting to ask you.'

'What?'

'Have you ever had a showdown with Muthalali?'

'Who told you that?'

'I overheard someone speaking once. He was stone drunk and spouting a tale . . . about a very rainy night. I never asked you about it, Uncle.'

'David . . . what do you mean?'

Like a coconut tree struck by lightning, my head went up in flames. Fire and smoke flowed through me. An unceasing rain scalded me further. I shut my eyes tight to loosen my taut nerves. Else those would have ruptured and I would have been washed away in a deluge.

'Uncle, if at all there was such an incident, today I extracted revenge for that too! I hacked off his life-tree. Now I shall leave the village. No one knows that I am the one behind Loppo's death. But it is better to stay away for a while.'

'Shari . . .?' I asked, trembling.

'I will take her along. She had a narrow escape only because of her pure heart! That bastard always used to say that she was like his daughter,' David breathed hard.

I felt tears welling up in my eyes. My children were readying to leave me orphaned yet again. Though departures were painful, I wished them well as they had done me the favour of a lifetime. Antappan would be extremely distressed. But it would all turn out fine.

When David got up to leave, his recklessness had faded. He held my hands tightly in his.

'I will never forget you, Uncle. I wonder if I will be able to see you again.'

I wished that he had never uttered those words. One afternoon, after the turmoil had settled, I was sure that they would appear again in my shop, hailing me heartily. When my will is read out after my demise, would they like to become the owners of an old coffin shop situated on a dilapidated piece of land?

'David, wait a minute,' I requested.

David stopped in his tracks. I extended to him the lone precious item in my coffin shop.

'Give this to Shari.'

David wept when he touched the golden chain which had graced Beatrice's neck even in penury.

Even while reminding him that men shouldn't cry, I sobbed with him. From now on, even if I wished to, there was no reason left for me to weep.

This is the last path of tears I have to walk.

Even after David left, my tears continued to flow unabated. When the last impurity was cleansed, there was a sense of repose.

I climbed on top of the stool and on tiptoe, planted a kiss on the Anti-Clock.

'You have proven your true worth. No one will drill holes through Aadi Nadu's mountains again.'

After bathing and changing my clothes, I started for St. Anthony's Church.

I want to cleanse my mind and pray till I touch the very skies today.

All the burdens lifted from my chest, I sat in utter tranquillity in the church. When Mother Gabriel started taking out that day's pleas from the box, I was indifferent. But on hearing the name of the first applicant, my heart wrenched painfully, torn from the roots.

It was a prayer that Philomenamma had written, beseeching for her husband's long life. Listening to that never-to-be-fulfilled prayer for the life of a man submerged under water, I stared at the One hanging on the cross, and restrained myself from shaking with laughter.

35

The Liturgy of the Hours

'Now the temple was crowded with men and women; all the rulers of the Philistines were there, and on the roof were about three thousand men and women watching Samson perform. Then Samson prayed to the Lord, "Sovereign Lord, remember me. Please, God, strengthen me just once more, and let me with one blow get revenge on the Philistines for my two eyes." Then Samson reached toward the two central pillars on which the temple stood. Bracing himself against them, his right hand on the one and his left hand on the other, Samson said, "Let me die with the Philistines."'

(Judges 16: 27-30)

I now know the torment of the man who sweated blood while he prayed in the Hour of Betrayal. If even the One, who was willing to suffer for the sake of sinners, had implored momentarily to remove the cup from him, how pitiable is the plight of a feeble-minded wretch like me!

The prayers of the Son of Man on the night of the Last Supper have always haunted me.

My childhood friend, who had turned out to be an unbeliever despite being named after Prophet Jonah of the Old Testament, had once baffled me by raising a vexing question in the church's Sunday Class.

'Just because the Lord died on the cross somewhere, how will my sins be forgiven? That's a load of tripe!'

Jonah's query hit the bull's eye and struck a chord in me. It was not a puzzle that could be resolved through the collective thinking capacities of Jonah and me! I could have accepted that simple logic, given up faith and turned into an atheist too. Yet, I used it to measure my Appan's wisdom. Hearing my question, my father burst into hearty laughter. When he stated that it was only a primary level question in the School of Spirituality, I was slightly miffed, probably being in the first standard myself.

It was by drawing my attention to the final night of the One who perspired blood while praying, that Appan handled my question.

'Like the Father and the Son in our hymn of praise, there is a stage when you become one with the Lord, my child,' Appan explained gently. '*That oneness reaches the soul, far beyond the body and mind.* Two strangers can never experience oneness with body or mind, but those connected with love can. That's what happens between spouses as well as between parents and children. The husband willingly indulges his wife, and parents undertake any sacrifice for their children due to that bond. A relationship which transcends the unity of body and mind will invoke a soul connection. But that phenomenon will be beyond the reach of those who cannot experience it. But for the one who can, the Son inherits the Father's riches. Even in daily life you observe how the father pays the penalty for his son's faults. Indri, after crossing the body and mind, when you reach the soul, *we are all one.* That is why the Lord advised us to love our enemies.'

Oh, that father of mine!

Appan explained with such simplicity that *man was nothing but distance from God*, and when the distance dwindled and finally became zero, *man became one with God*. The agonized prayer by the Son of Man, on the night of the Last Supper, to be one with everyone could be understood only after the separation of body and mind were overcome.

Those precepts are too elevated for me to understand. My worthless existence cannot claim to reach such heights. The toughest test for me right now is to pray for my deadly enemy. In the oneness which included him, my prayer for Loppo would turn into his salvation.

May my father's philosophical outlook be right, nay, be wrong.
Caught betwixt that conundrum, I matter nothing.

I realize the true aim of Mother Gabriel's prayer sessions now. It is an invitation to climb the tough rocks of separation and reach the pinnacle of oneness. Only then can one pray for another, without expecting anything in return.

Who trapped me into praying for my lifelong foe? God, devil, or my own self?

Perhaps, it was my conscious choice.

The Lord has laid the trap for me quite sardonically.

I started wondering about the timeliness of Philomenamma's prayer. She had obviously sought someone's aid to submit it in the Box of Appeals. In her mind, purified through constant prayers, there must have been a premonition of her husband's death. The loyal wife couldn't ignore the forewarning, though aware of her husband's philandering habits. That was why she had submitted the supplication.

By the will of God, in that gathering, nobody except me knew the sheer futility of that prayer. Satan Loppo was a lump of flesh flailing about in the depths of water. He could not survive for long without air. David had informed me that an alarm would alert the occupant of the suite to the reduced oxygen levels. Loppo would try to activate the emergency switch. Then he would realize that David had intentionally messed with it.

How would Satan Loppo's face look then?

I wished to witness judgement being pronounced on him for each of his misdeeds. When a man curses himself that there was no time left for rectification, his death becomes final.

My conscience pricked me; I was not supposed to celebrate my enemy's downfall. It was a sin against the Holy Ghost if one was implacable against a defenceless person. The Lord had prayed while sweating blood for the sinner and the depraved too. Right now, my task was to extend help through prayer for my enemy. It was an inimitable blessing offered to me.

Buoyed up with positivity, I joined the gathering in praying for Satan Loppo's long life.

'Our Lord of Compassion, hereby we submit the prayer of a lamb belonging to thy flock. May thy Holy Wounds accept it and answer her . . . Amen.'

It astounded me that I was praying with a sincerity that even the Lord could not turn his face away from! Surely, our prayer of lamentation carried Philomenamma's piety on its wings.

The One who taught us to love the enemy was teaching me to pray for him as well. Since a lot of my energy flowed into that effort, I couldn't focus on the soulful topics that followed afterwards. Meanwhile, the dark side of my mind argued vociferously, 'How will the Lord fulfil your prayer for granting long life to a dead man?'

I sprouted, blossomed and became laden with fruits while praying. My deepest sympathy was with Philomenamma. Yet Loppo's fate was inevitable, and encrypted in the scrolls of judgement like a prophet's voice.

When I prayed for the one whom I wished to kill, with the door of my heart wide open, peace started raining in on me as if the very heavens had descended. No anxieties troubled me. What was heaven, if not a peaceful existence devoid of worries? Since that possibility was hidden in every human being, the Son of Man had exhorted: 'The Kingdom of God is within you.'

I was famished like a man who had fasted for forty days. In the shop opposite the church, I broke the fast by wolfing down porotta and beef.

Aadi Nadu seemed to have undergone a total transformation. There was a spattering of silver light over the church's spire and the neighbouring houses.

Dear night, when more stars bloomed on earth than in the sky, I love you more than ever!

I floated lightly like a soul over the village path in the drizzle. It was not my bones or flesh that had weighed me down but the tonnage of my own mind. Life would henceforth be a joyous flight and not an unendurable burden.

In the assurance that Satan Loppo, who had eyed the Anti-Clock, had been snatched away by time, I had started for the church without locking the shop door. As if no other thief existed in the world, I happily embraced the universe as my home. The sky alone shall be my roof now!

The age of the children of hell was over.

The time of the angels has begun.

Having prayed for my enemy and seeing my wicked wish for him turn fruitful at the same time, I felt rather impressed with myself. Nobody could find fault with me. I was saintly!

I reached my shop brimming with satisfaction. How appropriate was the inscription 'Heavenly boxes for sale'! I thanked the heavens for making those words come true. Pundit's caution stirred in my memory. Affirming the truth of the Anti-Clock that shepherded earthquakes and tempests, many things had turned topsy-turvy in my life recently. It had erased the distance between me and my family. The blissful world of my Appan's clarinet and band music had been restored to me. Above all, it had torn apart the existence of my lifelong foe. An enslaved Aadi Nadu was freed from the mad interventions of a dictator. It was after the Anti-Clock's arrival that there was an upheaval. Glory to Pundit who foresaw every event!

With Shashankan having shut his shop earlier than usual, darkness loomed everywhere. The doubling of his workload due to Shari's absence might have tired him out. As the watch shop had been closed ever since Pundit's death, the street embodied utter desolation. The sole life existing here was that of Hendri!

No, I have Beatrice and my children with me.

This is a happy kingdom where the five of us reign joyously.

I had a sudden urge to stand behind the vertically placed coffin and gaze at the empty world outside. Since Loppo was dead, someone would arrive soon, asking for a coffin. That coffin should be sold from my shop and not from Joppan Memorial Shop. What if someone had already approached Gracy? The coffin that I had kept so long for Loppo would grieve like a barren womb!

Without stopping to ruminate, I found myself racing to Gracy's place.

'Please don't compete with me today,' I gasped.

Gracy might not have understood what I said. How could she gauge that my thoughts and emotions were confounding me?

'Loppo's coffin *must be* from my shop. If your love for me is true, please allow that.'

Yes, love should mediate in some of life's critical bargains.

Gracy would listen to what I said, since her love for me was true. Bolstered by my belief that love in all forms was true, I made my way back without uttering another word. Even without a backward glance, I knew once again that Gracy was gazing after me. Unrequited, innocent love was fated to gaze after the beloved until the end. Perhaps, even beyond death.

As I stood behind the huge coffin once again, I affirmed one fact. I shall not charge money for Loppo's coffin, made perfectly to his measure, but shall gift it instead. After that, I shall never be able to watch the world from behind it. Of course, there would be no further need. A few moments were all I had, to fill the deep hollow which Satan Loppo had created inside me with either tears or sweetness. I took the unilateral decision to fill it with sweetness.

When I stood happily behind the coffin, my eyes fell on a blurred shape moving towards me in the darkness. I was certain that it was the buyer for Loppo's coffin. He must have been sent away by Gracy. She was a good woman.

As I stared intently through the crevices, slowly the haze cleared. It was heading towards my shop for sure. When it stepped into the foyer, my breathing snagged between my chest and navel.

Satan Loppo!

My whole being was sucked into a hellhole that moment.

How? How could he . . . ?

I wailed inwardly, asking the Lord whether he had saved Loppo, answering my prayer against my own self.

To verify whether Loppo had returned as a ghost after death, I checked if that black figure had horns, tail and fangs; and also, whether its feet touched the ground. Trapped alternately between 'Yes' and 'No', I stood quivering. Loppo stopped in confusion at the front door.

He did not know that a ghost was hiding behind the coffin. There was merely half an inch of a wooden plank separating us both.

I did not move. Ghosts should not move.

Seeing no one around, Loppo knocked on the vertical coffin noisily. Akin to hailing a hollow man, his sound splintered my ribcage and penetrated through.

'Anyone here?'

It was the rumbling voice of someone who had returned from the dead. From the border dividing death and life, it inundated my senses. I could hear the pendulum swing of the Anti-Clock markedly ticking away the moments before the partition between us was breached.

Peering inside the room once more, Loppo called out:

'Anyone here? I want a coffin.'

36

The Final Judgment

'Then he told me, "Do not seal up the words of the prophecy of this scroll, because the time is near. Let the one who does wrong continue to do wrong; let the vile person continue to be vile; let the one who does right continue to do right; and let the holy person continue to be holy. Look, I am coming soon. My reward is with me, and I will give to each person according to what they have done. I am the Alpha and the Omega, the First and the Last, the Beginning and the End."'

(Revelation 22: 10-13)

It was impossible to continue the hide-and-seek game for long.

When the enemy appears before you and calls your name, even a dead man will lose his composure. Deciding to face anything, I emerged from my refuge. Like one whom death had renounced by the wayside, I stared at the face of my foe. Four eyes locked horns after a long time.

Loppo's eyes were bloodshot, like that of a crow pheasant. The venules of his eyes must have got inflamed in his desperate struggle under the water. How did he overcome that deathly tangle? Which secret emergency system, undisclosed to David, had come to Loppo's aid? Did David grossly miscalculate that a wily man like Loppo, who never trusted anyone, would divulge all his secrets?

Without any preamble, Satan Loppo said: 'I want a coffin.'

The tone of his voice was as if I owed him one. Truth be said, it was he who was indebted to me. I couldn't tolerate that unpardonable conceit.

'Measures?' I asked drily.

My vision was intense enough to pierce through a human body and see the internal organs. I could see Loppo's black heart, his twisted mind and his wicked brains. He was lost in thought for a few seconds. His eyes darted from coffin to coffin. As a wild exhilaration bubbled in me, Satan Loppo's eyes fell on the huge coffin designed for him. It was my pleasure and privilege to inform him that his desires were pointless.

'Those are not for sale.'

My voice was imposing enough to inspire myself! I wondered how an abject coward, who could not utter a word in defiance till now, had stood up so confidently. Not I, but someone else from within was speaking. As the Anti-Clock animated the springs and gears inside me, I underwent a modification too. It was Loppo who was astonished that I was no longer my ordinary self.

'If not for sale, what are they for?' he snapped.

'The largest one is for you to lie in! The rest are for those who hurt my Beatrice and children . . . from that nasty Rachel who grabbed Beatrice's hair for a few borrowed measures of rice, to the teacher who forbade my children from coming to school for not paying the fees in time . . .' That should have been the truthful reply.

I stifled the scorching heat within and answered thus: 'Those are meant for specific people.'

'But I need a coffin.'

'You will have to tell the measures first.'

Satan Loppo's countenance made it evident that the impudence in my reply was causing him consternation.

Glory be to destiny, which kept aside some small winnings for me. The little relief due to someone who was like the salt which lost its savour, and the lamp without its light.

Loppo, how dare you cover up your inner evil with a calm mask and enter these precincts? Did you presume that losing my mental balance, I had forgotten everything? Or are you confident of my lack of strength to fight you? You should have shed those misconceptions before stepping into these sacred premises. Know that this place is holy, where all footwear is forbidden. Here, in this pure sanctuary, dwell those who can see and hear everything.

Midway through my swarm of thoughts, Loppo answered hesitantly, 'Measures? Well, the measure of that David . . . of Konganchirra.'

Thud! Along with all ego, my heart was smashed to smithereens.

Dear Lord in heaven! Even as a frantic cry suffocated me, all the castles in the cloud came tumbling down and I was crushed underneath.

Unable to trust my ears, I muttered witlessly, 'David?'

'Yes, David.'

No, I distrust Loppo's evil words. Just a few hours earlier, I had placed Beatrice's golden chain in the hands of the one who had rushed to the bungalow with his battle cry and returned rapturous in victory! How could a disaster befall him in that short interval? I screamed at the sky silently: *Lord, after accepting my prayer, are you enforcing your despotism on me?*

Not getting a reply, as I stood unnerved, Satan Loppo spoke.

'First time I am booking a coffin before someone's death! After all, he was my handyman for quite a long time, wasn't he? Let it be an expensive coffin. Don't bother about the money. The father should dig the son's grave. It will all be arranged soon.'

Seeing the feral thrill on Loppo's face as he snarled the words, I lost my composure.

A terrible tempest, along with rain and earthquake, rushed through me.

O' Lord, my Antappan . . . my David!

My destruction was complete, with nothing left to be salvaged. As happened to those facing death, certain feverish vignettes started flashing before my eyes.

Exactly at that moment, that tailless mouse, squeaking raucously, streaked past the corpse-nests again. An instinct pulled me strongly in the direction where it sped, announcing the message of death.

Pointing at the bleak corner of the darkness-infested room, I asked Loppo, 'Will that coffin do?'

Satan Loppo looked at the blackness with his red eyes. To get a better view, he moved inside and leaned against the coffin which stood upright.

That was a savage sight to behold! A man leaning against a coffin designed especially for him.

Hey lucky man, destined to touch your own sleeping casket. Can't you see your name engraved inside it?

The Anti-Clock rang out then, proclaiming that the value of that moment was equivalent to the sum of all the moments in the universe. Satan Loppo seemed taken aback by that sudden declaration of time. He looked fixedly at the clock on the wall. He was seeing the contrary clock which had evaded his avaricious grasp for the first time. His eyes moved left and right following the clock's pendulum, which was swinging between the past and the future.

What had Pundit implied while speaking about the *still-centre* of time? If there was a silent midpoint in the sway of a pendulum, there would be one amid a man's eye movements too.

I smelled death.

The intoxicating scents of death and darkness came up to me in waves. Satan Loppo's odious breath, stinking of cigar, permeated my senses. Allowing that no man was fundamentally bad and it was the dirt that entered him which transmogrified him into a murderer, Loppo's life breath was possessing me demonically.

Pundit had foreseen all these happenings. I could now feel within me the spirited rebellion of those who had shed blood in the jungles of Burma.

This man, this evil man, had plundered and abased my motherland. The one who marred my woman's chastity and my land's worth should be answered with violence, not non-violence. No dictatorship would last forever.

A cyclone, having uprooted the past, started blowing through me.

The rattling, mourning night rain; the coffin maker who was busy working in his shop till midnight; drenched to the bones when he returned home, the sight of his wife weeping uncontrollably; the stink of Satan Loppo's expensive cigar on her bitten lips; the black hell hound which mauled a man in front of a bungalow . . . Finally, the cursed night of relentless rain when the tamarind tree, weakened at its roots, gave way and crushed a small house.

My nerves stretched tight. I could have toppled the world and drained away the oceans in my vengeance.

I stared at the back of Satan Loppo's neck with a surging fury. There was a profusion of thick, black hair around it. The crowing superiority of a golden rosary entwined his neck.

On the ground, amidst the coffins, a strong piece of rope, scalpel, sharp chisels, the thick measuring rod.

Nothing that happened afterwards was in my control.

During a sinful moment, I must have pounced on Satan Loppo. The measuring rod might have hit his left temple hard. A chisel might have stabbed his back. Or a rope might have strangulated him. The upright coffin tumbled, and Loppo lay whining inside, along with his doom.

I rushed to the front door and latched it, declaring Holy Sabbath.

'Now watch yourself getting buried alive in this coffin,' I bellowed ecstatically.

My savage laughter must have torn apart Loppo's remaining consciousness. I could hear him bleat, staring at the encircling boundaries, 'Don't kill me . . . for God's sake . . .'

Glory to the moment when the devil utters the Lord's name for help!

I felt like laughing aloud. In this moment, I owed nothing to heaven or hell. His entreaty should not provoke any compassion either. Not even in my dreams had I thought that the enemy would be annihilated so fast. The lascivious, roaming bull had been tamed finally by a simpleton's halter. Unleashing my repressed thirst for retribution, I yelled:

'Where is your blasted German dog? Whistle for it. Where is your famous goonda gang? Invite them! When it is time to die, no one will come to help! The end of every tyrant, adjudicated by earth, is this! Murder at the hands of the suppressed. Or a cowardly suicide. But you have no choice, do you?'

I felt resentful that the hell spawn would get away so easily with a simple death. He who harmed the soul more than the body should be subjected to an equivalent bout of torment.

'You are not going to get a dignified exit like others. You swine, all your luxuries will not come to save you now,' I gloated.

As if possessed by the devil, I grabbed at Satan Loppo's clothes. For every disrobing he has conducted in his evil life, let his covering fall one by one!

When I grabbed his mundu, Loppo could only object weakly; and I understood that in his utter devastation, his body was unable to reach where his mind desired. A revenge baptised by hell took over me completely. Making him experience the humiliation of being stripped naked, I mercilessly tore away his last piece of clothing. Seeing his scared and shrunken manhood, the same one which heralded its glory all through life, I felt like mocking the world. All flagpoles of arrogance were so short-lived! Unable to quench my wrath, I disgraced him by prodding his penis with a stick.

The despicable man did not deserve an honourable ending. Even death would spit out thick phlegm on his face.

'Water . . . water,' Satan Loppo pleaded, lying stark naked in his coffin.

'Not a drop,' I howled at him. 'You who turned Aadi Nadu into a wasteland, should realize the value of a drop of water! When you die, neither your status nor your money will wet your parched throat. You should die of thirst, cursed by water.'

Though I reviled him with foul words, it was fair to give a few drops of water to a dying man. From a clay jar, I poured water into a tumbler. I drank it with relish in front of him. I saw him smacking his dry tongue at the sight of the rivulets of water streaming down my face.

'I shall give you some water if you want! You are so shameless, aren't you? You choked the water supplies of this land and yet you feel thirst. If you have a semblance of pride, try spitting out the water I give.' Having disparaged him, I poured water down his throat.

If he had any bit of ego left, he would have spat it out. But he did not.

I felt gratified to see him lapping up the water shamelessly. He had sunk as low as he could. An immense satisfaction filled me.

Letting free all bottled-up feelings of retaliation, with lightning speed, I shut the top lid of the coffin and hammered in the thick nails. I was panting . . . *Now as soon as I can . . . without a moment's loss . . .*

With a shovel, I rushed to the backyard, wanting to bury the living corpse before anyone came searching for him. My weapon plunged into the earth's depths, throwing earthworms and crickets into disarray. I begged the earth to lend some space to put a dead body to sleep.

Finally, fatigue caught up with me. I perspired heavily. The earth lay guiltily in front of me with her womb open, ready to accept her sinful creation back. I stood staring for a few moments at the pit, and injecting myself with spiteful thoughts, returned to the one-room shop with its lifeless relics.

Binding down with a robust rope the coffin that held Satan Loppo's sturdy body, I dragged it to the edge of the freshly dug hole. Invisible hands came to my aid as I completed that onerous task. Yes, I knew my helpmates.

Even a murder should be done without any dishonesty. Here, as the last ritual for my sworn enemy, let me pray with closed eyes.

'Please take care of this soul.'

After the final prayer, with the entire universe as my witness, I briskly pushed the coffin into the grave.

The hole was filled.

Confined inside the dark coffin, Satan Loppo groaned, with whatever remained of his strength. 'Don't kill me! Please don't kill me . . .'

'Don't you remember the pleas of those whom you mercilessly murdered? Aren't you ashamed to cry now? Even if you try to get away in a German-made ark, your coffin awaits you finally. Be consoled, be consoled . . .'

I gave him wise counsel on meeting his death readily.

As the lid was shut, I could not see his face. I tried to envision it in my mind. Instead, I saw Beatrice and my children. *My blind Rosarios, my daughter Roselyn who was fragile as a fledgling, my brilliant Alphonse.*

My nerves stretched taut yet again. I was seized by an apoplectic frenzy.

Staring at the mud hole of death, I lamented, *'My Lord, My Lord . . .'*

Burning in the memory of four lifeless figures lying next to one another, I dived into the fresh grave like a manic bull.

Dislodging the coffin lid, I shouted at the top of my voice, 'Get lost, you filthy swine!'

The profanity, imposing as if carved in stone, washed over Satan Loppo. Life throbbed in him again. Stirring slowly, bloodied by the wound on his temple, looking like a naked devil, Loppo rose from his coffin. I threw a torn piece of cloth at the fiend.

He gave me a deadly look mixed with the blood stains of his humiliation. I stood staring after him, as he agonizingly limped his way out of the shop, with one last flaming look at me.

The distance between life and death is miniscule. There goes my easily defeated arch-enemy, with the life I have donated freely.

I felt proud; there could have been no better payback in either heaven or earth. There was no need for a coffin's plank between the world and me any more.

My arrogance was short lived. I was felled by a vicious blow on the head and went sprawling amongst a heap of coffins. When I turned my head, I saw my adversary, whom I thought I had defeated easily, standing in his torn clothes, with a wooden batten in his hand. His eyes blazed fire like that of the beast uttering blasphemies in the Book of Revelation.

He was aiming for a death-blow next. No, I could not have defended myself. Neither did I wish to.

My soul's revenge was complete when I let him walk away from death. If Loppo killed me, I would presume that my time to join my loved ones had arrived.

Desiring death intensely, I was gazing at him dismissively when the Anti-Clock proclaimed the new hour. Satan Loppo was transfixed by the Anti-Clock. Though he had bargained for it with lakhs of rupees, Pundit had disdainfully denied him and hung it on my humble wall.

'Damn you! Die after watching me take the Anti-Clock!' Satan Loppo bellowed.

What he was meting out to me was a revenge worse than death. Though he could have finished me off in a single knock, he wished to break my heart by seizing the Anti-Clock.

Loppo clambered up the old stool. It was the same one on which Pundit had sat, a relic from my Appan's time. The sight of those sinful feet perched on the ancient stool—which had lain loyally all these years without the least bit of attention or care—was despairing. I watched helplessly as Satan Loppo stretched himself and stood on his toes to reach the Anti-Clock. The searing pain of being unable to keep my word to Pundit, that I would keep his clock safe, spread all over me. In a death-like state, I cast a final glance at the Anti-Clock with its backward racing needles, before it was looted.

Exactly at that moment, the legs of the ancient stool lost their balance and swayed. Satan Loppo struggled to regain his balance. One of the stool's legs gave way and I saw Loppo falling. A bloodcurdling scream swallowed up my coffin shop. I didn't know that a razor-sharp chisel, fixed upright in the toolbox down below, was waiting with more thirst than me.

For a moment I felt that my soul had escaped the universe. How quickly . . . how quickly had death stepped in, with its incontrovertible power to assert its final authority. While recollecting that it could knock at the door of anyone, any time, with absolute liberty, the writing on the wall of time became visible to me—the need for a new coffin.

A grave once dug, demands its due.

My nostrils can smell the presence of the invisible spirits. They are forcing me to yet again read Pundit's sheet, with its translation of the German words, pasted on the nearby wall.

Make good use of time
that is given,
while each hour
adds to life.

And with each
pendulum swing
you will be closer
to your last
resting place.

Before diving into the riveting assortment of rats, chisels and mallets to create a coffin adorned with art and lace work in the shortest possible time, I measured the boundaries of my pitiful body. While noting down the measurements with a pencil, I could not help sniggering at the thought that in this boundless universe where billions and billions of solar systems revolve, a man could be summarised thus:

62" x 16" x 9"